INNER CITY JUNGLE

INNER CITY JUNGLE

SANTANA SOKOLOV™ BOOK TWO

MICHAEL ANDERLE

LMBPN Publishing
PMB 196, 2540 South Maryland Pkwy
Las Vegas, NV 89109

Version 1.00, November 2021
ebook ISBN: 978-1-68500-571-9
Print ISBN: 978-1-68500-572-6

THE INNER CITY JUNGLE TEAM

Thanks to the JIT Readers

Rachel Beckford
Zacc Pelter
Dave Hicks
Deb Mader
Dorothy Lloyd
Diane L. Smith
John Ashmore

If I've missed anyone, please let me know!

Editor
The Skyhunter Editing Team

DEDICATION

To Family, Friends and
Those Who Love
to Read.
May We All Enjoy Grace
to Live the Life We Are
Called.

— Michael

CHAPTER ONE

The pre-dawn glow of red lingered on the horizon, the foggy black yielding to the rising sun.

Santana sat on the dewy grass, her shorts soaking up the moisture as she smiled at the creatures surrounding her legs. Her mother used to tell her that "the early bird catches the worm," and here she saw the evidence. The soft, loamy soil gave way to long pink creatures. Crows, sparrows, and starlings danced around her leg, beaks alternating their pecks between the bird feed in her cupped hands and the long slimy heads emerging from the dirt bed.

Around her, the trees stood tall, their trunks like guardians lining the long paths of the inner city park. The landscaping silhouetted a tall, round fountain in the distance, and later, when the sun rose, this place would fill with human activity.

But not now. Now it was Santana and her beasts. More than birds, squirrels nestled beside her, their paws cupped as they fed on the nuts and fruits that Santana provided. There was even a stray fox nearby and a couple of raccoons, all creatures preoccupied with their hunger and ignoring the others around them.

Santana smiled. It was easy to befriend the creatures of this world. All animals needed was food, drink, and security. When the humans built their metropolis and claimed the land for their own, the animals grew to mistrust, and things had changed. Children terrified the pigeons. Adults shot at the foxes and raccoons.

In reality, all could get along if they tried. Animals and humans alike wanted the same thing. To live and thrive.

Was that so hard?

"Except snapping turtles," Santana muttered so she didn't upset the creatures dancing around her. "Snappers can fuck off."

She laughed at her little outburst and flushed. Out of all the Earth's creatures, snapping turtles were the ones she understood the least. Deadly bastards with a powerful bite that she'd had several run-ins with in the past.

She'd heard that all explorers had one breed of animal that disliked them. One of her mother's friends had sworn that parrots took a natural disdain to her and swooped at her head with raucous screeches.

For Santana, it was snapping turtles. The moment they saw her, they were unrelenting, streaming her way with jaws clapping loudly. At first, it was funny. After her tenth encounter, she couldn't shake the feeling that they simply didn't vibe with her mojo.

Santana tossed a handful of birdseed in front of her, emptying her container onto the grass. The raccoon flinched, then tucked back into his treat. For a long while she sat there watching, head cocked and a smile on her face in vacant amusement.

They were incredible creatures to advance in their behavior to survive in a human city. Once, they were wild, not all that long ago. The city had only stood for seventy years, and here they were, thriving.

A nearby pigeon took wing. A dozen others swiftly followed it. The world in front of Santana's eyes turned to a whirlwind of feathers and rushing wings. She closed her eyes, shielding the worst with her arms. Squeaks and rustles sounded around her as the animals darted into the bushes and trees.

Silence followed.

Santana lowered her arm, adjusting to the pre-dawn light. The grass was empty around her with only a scattering of seed left where there had been much activity.

"Didn't mean to crash your party," a voice crooned from behind.

Santana rested back on her arms, craning her head back until the woman appeared upside-down in her vision. A blood-red jacket caught the glimmer of pinks from the sky. Santana sighed. "It's okay. Things were due for a wind-down. The foxes were getting a bit raunchy, and kick-out is at four a.m."

Valentina Winters chuckled, stood beside her, and offered a hand. Santana accepted, and the other woman pulled her to her feet. She brushed off the blades of grass and peeled the sodden cloth from her body.

Valentina cast a judgmental eye her way. "I thought pissing yourself was a good way to mark your territory. Didn't realize it attracted the wildlife to you too."

Santana chuckled. "Good one."

"Thanks." Valentina stood straight, gaze fixed on the growing arc of light on the horizon. Buildings stood like dark teeth jutting from the ground, birds flying in flocks across the sky. "I wouldn't think you'd have time to play with your friends when there are more pressing matters underway."

"Didn't take you long to get to the point." Santana dug her hands into her empty pockets and joined Valentina in gazing at the sky. "If I had news, you would be the first to know."

Valentina drew a long breath. There were worry lines on her brow, although there was no tiredness in her eyes. "I want him back, Sokolov."

Santana nodded. "I know."

"Do you?" Valentina shot back softly but with an edge to her words. "Because from where I'm standing, my brother remains lost out there somewhere in the Atlantican wilds, and you're my only hope to find him. Yet still we stand here while you play house with your little critters like a twenty-first-century Snow White."

She shook her head, casting her gaze to the ground. "I need him back. The longer we leave him, the higher the chance that it's all over."

Santana narrowed her eyes. She remembered it well, the chase into the wilds, a man named Archie Fontana stealing away into the unknown with Valentina's brother. The whole ordeal had been chaos. They'd been lucky to get out of there alive together, but ever since then, things had fallen quiet.

"My benefactor is hunting," Santana replied at last. "We can't rush this kind of operation. Do you know how large the wilds here are? How many square miles of dense tropics and foliage there is to scan? The network of underground caverns? There's a reason that few explorers are brave enough to survive the wilds. Most don't return. We're doing what we can—the *right* way."

She turned to face Valentina. "The moment I know, you'll know. I'll chase my source and see where we're at. If I have news, you'll know."

Valentina's lips thinned. She opened and closed her fists, eyes shimmering. When she met Santana's eyes at last, her gaze was cold and hard. "One more week. Tops. Then I'm intervening and getting involved in the best way I know how."

"How's that?" Santana didn't really want an answer. She'd seen the media articles. She knew what Valentina Winters was capable of—a ghost in the machine who extracted answers and eliminated targets by any means necessary.

Valentina shrugged one shoulder. "I don't think you want to find out." She turned back to the sunrise, the first hints of gold shining through the milky haze over the city.

"The only thing we've got going for us is that they won't eliminate Kit if they can help it. They've invested too much money into sustaining his health and employing the AI to keep him alive. There's too much money on the line to drop a project dead."

Santana thought back to her conversations with Valentina, trying to understand the significance of all this. From what she could glean, Archie Fontana held Valentina's brother on a life support system. He was trialing experimental neurobiological artificial intelligence to heal his system and bring him back to health.

If what Valentina had said was true, there would be a large amount of money at stake. To have a technology capable of self-healing the human body, to repair deadened nerves and restoring neurological wiring in humans, now that would be highly coveted indeed.

"We'll find him," Santana reassured. "We need to zero in on any technological hotspot activity."

"You've been saying that for weeks," Valentina shot back. "Yet, here we are."

"It's not my technology," Santana explained.

"No." Valentina wrinkled her nose. "It's not. It's Taylor Yungheim's."

Santana sharply glanced her way. "You know?"

"I know. It's my job to know."

She turned on her heels, taking a few steps from Santana before adding over her shoulder, "Time is a ticking clock, Sokolov. I'll destroy all of those in my path to retrieve the ones I love. I've given you more patience and time than I'm accustomed to and I'm quickly losing what little remains."

Santana turned to face her, but when she did, Valentina was gone.

She stood in the park, the steady hum of the morning traffic rolling nearby. Birds chirped overhead. The raccoon returned in Valentina's absence, bumbling along the grass toward the forgotten fruits and berries.

Santana looked back at the rising sun, the sense of urgency rising within her. She'd made a promise to Valentina, and it was one she needed to uphold. If she didn't, she feared the fate that would befall Taylor.

"Looks like I need to visit someone." She spoke to the raccoon.

The creature looked up at her with glistening black eyes, a sparkling intelligence behind them.

Santana crouched to one knee, running her fingers through the creature's coarse hair. The fox lingered in the trees behind, awaiting its calling toward its food.

CHAPTER TWO

"I told you, these things take time." Taylor Yungheim sat behind a pile of ancient tomes, the yellowed pages frayed and breaking. Behind him, the floor-to-ceiling window allowed daylight to cast the room in an incandescent glow.

Santana sat back, feet resting on Taylor's desk. Flakes of mud flecked down from her boots and littered the polished walnut surface. "We're running out of time," she returned. "I don't think you understand the urgency of the situation here."

Taylor scoffed, casting a wondering eye to Santana. "I think, of all people, I understand the situation rather well."

Santana glared at him, but he didn't return it. His face was kind, softened at the edges, with no sign of malice in his eyes. A bubble of guilt popped in her stomach. Where did this annoyance come from inside her? It was like being angry with a kindly old grandfather. "If that were the case, wouldn't we be out there? Couldn't you at least provide some coordinates for me to explore? I need information. We need *something.*" She didn't want to say what she was thinking. *Before Valentina gets her claws into you and uses any means necessary to extract the information.*

Taylor finally looked up from his book. Beside him, scratchy penmanship filled a large sheet of paper. Despite the extraordinary technological advances in Atlantica and the wider world, Taylor still opted for quill and ink. There was something romantic about that. Taylor was a fan of the Old World, hence his profession.

"Santana…" He smiled warmly. "You have to trust the process. You know how much out there is still undiscovered. You know how much of the wilds are still to be examined and tamed."

"If you send me…" Santana began.

"I will not," Taylor replied firmly. "You're a rare specimen, and I will not risk your safety for the sake of this hunt. Once we've zeroed in on the location, I'll set you loose, but I will not send my greatest asset into the field until we have more intelligence. I almost lost you a few days ago. I won't risk that again."

Santana's mind filled with a bright white light, the smell of explosives, and the image of Sasha Chechik as she succumbed to the wrath of the gods in the temple—if gods they were. Despite her talks with Gyles in her apartment, she couldn't fathom the truth of what had happened out there.

"Well, time isn't on our side," Santana replied. "I need news. I need momentum. A woman's brother is at stake."

Taylor sighed, resting back in his motorized chair. Beneath the cradle of his seat, a blue light glowed from a ragged core that made Santana think of the perfect orb she'd stolen from the temples. The Atlanticore pulsed as it powered the chair with boundless energy.

Taylor wiped a hand across his brow, the daylight beginning to warm the room through the glass. "Fine. You want an update?"

"Yes." Santana lowered her feet and leaned forward attentively.

"We believe we're homing in slowly. There is a disturbance in the northwest region of the wilds, around the base of Mount Garbet. At this point, we're unsure if it's seismic or manufactured. Any attempt we've made to fly drones or helicopters to scan the location, some kind of frequency has disrupted our technologies and scattered the feeds." He raised his eyebrows. "As you know, this isn't all that unusual in the open airspace above the jungle."

Santana nodded. There were always reports of attempts to scan and analyze the Atlantican tropics. All of them came back as wasted ventures. Theories surmised that residual activity from the Atlanticore fragments was enough to disturb the technologies in the sky, but that was yet to be proven. There was still much to understand about the strange glowing rocks that expelled seemingly infinite, clean energy.

"Still, I've sent a team out there," Taylor continued. "They left two days ago. The expedition should take four to five days. I will hopefully know soon—provided they return in one piece."

He leveled his gaze at Santana, the pair both thinking the same thing. Their odds of return were slim at best, even without the added danger of stumbling across a hidden underground colony of tech geniuses and henchmen.

"Fuck..." Santana shook her head, reaching for the glass bottle on the counter. She poured herself a drink, the sour tones hitting her nostrils and bringing to her mind thoughts of a private investigator by the name of John "call me Dick" Chambers.

Taylor cocked his head. "I know it's difficult, but we're making progress. Keep yourself busy. Find something to keep you distracted while I do this. Trust me. I want what you want." He sat back, accepting a drink offered by Santana. "Little early in the morning, wouldn't you say?"

Santana downed her drink without flinching. "It's always drinks o'clock in Russia."

Taylor grinned, wincing as he drank his. He set his glass down and stared at Santana. "Why don't you have some fun in the city? Find something to entertain yourself. You know, enjoy a movie, see a play... You're in the greatest land in modern living. Make the most of it."

Santana rolled her eyes.

Taylor extended a wrinkled hand across the table and laid it on top of hers. "It's worth a try. Who knows, you might have some fun."

Santana walked through the streets, restless and concerned.

She'd asked Taylor for a new assignment, something to take her back into the jungles, but he'd dismissed her, emphasizing the need for some R&R.

Santana balked at this, but even after several shots of whiskey, Taylor hadn't budged.

She decided to abandon the idea of a driverless cab, opting instead to head into the city on foot. She was used to walking and climbing long distances so by the time the metropolis swallowed her, she was a little hungry but not too fatigued.

She strode past unique boutiques, storefronts that sported tourist items, and several fast-food restaurants. Snaking along the roads reminded her of why she disliked the city, the bustling crowds, the grim expressions on citizens' faces as they rushed toward their place of work. The air felt closer, smokier, as she trotted along the paved sidewalks. There was less room to breathe, less room to stretch. Everything was so…manufactured.

"Hey, watch it!" a man grunted, whipping around to face her, one finger pressed to his ear as his nano cell phone utilized the tiny bones around his ear canal to magnify the sound.

Santana rubbed her shoulder and glared at him. Without a word, she stuck out her middle finger, eliciting a huff from the suited man as he turned and strode up the street.

It wasn't all gray-stone misery in the city. Santana kept an eye out for those around the city who still admired the greenery of nature. Several buildings along her route encouraged the ivy to scale the brickwork. Some had stacks of flower pots, and lofty herb gardens fixed to the sides of their apartments. A short distance farther and she came across the Atlantican Garden of Eden, a large glass-fronted building that displayed exotic foliage from around the world. Inside was a butterfly conservatory, as well as several exhibits with turtles, crocs, and Eastern fish species.

She paused outside the building, tempted to head inside and explore. The sudden smashing of glass from a nearby building pulled her attention away.

She turned to face the small tavern, a tiny one-story room set beneath a towering block of apartments. Inside was dark and dank, but Santana knew that sound anywhere. A bar fight had broken out.

A grin spread across her face. While bar fights weren't unusual in the city, most of the ones she'd encountered had led her to meet a familiar face.

She thought of Dick Chambers and rolled her eyes. When she entered the bar, it was hard to identify anyone except for the flash of blue.

Patrons cowered at the edges of the room. The bar staff was absent as several bodies collided and scrapped at the end of the room by a series of roulette tables. Santana moved her hand to her whip, looking around for Dick Chambers.

She grinned. There was no Dick. There was, however, a trio of Atlantica Justice System officers, one of whom she recognized even in the dank gloom.

Terra Kris ran toward a towering brute as he peeled himself off the roulette table. Streams of blood ran down his head, his eyes hazy as he swung meaty fists and looked for a target. Another officer stood nearby, pistol aimed at a thin woman with hair that reached her ass. The woman was scrambling for a weapon, the officer roaring at her to put her hands in the air. A second brute tossed brown glass bottles at the officers, one of them missing by a clear mile and smashing at Santana's feet.

"Piss off, filth," the second brute roared. "This is an AJS-free zone. Private, init."

Terra ducked under the man's fist, slamming her shoulder into his soft gut. He exhaled a gust of air and fell backward. Terra used her momentum to climb on top of the man and slap a pair of cuffs on his wrists.

The officer with the gun fired a warning shot at the woman's feet. "Not when we have permission from the property owner. Now, all of you, hands up."

The woman flinched, raising empty hands into the air. The second brute tossed another bottle. The officer shot the glass in mid-air, raining shards around the group.

Santana stepped forward.

Terra sat back, moving a lock of stray hair from her face. She called at the top of her lungs, "You all have the right to remain silent. Anything you say can and will be used against you in a court of law. You have the right to speak to an attorney and to have an attorney present during any questioning. If you cannot afford a lawyer, we will provide one for you at government expense—"

"Kris! Look out!" a third officer called.

Terra whirled as the second brute raised a bottle and swung it down at her head. There was a smile on her face as she brought her arm up to shield against the *thwack*. A glimpse of a silver thumb shone in the dim light.

Before the glass could smash, a loud *crack* sounded. Santana flicked the whip, the end coiling around the bottle. She tugged toward her, causing the glass to shatter in the man's hand. He howled in pain, blood leaking between clasped fingers.

Terra turned her gaze to Santana. "Oh, hey, bud. Didn't see you there." She grinned.

Santana cracked the whip beside her, nearby patrons shrinking away. The officers looked at her dubiously.

"She's with us," Terra reassured them. She rose to her feet, then swept a kick at the second brute's shin. He collapsed to one knee, still nursing his pulped hand. "Stay down, prick. You're done for today." She jerked her thumb at the third officer. "Cuff him. Don't be gentle." Another nod to the officer with the pistol. "You get her."

She sauntered over to Santana, extending her arms as if nothing much had happened. Santana hugged Terra, then they both turned to face the chaos.

"Funny," Santana commented. "I wasn't expecting the guys in blue to be behind a bar fight."

Terra chuckled. She flexed her hand in front of her face, Santana locking onto the biomechanical parts of Terra's anatomy. "Honestly, it's rare we're able to get involved. Most of the time the owners refuse us entry and all we can do is stand on the sidelines." She shook her head. "It's bullshit. Still something we're trying to rectify, but that's Atlantica. A city that's half ass-backward and always working in favor of the asshole."

"That's a whole lotta ass," Santana replied.

Terra glanced at Santana's shorts. "You're one to talk."

They laughed. The other officers busied themselves getting the perpetrators to their feet. For the first time, Santana noted the APRIL glasses on their faces. "Are they standard to every officer now?"

Terra gave a sad nod. "Unfortunately so."

"Why unfortunately?"

Terra drew a long breath. "Something to catch you up on over lunch, perhaps?"

"Works for me." Santana checked her watch. "I'm free now."

"Eager."

"Always," Santana agreed.

The officers dragged two perps to the door. Terra glanced pitifully at the woman with long hair. "Tell you what, let me get this shitbag to the station. Then I'll contact you and sort out a dinner date." Her eyes lit with sudden enthusiasm. "Actually…

This is good timing. I may have something that you could be interested in."

Santana raised an eyebrow. "Intriguing…"

"You don't know the half of it."

Terra pulled the woman up by the crook of her elbow. As she passed Santana, she added, "I'll call you shortly. Looking forward to a catch-up." She laughed. "Small world, right?"

"I wish." Santana thought back to Taylor and his struggle to locate their enemy in the jungle.

When the officers left the bar, Santana stood in uncomfortable silence. She glanced around the room of patrons as they slowly came out of the shadows. When she turned to the bar, an older woman stood in a doorway leading to the back with a rifle in her hand. "You're a little late," Santana stated. She coiled the whip at her side and sat at the bar. "Your best espresso, please."

The woman gave her a strange look, then moved to a dusty coffee machine in the corner.

CHAPTER THREE

"I'm bored," Gyles complained as he slouched on the couch.

Santana busied herself in her kitchenette, pouring herself another coffee. It was late afternoon, the sun descending and filling the apartment with dazzling golds. "Then go outside and get some fresh air."

Gyles leveled his gaze at her, lowering the PlayStation controller. Santana didn't like the idea of having video games in her apartment—her father and mother had always taught her the importance of the real world over the digital—but still, what was she to do? Since she'd brought Gyles to the safety of her apartment, he wouldn't leave.

"You know I can't do that," Gyles replied. "The Order of the Scythe is still out there. Just because we severed one hydra head doesn't mean they won't still hold a grudge and find me. You remember what they did out there, right? They're ruthless with their enemies, and I'm a *traitor*, remember?"

Santana wiped a hand down her face. She needed a shower before heading out to meet Terra, but now she was caught once again in this conversation.

She turned to Gyles, coffee steaming in her hand. "It's been a week. If they were coming for you, they'd have made some kind of progress. They're a smart group of people. They stole the artifact from my employer and hunted down the locations of the temples in the jungle. That wasn't all their leader. That was their *team*. If they wanted you dead, you'd be dead."

Gyles scoffed and turned his attention back to the TV. In fairness, Santana approved of his game choice. A digital Lara Croft ran through the jungle on the modest screen, bow and arrow ready in hand, chasing down enemies as she zeroed in on some rare artifact. It would no doubt sell for millions and potentially change the understanding of history as they knew it.

She sighed, moving over to the coffee table and taking a seat in front of the TV. He rolled his eyes and paused his game. "Yes?"

Santana softened her voice, speaking as a mother might to her child. "You can't hide here forever, Gyles. You know that. Just because I'm out a lot of the time doesn't mean you can make it your home."

Gyles lowered his gaze. "I know."

"You'll be okay." Santana sat straight. "How about one day this week we go out together. Something simple. The corner store? The Garden of Eden? Somewhere to get you outside and back into the world, show that you no longer have a target on your back?"

Gyles chewed his lip. "I don't know."

"You can't remain caged in here forever," Santana enforced. "The wallpaper is beginning to peel from your stink."

Gyles glanced at the walls. "They're painted."

Santana raised an eyebrow.

"Fine." He gave in. "One day this week. Now, would you mind? Lara needs to go for a swim."

"Perv."

Gyles laughed. "Not like that."

Santana hopped into the shower and cleaned up. When she was

dry, she donned a pair of cargo pants and a fitted black tee. She tied her hair back into its customary ponytail and stocked her provisions in her pockets. She was going to dinner with Terra, but it never hurt to be prepared. Life had shown her that much, at least.

Leaving Gyles to the harsh glow of the TV, she headed into town. The driverless cab was silent, and soon she arrived outside Angus' Steakhouse.

Terra stood waiting for her, clad in a pair of dark blue jeans and a black leather jacket. She grinned and kissed Santana on the cheek. "After you."

They were seated by a man with a ponytail that put Santana's to shame. He offered their menus and fetched them a bottle of wine to share.

"Swanky place." Santana looked around at the lit candles in their glass containers, pristine white tablecloths, and gleaming silverware. In the corner of the room, a nine-piece band played softly, sweeping melodies across the room. "If I didn't know any better, I'd say you were trying to get into my pants."

"Don't flatter yourself." Terra smirked. "I figured that a girl born from the wild such as yourself hadn't experienced the finer side of living in the city. Notice there are no traces of mud or dirt on the floor. The plants are in pots and emerald green. Water is filtered, and over there is a small koi pond with unblemished fish."

Santana nodded. "All fake. All manufactured."

Terra's grin remained. "Yeah, I didn't think you'd take to it. Still, it's something different, and we all need that sometimes."

Santana thought of Gyles, bored in her apartment. She thought of Taylor, encouraging her to try something new. *Well, here it is, old man. You got your wish.*

They each ordered steaks presented on thick slabs of wood with baskets of fries and vegetables. As they tucked into the juicy and tender meat, they spoke of old times, swapping past experiences of school lives, laughing over how much things had changed, but also how much they hadn't.

"There was no question you'd make it in the AJS," Santana remarked, dabbing her lips with her napkin. "From the moment you stopped Kiera Kurshner from beating down on Lily Abbott, it was clear."

Terra's eyes swam with nostalgia. "Yeah...I couldn't stand the injustice. Lily was a sweet kid. Kiera was a bitch. She'd been stealing Lily's toys for weeks and keeping them for her own. I'd had enough."

"Then you graduated to older kids." Santana chuckled. "Three grades older, and you were scrapping with them, getting covered in bruises as you got involved in things well above your pay grade."

"Nothing has changed there." She finished her final mouthful of steak. "What about you? Jungle kid, that's what they used to call you."

"That and 'Eliza,'" Santana commented.

Terra frowned.

"Thornberry," Santana explained. "It was an old TV show. A girl who could talk to animals."

Terra gave Santana a strange look. "You can't, though."

"No," Santana confirmed. "I can't talk to animals."

"Just checking." She sat back as the server collected their plates and offered a dessert menu. When he was gone, she added, "You used to crawl through the playground looking for insects. Anything furry or with wings that moved, you tried to lure in. Any biology question asked, you had the answer. It was impressive."

"What can I say? My parents raised me well."

Terra nodded.

"As did yours," Santana continued. "They did well to raise us as good civilians in a place like this. Atlantica is a dirty place, marked by the assholes who take advantage of its backward rules and policies. Is it any wonder that I fight out in the wilds…"

"While I fight on the side of the law," Terra finished. Her face grew somber. "It's a tough fight. I'll give it that. Things have improved somewhat in the last few weeks." She tapped her temple, and behind her eye, Santana spotted a flicker of a green LED.

She thought back to their last conversation over drinks, Terra telling Santana of the advanced artificial intelligence wired inside Terra's head. The system linked with the AJS, connected with her neurobiology, and spoke to her inside her head. Santana had seen *Robocop* before, knew the kinds of things that could go wrong with this kind of technology, but as much as the hairs on her neck bristled, she was sitting with Terra. Not a manufactured Terra, but the real deal. The tech hadn't changed her one bit.

"Go on…" Santana encouraged.

Terra considered her response. "After dessert. Let's at least have one mortal meal before we dive into the strange and the scary."

"Fine. But you're paying."

"No." Terra grinned. "The AJS is. This is a business dinner."

Santana laughed, sliding a finger down the dessert menu until she settled on a Baked Alaska. Terra selected a chocolate fudge cake that looked like it could feed a family of four.

They joked and listened to the music, occasionally pointing fingers toward nearby patrons as they enjoyed their food, oblivious to the two underdressed women. At one point, a man fell to one knee and held out a ring to an enthusiastic buxom woman. Polite claps rattled around the restaurant. A minute later, the band took a break, their orchestral sounds replaced with soft piano instrumentals played through the speakers.

Their desserts arrived, presented on immaculate plates. Terra cast a curious eye at Santana.

"Ice cream, sponge, and meringue," Santana explained. A thick layer of sugary meringue covered the treat; the swirls tipped with brown scorches from a handheld blowtorch. "The impossible dessert."

"I don't understand." Terra arched her neck to see better. "I've always wondered how you can bake ice cream without it melting."

Santana shrugged. "There's magic in the world."

Terra scoffed. "No. It's science. I just don't understand the science of it."

Santana chuckled and sliced through the center. She sliced again, removing a triangular section to reveal perfectly perpendicular blocks of ice cream inside. "I can tell you the science, or you can believe it's magic."

Terra grinned, mouth stuffed nearly full with fudge cake. "Science," she stated through the food, earning a disapproving look from the couple at the closest table.

"It's surprisingly simple," Santana began. "The meringue and the sponge are filled with several air pockets at the cellular level. Meringue and sponge are naturally poor conductors, so they form a protective shell around the ice cream. Even when blasted with heat, the ice cream remains protected and safe from melting."

To punctuate her point, she scooped a spoonful of ice cream and plunged it into her mouth. "Delicious," she managed through the food.

The couple turned up their noses.

Terra laughed. "See? Science is always the way."

Bright white light flashed into Santana's mind. A glowing blue orb and a crumbling temple shuddered in her vision.

"Not always," she murmured.

"I'm sensing there's something you're not telling me," Terra muttered.

Santana nodded. "A story for another time. Now, you tell me yours."

Terra's plate was nearly empty already, only a small smear of chocolate sauce remaining. She laughed, then put the last mouthful between her lips. Replete, she dabbed her mouth with a napkin. "I suppose you're right." She took a long sip of her drink, then relaxed into her chair.

Santana continued eating.

"I think the first thing to tell you is that things have changed at the AJS," Terra offered. "In all honesty, only a few weeks ago I was in hiding, running from assailants that were after the APRIL technology they'd inserted into my head." She tapped her temple with a finger.

"What happened?" Santana asked.

Terra drew a long breath, then proceeded to tell Santana the full story. It was a winding tale, with twists and turns and unseen enemies. Terra had remained true to her principles, wanting only to see justice prevail, but the enemy was hiding around every turn.

She'd hidden low, dug into the history and the technology's developers, and uncovered a hidden plot to use the APRIL glasses to orchestrate and direct the AJS for nefarious purposes. Somehow, despite it all, she'd prevailed.

"I have protection behind me," Terra replied. "The AJS reinstated my office, and now I have something of an...I guess you could call it immunity from the public versus private protocol—in certain circumstances. Even this city wouldn't want a solitary AJS officer going rogue. They would never want to see the Executioners reinstated."

"The Executioners?" Santana thanked the waiter as he cleaned up the items on their table.

"Another story for another time," Terra replied.

Santana laughed. "We have a lot of them. We should catch up more often." She took her drink.

"No argument there," Terra agreed.

"So you're back in the inner city HQ?"

"No. I chose to stay in the outer city." She held up a hand at Santana's quizzical look. "There's more opportunity there—more chances to help people. The corporal and I have an understanding. Trust me. It's for the best. It's there I can have the greatest impact…for now."

"So what's all of this got to do with me?" Santana asked.

Terra grinned. "I'm glad you asked." She leaned forward, casting a suspicious glance around the restaurant. The hour was wearing on, and many of the patrons who'd been there when they'd sat had moved on. "I have a case sitting in my inbox that I have *zero* clue how to deal with it."

Santana frowned. "Don't you have Wikipedia installed into your brain?"

Terra laughed. "I do. Just because I have the information doesn't mean I'd be the best marine biologist or the greatest architect. It's supplementary, not all-powerful."

"Animals," Santana stated.

Terra's eyes narrowed. "Animals."

The band started up again, music sweeping through the stilled restaurant.

"Are you familiar with the ICG?" Terra asked.

A flicker of recognition crossed Santana's face. "I am. The International Cloning Group. A group of overly eager scientists working together to bring back to life creatures that have been declared extinct."

Terra nodded, her smile fading.

Santana cocked her head. "Wait, they're in trouble with the AJS? I thought the ICG were under strict UN regulations and could only bring back one of each creature for historical and biological advancement."

Segments of news articles sprang to Santana's mind with pictures of Tasmanian tigers, dodos, and extinct butterfly species. They'd all been dragged back into the realm of the living in the last few years. After a rogue team of biologists in Japan had forgone all international regulations and brought back the first real-life dodo seen on planet Earth in over three hundred years, interest in cellular biology, and cloning in particular, had skyrocketed.

The world had fought to control the advancement. Rumors of woolly mammoths, saber-toothed tigers, and other larger primitive creatures nearing entry into the present world had begun to fly. A failed attempt at restoring the marsupial lion—an ancient species of big cat that had been incredibly agile in trees and jungle environments—resulted in the slaughter of an entire family as the creature escaped the basement and strove for freedom. Lithuanian authorities soon hunted it down.

Strict rules had been brought into play, allowing only a singular group—the ICG—to play with DNA and the restoration of the world's lost creatures. There'd been speculation over whether they'd create a park or zoo to house the creatures and show the world the group's efforts, but the ICG hadn't confirmed anything yet.

It took a long while to clone anything at all.

Terra sighed. "It's not the ICG. Those fuckers would be stupid to do anything outside of their jurisdiction. Do you know how much funding Atlantican moguls have sent their way? Do you know the types of protection and security measures are put on that group to ensure they stay safe and we don't end up with a real-life version of *Jurassic* fucking *Park*?"

Santana chuckled.

"There's another group," Terra continued. "Here in Atlantica. Or, so the reports say."

Santana's ears pricked up. "A cloning group? It wouldn't surprise me. People can get away with murder here."

"We've had reports of roars and late-night growls," Terra elaborated. "A series of attacks have been recorded over the last few months, apartment rooms where no human break-ins have been detected, but in which people have found the bloody remains of victims."

Terra took a tablet from her inside pocket and handed it to Santana. "APRIL, show Santana the images."

Something flashed behind Terra's eyes. For the first time since she'd arrived, Santana noticed something on Terra's chest. Another light flickered. Was she wearing a chest plate beneath her shirt?

A feminine, robotic voice responded, **Communicating with remote device. Displaying images.**

"What was that?" Santana's mouth fell open.

Terra handed her the tablet. "APRIL, of course. Here."

Santana studied Terra's chest, looking once more for the light. When she couldn't find it, she took the tablet and studied the screen.

A grisly series of images filled her view. She scrolled through the montage, most of the rooms shown in the pictures splattered with blood. A few shots showed the close-ups of bodies with chests slashed open or heads torn off. Whatever had made these attacks, the blades weren't sharp.

You've seen animal attacks, Santana. You know these aren't human cuts. Her eyes lingered on the half-chewed intestine trailing across a wooden floor near the window.

"Hard to digest, isn't it?" Terra asked.

Santana nodded and handed the tablet back. "You've got yourself an animal there. What makes you think you're dealing with an extinct creature, though? Any number of cats could do this. Just a few weeks ago I was…invited into a manor where they hosted a tiger in a cage."

"Invited?" Terra smirked.

"I found an entry," Santana shot back. "Point is this could be anything. Leopard, jaguar, panther. It's easy to train a cat, lead it to food. Hell, it could even be a pack of wolves for all we know."

Terra nodded knowingly, then fished inside her pocket. She

drew out a small glass vial the length of her finger. Inside the tube was a single hair.

She handed it to Santana.

Santana rotated the vial as Terra spoke. "No DNA match to any creature living on this planet. I've run it through APRIL's system, and while we can get close relative matches, we're a long shout from anything alive and kicking today."

The hair was coarse and long, around the length of Santana's finger. It was a dirty blonde in color, with speckles of black. *Could be a leopard? Possibly a jaguar of some type. I doubt it's a cheetah or anything more slender and used to warmer climates.*

She turned the hair over in her hand, then offered it back to Terra. Terra declined politely. "Yours. We have another at HQ. A few of them."

"But you're having trouble tracing the target?" Santana asked. "Can't you use your…" she waved a finger at Terra's face, "AI friend to help you?"

Santana knew very little about the AI hiding in Terra's head, what its capabilities were or what it offered, but despite what little Terra had told her, she guessed that there was much more than met the eye.

Terra chuckled. "You're finally interested in the tech?"

"I was last time," Santana replied. "A crowded bar and plenty of drinks don't make for the best environment to probe." She waited expectantly.

Terra held her grin. "APRIL is…advanced. She can scour the entire AJS database. She allows my vision to switch through heat, to dark, to normal."

Her gaze shifted to a waiter idly standing by the counter, waiting for someone to serve. "I can tell you that man is James Maddow, and he's twenty-three years old. I can tell you that AJS has brought him into the station fifteen times in his life, mostly for small dealings associated with drug peddling. Only one serious event, which saw him take six months of house arrest with a five thousand dollar fine."

Santana's eyebrows raised. "Impressive."

Terra nodded. "Irritating, too. It's hard to get her to shut up."

"So with all this technology lingering in your skull," Santana started, "what do you need little old me for?"

Terra frowned. "You're not up for the job?"

Santana scoffed. "Oh, I believe I'm more than qualified."

"I agree. My team, however, are not." Terra played with her thumbs. "Plus, as intelligent as APRIL is, I need someone who has a way with creatures. Someone who can stop me from accidentally getting mauled by tigers without me having to blow their brains out. I may have a special pass to break into private residences and for the top honchos to turn a blind eye, but that doesn't mean I can be loud."

The smile returned to her face. "Plus, it might be like the old days."

"Fooling around with insects in the playground while you stop the bigger kids shaking down the smaller kids' cash?" A nostalgic shine found Santana's eyes. "You might be in luck. I have a little downtime."

"You still sound hesitant," Terra offered.

"Does it pay?" Santana asked.

Terra smirked. "Yes."

Santana nodded. "Then I'm in."

CHAPTER FOUR

With dinner concluded and Terra dutifully picking up the check, they headed out into the evening air.

A fine mist fell from the sky. Atlanticans strolled by quickly, cowering beneath their umbrellas. Streetlights turned to fuzzy orbs as Terra took Santana around the corner to where she'd parked her AJS motorcycle.

Santana hesitated, tilting her head. "What happened to your Ducati?"

She remembered it well, the sleek machine Terra used to race around the city on. It had been her pride and joy, a remnant of the old world. Petrol-fueled and noisy as all hell—a stark contrast to the quiet hum of many of the electric engines that occupied Atlantica's roads.

This bike was, somehow, even sleeker. There were no hard edges. The machine's design would rip through roads with minimal drag. The body was a midnight black that seemed to absorb light, and the only true flash of color came from the glowing Atlanticore orb set into the machine's heart.

"A long story," Terra replied. "Maybe one I'll tell you someday. Suffice to say that this was a gift from some powerful friends."

She straddled the cycle and stroked a hand along the bodywork. "She's a beauty. Can tear through the city like a machete through paper. But boy do I miss that roar of the engine."

Santana climbed on behind her. "Doesn't it make the bike better for stealth?"

Terra sighed. "Yeah…"

She twisted the accelerator, and Santana had to grip Terra's jacket quickly to stop herself from being flung off the back.

The bike *was* fast. Terrifyingly so. Terra handled the machine as though it was an extension of her, the city turning to a blurry image on either side. They leaned hard around corners, Terra's knees almost scraping the blacktop. Santana gritted her teeth as the wet misty spray cooled and dampened her face.

Still the bike was silent. Terra wove through the late-night traffic with stealth-like precision. The gentle vibrations beneath Santana's ass were the only other indications that the motorcycle was performing. There was no smoke filtering out of the back, no growling engine. Whatever magic existed in the Atlanticore fragment, whatever technology harnessed its power, it was a miracle of modern-day craftsmanship. Santana knew frighteningly little about the Atlanticore found on the island, other than the fact it kicked out tremendous amounts of green energy. Huge areas of the city ran on Atlanticore, the blue fragments the envy of the world. She had encountered several across her adventures in the wild, although many city-dwellers believed their supply to be running thin.

So many mysteries. So little time.

After what seemed like only seconds of driving, Terra pulled the bike up to the curb of a quiet little neighborhood on the south side of the city. The roads were narrow, the buildings towering above them. Terra waited for Santana to dismount, then climbed off. She patted the bike affectionately. "Not bad, eh?"

Santana worked her hair back into some kind of order. Her

ponytail had kept most of it straight, but a few stray locks had worked their way free along the journey. "She's quick…quiet."

"Silent," Terra replied sadly. "That's the thing I miss the most. The roar of the engine. The rumble of action underneath your ass."

"Guess you'll have to find that fix another way." Santana winked. "I have some friends who might be interested. How about a bored, paranoid squatter who has a thing for gaming?"

Terra raised an eyebrow.

"Doesn't matter," Santana reassured her.

They stepped toward an awning that stretched over the sidewalk and provided shelter from the rain. Glass double doors barred their way. Cracks in the lower corners appeared to be evidence of previous gunshots.

Terra moved to a security panel and pressed her metallic thumb to the scanner. Something whirred, and Santana could've sworn she noticed the thumb change shape before a green LED light and a *beep* confirmed their entry.

Terra smirked.

They strode inside to a marble reception area lit by dull, gloomy lights. The place looked like it was trying to be upper class but didn't have the budget. A threadbare couch sat on the wall beside them, a large walnut reception desk stretching along the far wall as they headed inside.

There was a layer of dust on the desk, papers strewn with people's private information across its surface. In the corner, chuckling sadly, was a stone pond with golden koi gasping beneath its surface, a layer of green algae starving the poor creatures of oxygen.

A dozing balding man rose as Terra and Santana approached. He wore a white shirt that was three sizes too large, his sunken eyes tired and haggard. He placed a clammy hand on the table, eyes twinkling as he studied them up and down. "Can I help you lovely ladies today?"

Terra flashed her badge. The twinkling in the man's eyes died. "AJS business. I need access to room three-oh-five."

The man cast an uncertain look toward a rusting elevator. "I thought you pigs had finished with the examination—"

His words cut off as Terra aimed her pistol at his face. His hands rose into the air.

"Three-oh-five," Terra repeated.

The man swallowed, then carefully lowered himself to a drawer beneath the desk. His eyes darted back to Terra as he scooped out a set of keys and laid them on the desk.

Terra offered a sarcastic smile. "We don't appreciate 'pigs' on the force. I'd watch your mouth if I were you." She lowered her gun but didn't holster it.

The man grumbled beneath his breath as they swept around the desk toward the elevator. Terra pressed the button, then whirled toward the shocked receptionist. A whipcrack accompanied the pistol spinning out of his hand and arcing through the air. It landed nearby with a clatter.

Terra scoffed, her pistol aimed at the clerk. "You chose the wrong ladies to fuck with."

Santana looped her whip back at her hip before scooping up the man's weapon. "Shooting at an AJS officer? That's surely a long sentence in jail."

Terra shrugged. "A private business owns this place, ain't that right, Frank?"

Frank's face drained of color.

The elevator *dinged*. The doors opened. Terra stepped inside, ushering Santana with her. "I'd think twice about calling for backup, too. Just because no one's convicted you for those multiple DUI's and the family you mowed down on Fifth doesn't mean I won't find a way to get you."

The snarl returned to Frank's face, disappearing from view as the doors slid shut and the car began its ascent.

The apartment they were looking for was on the third floor.

They stepped onto a long rug caked in dust. It was a deep red under the gray, but that didn't do much to hide the dried blood-stains that peppered its length.

"This place is a shithole," Santana observed.

Terra nodded knowingly. "You haven't seen inside yet."

Terra unlocked the door, then swung it open. A thick, musty scent poured out, causing Santana's nostrils to wrinkle. She coughed, covering her mouth with her sleeve. "Jesus."

"Mmhmm," Terra confirmed.

The place was dark, the curtains closed and blowing gently in the wind. Terra clicked the light on, bringing the full room into view. Shithole wasn't the right word. The place looked as though a tornado had hit it. Furniture had toppled, objects had smashed, the frames of items that might once have contained glass that the AJS had since cleaned up lay around like old skeletons.

Then there were the prints on the floor, painted in the blood of the fallen victim. The AJS had shipped the body away, but a clean outline remained on the carpet. A few strands of AJS tape remained on the walls and the nearby doors.

"This is where they fell," Santana stated.

Terra nodded. "Jermaine Brixton. A real estate agent, origi-nally from Barbados. Forty-three years old, and now rotting in the ground—or, what remains of him is."

Santana strolled toward the window. "The point of entry?"

"It's assumed." Terra's eyes glazed over as though she was reading something that no one else could see. "There was no other sign of entry. The officers leading the case found the window open like this. A few bloodstains trailed across the carpet toward the glass. No in, only out."

Santana crept closer to the window, following the small blood splatters on the floor. "Well, you've certainly got yourself a big cat."

Terra drew by her side. "Yeah?"

Santana pointed. "Yeah. Pawprints." They were ill-defined, but she'd seen enough evidence of large cats in the jungle to know what their feet looked like. "Unmistakeable."

Terra grinned. "Confirmed."

Santana got the impression she wasn't talking to her.

"They came in through this window," she trailed her finger along the carpet toward where the outline of the body remained. "You have clear signs of disruption and a struggle." Her eyes went to a blood splatter that painted the wall. Some of the wallpaper had peeled off and hung like loose fingernails. "And back. Entry and exit through the window." She nodded, frowning.

"Entry and exit confirmed," Terra repeated again.

Santana cocked her head. "Who are you talking to?"

"AJS database," Terra replied. "Updating the case files as you go."

Santana shook her head, annoyance building within her. "Can I ask you a question?"

"Sure," Terra replied.

"Is this all a fucking joke?" Santana asked.

A silence hung in the air.

"What do you mean?" Terra asked at last.

Santana swept her arms around her. "What I'm telling you isn't rocket science. It's clear from the evidence around here." She pointed back at the window. "A huge bloody paw print is on the window frame. The creature jumped out after attacking its victim."

She pointed at the wall. "Over there, that's where the bullet landed, missing the cat." She shook her head. "I don't understand what I'm doing here, Kris."

Terra smirked. She nodded in agreement. "Kris."

"Kris." Santana stood firm.

Terra lowered her gaze then wandered to the wall. "I agree with you, Santana. Had this been my case, I might've picked up on a load of these clues. It's all pretty obvious if you've been studying this kind of thing for years. Or if you've got technology built inside your skull, which allows you to filter out and highlight the parts of a crime scene that need examination." She placed a hand between the cushions of the couch, then pulled out a human finger. "This, for example."

She held it up to Santana, the golden ring around the finger catching the lights.

"How did you know that was there?" Santana asked.

"I told you." Terra tapped her temple. "I'm not bullshitting. It's not only information recall this AI gives me. It enhances my senses. Plays with my synapses. Couples tech with bio and allows me to become…"

"Robocop," Santana finished with a smirk.

"Hopefully not," Terra replied. "Did you see that guy's outfit? No thanks." She removed the golden ring and took a moment to study the inner circle. Satisfied, she tossed the ring to Santana.

"Check the hallmark. It was manufactured here in Atlantica. A little-known place by the name of Luxury Frost. They have places across Atlantica, but this one shipped to the store on Kingston Avenue four years ago."

Santana looked stunned.

Terra tapped her head again. "AI. I have access to a *lot* of public—and not so public—records." She turned her attention back to the room. "You're here to confirm for me the things I might've missed. You're here because you know animals, and you might have leads that the AJS doesn't when it comes to this kind of thing. You're here because…well…"

"Well, what?" Santana asked, bristling.

"Because we don't hang out enough." Terra winked.

Santana laughed. "You're kidding."

"I am." Terra walked closer to Santana. "In all seriousness, you're here because I can't do this alone.

"The rest of the AJS team won't have clearance to crawl into the dark spaces where we'll find our answers, and as great as APRIL is with humans, her makers didn't design her for wild creatures. She can tell me a puma is attacking, but that's about it. I've seen you bring a four-thousand-pound rhino to its knees with its cheek cupped in the palm of your hand. Tarzan, George of the Jungle, they ain't got shit on you."

"They're men," Santana replied. "Of course they haven't."

Terra looked at her expectantly.

"So I'm your partner in all of this?" Santana offered eventually. "Just a sidekick?"

"That such a bad thing?" Terra grinned. "You got better things to keep you busy?"

Santana rolled her eyes, then wandered over to the window. She ran a finger along the stained red glass, but none of the residue shifted. It was dry as a bone. "You want to know the one thing that none of your crew have deemed fit to ask throughout this investigation?"

Terra waited expectantly.

Santana turned to look out into the street. Through the open window was a nearby fire escape. From here she could see into the narrow street. A couple of older gentlemen were walking on their way back home. A couple of cars idled nearby. "The question is: how did the cat get in?"

Terra's eyes glazed over. "The notes have it. They say 'through the window.'"

Santana rolled her eyes. "Yes, through the window. But who opened it? Who allowed the kitty-cat to crawl through?"

"Maybe the window was already open?" Terra asked.

Santana chewed her lip. "That climb is rough, even for a big cat. It would've needed help to clamber inside. Not only that but what about when it got out? You think an animal handling crew would be smart enough to train a big cat to climb and return on command? They're feral creatures. They live by their own code. They don't play fetch and attack."

"You're saying someone was out there with some kind of pen

or cage, drawing the creature back in when it finished?" Terra asked.

"Maybe. It's all speculation at this point." She held up the ring she'd palmed. "Whose ring is this?"

Terra closed her eyes, drawing inward. After a few moments, she stated, "Hilary Hopkins."

Santana lifted her eyebrows. She turned to the area on the floor where the victim had laid. "And their name was?"

"Brian Felkins," Terra answered quickly. Realization dawned on her face.

"Are you thinking what I'm thinking?" Santana asked.

Terra nodded. "We need to find Hilary Hopkins."

CHAPTER FIVE

Frank ducked behind the desk as they exited, hiding from sight. Their footsteps echoed around the marble reception, and Terra didn't bother looking back. Only Santana threw a furtive glance, placing a hand on her bullwhip to send a message to the clerk.

They sped back through the city, Santana's grip loosening on Terra as she grew used to the vehicle. It was exhilarating, the cold air igniting her senses. Tiredness slipped from her as they passed through the neon city until they arrived in an area lit with glass storefronts and egregious displays of wealth.

Bon Vivant Valley was the shopping capital of Atlantica. Every window displayed diamonds, jewels, and high-end fashion not seen anywhere else on the earth. After claiming its mantle as the most advanced civilization on the planet—what else would you get when you gave the world's richest people a playground where the law didn't apply to them?—Atlantica was swift to consume the fashion market, too.

There wasn't a bulb that wasn't working. The streets were immaculate. In the center of the main commercial square sat a large open park with manicured grass and decorative fountains.

Santana smirked. The clientele that walked past her was

vastly different from the Franks where they'd been. Women looked like runway models. Men were suited and sharp. Not a hair was out of place underneath their umbrellas, both men and women with hands laden with bags.

"You wouldn't think people would be shopping at this late an hour," Santana offered as Terra took her around the corner to another wide street that reflected the square. Exotic cars lined the curbs on either side of the road. "Who needs to buy Versace in the middle of the night?"

Terra shrugged. "Those who sleep all day and party at night. I remember a time when the commercial districts weren't twenty-four hours. Once they learned that there was an entire portion of the population who would rather wake with the owls, that was it. Profit over sense. Makes our job surprisingly more difficult. More people means more traffic. Also means more chances for shoplifting, too."

"I don't envy your job," Santana stated.

"Nor I yours." Terra smirked.

The next street was alight with glowing signage, the lights shining so bright it was almost like walking in the daytime. Terra broke through the crowd ahead, steering Santana to a megastore with an arching glass front door. The words "Luxury Frost" arced over the front in giant letters emulating diamonds.

"Way to keep a low profile," Santana muttered.

Terra laughed and stepped through the door.

The place wasn't too busy inside. Islands of jewelry counters stretched as far as the eye could see. Santana's skin bristled, a chill sweeping over her as the A/C cooled her down. There was nothing warm in this place, only thousands of gleaming precious gems that left glittering afterimages in her eyes.

A woman in a white shirt and a waistcoat spotted the newcomers and approached with a practiced smile. "Welcome to Luxury Frost. How may we be of service to you today?"

Terra flashed her badge. Santana had to give it to her. The woman's smile didn't falter.

"Is there a problem, officer?" She clasped her hands. Santana spotted three almost identical workers glance their way.

"No problem," Terra replied. "I would love to ask a couple of questions, if I may?"

"Of course," the woman replied.

Terra turned to Santana and held out her hand. Santana handed Terra the ring.

"Someone purchased this ring from this store," Terra stated. "I was wondering if you could point us in the direction of the original purchaser."

The woman held her gaze.

Terra continued. "I understand that it's not within your remit to provide the AJS with information regarding your wares, but you'd be helping out the city. There's a possible threat out there that needs bringing to justice, and you'd be doing a lot of people a massive favor by providing us with what we need."

The woman drew a long breath, glancing over her shoulder to a man who was standing at the bottom of a set of golden stairs. He was double her width, and a thick beard hid his mouth. He wore shades indoors which, ordinarily, Santana might have found a little suspect, but in a place like this, she couldn't blame him. Her eyes were stinging from the brightness of the lights.

Terra reached out and touched the woman's arm. "Veronica… Not to lay it on too thick, but wouldn't you feel better knowing that little Charli would be safe enough to sleep at night without fear of an unwarranted attack?"

Veronica's trained mask slipped. "How do you…How *dare* you threaten my…"

"We're not threatening." Santana held her hands out placatingly. "We have information on a vicious killer, and we want to bring them to justice before they can do more harm."

Veronica glanced back at the man, then eyed Terra suspiciously. "Have we met?"

"No. We haven't had the pleasure."

She considered Terra for a moment, then turned and walked toward a nearby counter. The glass surface was angled, a series of lights creating a touchscreen display as she scanned her fingerprint and opened the database. She typed on the screen, nails clicking against the glass. After a few moments, her eyes gave her away.

"Something interesting?" Terra asked. She glanced back at Santana with a knowing expression.

"It's…" Veronica composed herself, standing straight. "The ring belongs to a former member of our staff."

"Former?" Santana asked.

Veronica nodded. "Hilary hasn't been to work in the last five days. She skipped her shifts and…" Her eyes darted to the man on the stairs, who watched them carefully.

"I've heard that management has been sending her letters, trying to contact her but…nothing. She disappeared." Her eyes narrowed on the pair. "Where did you get this ring?"

"Do you have information on her family? An address? A next of kin, perhaps?" Terra pressed, glossing over the woman's question.

Santana watched the man bring a finger to his ear. He turned and climbed the stairs, disappearing.

Veronica hesitated, then typed on the keyboard again. "She has an address here, Finnley Street. Number thirty-four."

"Perfect," Terra snatched the ring back from Veronica, then turned on her heels. She marched across the store, Santana jogging to keep in her wake.

"That's all you needed?" Santana asked.

Terra didn't talk until she'd left the store. The cold night air chilled their skin. "That's all we needed."

"What about your supercomputer brain?" Santana asked. "Couldn't you have gleaned that information through APRIL?"

Terra sighed, turning left and walking back toward her bike. "It's complicated. We're on an official case. I need to prove that I've been able to do certain things by the book. Not only that, but someone erased the records for Hilary Hopkins and her kin from public files. Someone has tampered with the records, and I needed to confirm the details."

They reached the bike. Terra straddled the saddle, hands in place, the engine already started.

"Wait," Santana instructed.

Terra turned her way.

"Terra, what's going on here? None of this is making any sense."

"What do you mean, jungle girl?" She offered a sly grin.

"The finger. The attack. The ring. The unidentified hair." Santana ran a hand across her head. "I need something solid to stand on if you'd like me to help in some way. I feel like I'm holding onto the back of your bike with two fingers."

The mirth in Terra's expression disappeared. "You're right. I'm sorry. I'm not used to working with a partner."

"*You* contacted *me*," Santana reminded her.

"I know." Terra chuckled. "Look, here's what we need to do. You still have that hair?"

Santana confirmed by patting her jacket.

"Identify the creature. Do your jungle thing and find out what exactly we're dealing with here." Terra sat back, eyes thoughtful. "If you can approach from the animal side, I'll approach from the side of the law, and together we can close in on our killers."

Santana glanced over her shoulder as feet scuffing on the sidewalk pulled her attention. "You might want to get involved now, then. Because those men don't look any too happy.

CHAPTER SIX

Terra dismounted her bike, standing side-by-side with Santana as the men approached.

There were four of them. Burly, brutish men with grim-set faces and dark shades, despite the late hour. They wore suits, the shoes so clean they reflected the nearby streetlights.

"Evening, gentlemen," Santana offered, hand moving reflexively to her bullwhip. She recognized the man at the front of the pack as the man who'd been standing on the stairs watching them.

The man brought a hand to his lips and took a drag of his cigarette. The cherry tip lit red, a ribbon of smoke curling. He exhaled a small cloud, then announced, "You two need to be careful."

Terra bristled at Santana's side. "Right back at you. You're out in public, talking to an officer of the law."

The man held up his hands in mock placation. "We don't want no trouble."

"Sure seems that way," Santana returned. "Four apish men advancing on two women in the streets. It sure screams children's tea party."

One of the men chuckled. It was hard to make out their age in the light or the intent behind their eyes.

"I'd recommend that you stop chasing," the man offered, voice steady, confident. "You might not like what you find."

"So there is something to find?" Terra asked.

Santana narrowed her eyes, noticing movement from the other's hands.

"Like I said…" The man interrupted himself with another drag of the cigarette. "It's better that you stop. For all we know, something bad might come your way if you choose to pursue this line of questioning."

Terra grinned. "You know that I could take you in for questioning right now? You seem to have some knowledge of what we seek."

The man shrugged. "Try if you like. Just saying… It might be best to avoid the thing you're looking for."

"Specific." Santana nodded. "Thank you for your warning."

They stood in a silent stalemate for a moment, both parties holding the other's gaze. After a long pause, the men bade their goodbyes, then headed back to the store.

"What the fuck was that about?" Santana asked when they were gone from sight.

Terra chose not to answer. "Here, come on. I'll get you home."

They mounted the bike. Terra pulled away down the narrow street. Before they reached the end of the street, something *tinked* against the bike's metal body.

Santana glanced down by her ankle but couldn't see anything. She looked back, finding the wink of dark eyes in the distance.

When Terra soon pulled back up near Santana's apartment, she kept the engine running. Santana dismounted, pausing before entering the building.

"Thank you for your help tonight," Terra offered.

Santana waved it off. "I didn't do much. It was all you and your computer." She frowned. "Who were those guys?"

"Bad men, according to my database. People associated with charges of arson, grievous bodily harm, and a few counts of dealing in narcotics."

"Why didn't you book them there?" Santana asked. "Bring them in for questioning?"

"Because I couldn't find any link to any kind of animal groups," Terra offered. "Besides, it would've been more hassle than it was worth to bring them to the station. They didn't do anything wrong."

"They could've," Santana returned. Her eyes drifted to the bottom of the bike. She crouched.

"What you doing down there, sailor?" Terra asked.

Santana studied the strange silver object with her head cocked. She pointed. "I'm fairly sure that doesn't belong there."

Terra climbed off her bike. She tugged away at the small device and examined it in her hands. "A tracking chip. They want to see where we're going. Where we are."

Santana's skin prickled. "I'd rather my location remain anonymous." She walked toward the road as headlights shone her way. As the Chrysler sped on by, she rolled the device into the road. Its magnets drew it toward the body of the car, and the Chrysler drove away. "That'll confuse them."

"That was evidence," Terra complained.

Santana shrugged.

"You might've put others' lives in jeopardy."

"We'll find out. I think they'll realize they've got the wrong people before they do any harm."

"You hope," Terra stated.

"I do." Santana hugged Terra. "Thanks for a fun night."

"You bet." She mounted her bike once more. "Find out what you can about those groups. You have some names, and you have the hair. Do your wild girl thing and report back to me as soon as you find anything useful."

Santana nodded. "Gotcha."

Terra sped away, the back wheel drifting as it fought for purchase with the sudden acceleration.

Santana turned toward her building, looking up to where her room hid behind the low-hanging clouds. She only hoped that Gyles was asleep when she entered her apartment. She yawned and stretched before stepping inside.

Santana awoke to the smell of cooked meats and smoke.

She sat up sharply to see a thin haze of gray blanketing her bedroom. She'd disabled the fire alarms some time ago—after a chaotic night in which even though she'd installed new batteries, the damn thing had continued bleeping—and hadn't gotten around to replacing them since.

Now, she was regretting that decision.

"Fire!" she called, springing from bed and running to her bedroom door. She wore only a pair of night shorts and a tank top.

Inside the living room, the smoke was even thicker. Someone moved in its depths, coughing and animatedly waving a hand.

"Gyles?" Santana moved toward him, ready to help the poor bastard from the place. Her mind spun a thousand revs a minute, wondering if the men who'd threatened them had already found her and were executing their attack, trying to smoke the pair out and starve them both of oxygen.

No. My traps...

But there were no traps, were there? At least, not as many as Santana usually set before she went to bed. Gyles was in her apartment. Gyles was her Doberman, ears pinned to the door, her alert for if anyone broke in.

"Gyles?" She coughed into her fist, sweeping the smoke with a hand. She clutched the man's hazy figure around the waist and dragged him toward the glass double doors of her balcony, where the worst of the smoke rushed out to belch into the city.

"Hey! What?" Gyles protested, kicking and flailing his arms. Something hissed. Metal *clanged* to the floor.

Santana didn't let go until they were on the balcony. She took long gasps of clean air. Gyles turned to her. He was disheveled, his eyes wide, and his hair a mess of tangles. "What the hell?"

"What do you mean, what the hell?" Santana shot back. "The place is on fire!"

"No, it's not," Gyles argued and bent to pick up the piece of metal he'd dropped. The pan was black. The remnants of four strips of bacon had turned to ash and melded to its surface. He looked abashedly at Santana. "I forgot about the bacon."

Santana's lips curled as she growled. "So what's still pouring the smoke?"

"English muffins," he replied guiltily. "I left them in the oven. Was about to open them and get them out when you pulled me out here."

Santana waved. "Then what are you waiting for? Get that oven turned off!"

Gyles nodded and pulled the collar of his shirt to his mouth. He disappeared into the smoke.

Santana followed swiftly, not quite trusting him not to mess up again. She swept around the apartment, opening all the windows. Smoke filtered up the side of the building, escaping into the heavens. Luckily she was on the top floor. Otherwise, her smog might've triggered the alarms in any apartments above hers.

The smoky haze faded. Soon only the smell remained, lingering on their clothes and everything in the apartment. Ashy smudges lined their cheeks as Santana stood in the kitchen and turned to Gyles. He stood by the trash basket with his head hung low and a sad expression. "I'm sorry," was all he managed.

At that moment, the anger, confusion, and urgency that had

consumed Santana melted. She guided Gyles to the couch, then gave him a glass of water. He drank it greedily as the ash from his clothes fell onto the couch.

"I wanted to do something nice for you," Gyles offered. "You've been so kind to take me in, and when you hadn't come back last night, I figured I'd plan a surprise. I went down to the local and got the ingredients. Thought I'd get a decent breakfast for you as thanks."

"Instead, you nearly burned down my apartment."

Gyles looked as though he was going to argue, then stopped himself.

"I'm kidding," Santana soothed, glancing around the space. Black scorch marks painted the oven. They'd spread to some of the surrounding cupboards, and there was some staining on the ceiling, but luckily that was the extent of the damage.

The smell would linger for a while, but that was nothing she couldn't fix. The only thing that was beyond repair was the pan. "You can buy me a new one of those, though." She nodded at the charred metal object left on the balcony.

"Deal." He grinned, although it quickly faded.

"Still, you hit the corner store?" Santana asked. "That's pretty big news. I thought we were going to do that together?"

"You were right," Gyles replied. "I can't just sit and mope here. I have to start living my life, getting out there into the big wild world."

"You might need some cooking lessons first."

Gyles laughed. "I'm sorry."

"You've said that."

"I know, but I am." He rose to his feet, looking around the room. "There's got to be something salvageable from this mess."

Santana raised an eyebrow. "How about we look at an alternative?"

Gyles met her gaze.

"You clean up," Santana ordered, "and I'll grab us something from Starbucks."

Gyles grinned. "You got it."

The Starbucks run took twenty minutes. By the time Santana was back, Gyles had set most of the apartment straight again. The pan's handle poked out of the trashcan, the cooking utensils were tidied away, and a faint smell of lilac hung in the air from the bathroom spray Gyles had used to freshen the place.

He was busy scrubbing the cupboards when he noticed Santana set down her purchase.

They drank their coffees on the couch, soon moving on to the breakfast muffins in the brown paper bag. Santana did her best to cheer Gyles up, but she could tell it would take a while for him to get over his mishap.

"You got bored with gaming?" Santana asked.

Gyles swallowed his mouthful. "Kind of. After your fourth run through the latest Tomb Raider, you realize you're wasting your life in fear of something you don't know to be true or not."

Santana nodded.

"Besides," Gyles continued. "I'd like to see my family again."

"They're in the city?" Santana asked.

"My brother is," Gyles informed her. "Parents are off in Cuba. Retirement home. They visit occasionally. I'm not close with cousins or other relatives."

"What's your brother do?" Santana pressed.

"Bioengineer," Gyles replied. "Does some work running DNA sequencing and something or other about decoding the general script of the human form."

Santana's ears pricked up. "Bioengineer?"

"Yeah, sounds like super boring shit." Gyles gazed at his coffee. "His team contributed to some…unknown…something with cancer. I don't remember."

"You're a great brother."

Gyles raised his cup. "Thank you."

Santana mused on Gyles' words. "I don't suppose your brother knows or has anything to do with the ICG, does he?"

"The who and the what?"

"Does he do anything with animals?" Santana clarified.

Gyles' brow wrinkled. "I'm not sure, to be honest. I'd have to ask him." He turned to Santana. "Why are you looking at me like that?"

Santana shrugged and smiled. "Would be useful to know." She waited expectantly.

"Now?"

"When better?"

"Well, okay." Gyles added, "Then we're working out where you're taking me on our date."

"Date?" Santana laughed.

"Yeah. You said you'd take me out." Gyles grinned.

Santana playfully punched his arm. "You've already been out this morning. Job done."

"I went to the corner store!" Gyles protested.

"Then burned down my apartment!" Santana motioned to the room.

Gyles folded his arms. "You still promised."

"Make the call," Santana instructed.

"Fine..." Gyles gave in with his smile intact. "While I do that, you figure out where you're taking me. I want to go somewhere nice."

CHAPTER SEVEN

Kealan Forde approached Santana and Gyles with a grin that stretched ear-to-ear.

Around them was the open glass foyer of the DN-Armada building, a huge laboratory filled to the brim with space for the researchers to conduct their experiments. Santana looked up at the ten floors that rose above her, the balconies encircling them and making her feel like an ant. Large green leaves twisted along the beams and girders, and a smattering of small birds and insects chirped around the space.

He approached from a glass elevator, walking past two rectangular ponds that lined either side of the walkway. His focus remained on his brother with his arms held wide, ready to embrace him.

"Hey stranger," he bellowed, wrapping him up. "Long time, no see. Where the hell have you been hiding?"

Gyles and Santana exchanged a glance. "Hey, bro. I'd like to introduce you to Santana Sokolov."

"Your new bit of action?" Kealan gave a hearty laugh. "Not bad. Not bad at all."

"His work associate," Santana corrected.

Kealan raised his eyebrows, looking over the arch of his eyebrows at Gyles. "Sorry to upset your friend." He turned his attention back to Santana. "You could do a lot worse than my brother."

"I have." Santana's reply elicited laughs from both gentlemen.

"Come, sit," Kealan commanded, ushering the pair toward a nearby cluster of brightly colored couches. "You said you have some questions."

"I do," Gyles stated. "Well, she does."

"That's all I am to you, lil bro? A walking Wikipedia?" He gazed at Santana, talking behind his hand. "I got the lion's share of the brains from our parents. Gyles got the looks and brawn."

"I'm the looker?" Gyles asked.

Kealan rolled his eyes, then sipped from a flask he produced from his bag. "What's the question? I have ten minutes. Then I have to get back to crunching data. The human body doesn't unravel without Kealan Forde on the team."

"I hope to find a connection with someone who works in animal biology," Santana explained. "More specifically, someone who deals with the biology of extinct animals."

Kealan nodded thoughtfully, alarmingly serious in the wake of the question. "You looking to infiltrate the ICG?"

Santana sat back. "What? No."

Kealan narrowed his eyes at his brother. "What the hell have you gotten her into?"

Gyles raised his hands. "I don't know what—"

"Oh, bull." Kealan waved him silent. "You told me about your situation with the order of the shite."

"The scythe," Gyles corrected.

Kealan steamrolled on, turning his attention to Santana. "Did you know my little brother here got himself involved with a cult? Yeah. A group of psychotic historians looking for some piece of weaponry. Ain't that what you told me?"

He jerked his thumb toward Gyles, whose mouth flapped open and closed. "Called me up a couple of weeks ago." He did his best impression of Gyles, which entertained Santana greatly.

"'Help me, brother. I don't know what to do. I can't leave. If I do, they'll come for me.' Have they come for you yet? I'm guessing you're out because why else would you be sitting here today? Or, it's because you're in deeper shit and she's one of them. In which case, get the fuck away from my brother, and tell your loser friends he stays with me."

He glanced between the pair of them, waiting for an answer. When a balding man in his early sixties walked by and waved, Kealan offered a bright smile and returned the wave.

He turned his attention back to the pair. "Well?"

Santana looked at Gyles. "Your brother. You explain."

"Six minutes," Kealan stated.

Gyles gave a quick overview of the situation, omitting a *lot* of information that no doubt would've raised further questions from Kealan. Kealan nodded thoughtfully—to his credit—waiting until Gyles finished.

"So, you're out?" Kealan asked when Gyles was done.

Gyles nodded.

Kealan leaned forward, smacking his hand across Gyles' head. "You fucking idiot. What the hell did you join for in the first place? That kind of shit will get you killed."

"Hey," Gyles complained.

"Please." Santana offered some help to Gyles, but not enough for it to deter Kealan. "We're here for a reason."

"Two minutes," Kealan stated.

"Animal biology contacts," Santana prodded.

"Right," Kealan replied, eyeing her cautiously. "What we talking here?"

Santana drew out the vial with the unknown hair inside, noticing the curiosity that filled Gyles' eyes. "I have a hair here that isn't from a creature currently known to be alive. I need to find out what it belongs to. Sooner rather than later. Can you help or not?"

"One minute." Kealan punctuated with a glance at his watch. "I might know of someone who can help you. I'll be honest. It's been some time since I've spoken to them. Last I heard, they'd gotten involved with a pretty murky crowd." He side-eyed Gyles.

"Who?" Santana asked.

Kealan grabbed a pen and paper from his pocket and scrawled down the information. After handing it to Santana, he quickly stood, his initial chirpy demeanor returning. "Well, it's always a pleasure to see you, bro. Don't leave it so long next time." He saluted Santana. "Miss Sokolov, a pleasure also."

"You too." Santana couldn't hide her mirth and disorientation from Kealan's sudden changing moods.

Kealan strode toward the glass elevator, waving to colleagues as he passed. When the car arrived, and he ascended back into the building, Santana looked at Gyles. "Well, he's…"

"A character?" Gyles finished.

Santana shook her head. "An ass."

"Yeah…" Gyles glanced around the room, suddenly uncertain.

"What is it?" Santana asked.

Gyles blushed.

"You were checking for assassins?" Santana queried.

Gyles nodded. Santana gave the space a cursory look. "I think you're fine."

"I hope so." Gyles looked at the paper Kealan had handed over. "What's that say?"

Santana read the paper, finding only a first name and an address written on the front.

Gyles kept his hood up as they entered the driverless cab and made their way across town.

Stevie Wonder played in the cab, an upbeat song that reminded Santana of long car journeys with her father. Gyles was quiet for the most part, his eyes darting around the city, occasionally looking behind them for signs of following cars.

Santana let him be. She could spend her time telling him that things were okay and he didn't need to worry, but the truth was that she wasn't convinced. Sasha Chechik was gone, but that didn't mean the Order of the Scythe had disbanded. They could still be at large, working on their next big discovery.

It all depended on how much of an influence Gyles had been on their cause. Judging by his state while staying in her apartment, as well as the burning pan incident, she didn't think it would rank too highly.

"Holding in there, soldier?" she asked as the cab neared their location.

Gyles nodded, choosing to remain silent.

She took him into a small diner located beneath a block of apartments. They took a booth in the back, one with a full view of the diner, while still allowing them to remain tucked away in the corner.

Gyles greedily ate his all-day breakfast, Santana quipping and making jokes the whole time.

"How's your first day trip in freedom going?" she asked when he pushed the empty plate away.

"It's okay." Uncertainty filled his eyes. "It's just… What if… You know?"

"I know." Over the years, Santana had upset enough people in her profession to know that a day might come when someone finally used the target on her back. Still, you couldn't live your life that way. Be careful, sure. But living in constant fear was living half a life, and Santana wasn't about to give up half of hers to the people she disliked most. "It'll get easier."

"They'll come when I least expect it," he fretted.

"Then that's best, right? If they kill you when you least expect it, you'll have lived your life without worrying. You'll die without the knowledge of who it was or that it happened."

Gyles offered a weak grin. "That's one way to look at it."

They stepped out of the diner a little after midday. Santana looked once more at the address, then put the zip code into her phone. The cab should've dropped them off at the place, but she couldn't see it anywhere. Buildings enshrouded them, all commercial. She wasn't looking for commercial. She was looking for…

"There?" Gyles suggested, looking at Santana's phone over her shoulder. He was pointing at a small cluster of trees that occupied the space between two skyscrapers.

Santana wasn't sure what exactly was happening over there, but it wouldn't hurt to investigate. She made her way to the trees, eliciting an angry horn blare from an impatient driver. When she drew closer, she saw the stairs planted in the shadows of the trees, a walkway leading down as if a subway station lay under the buildings.

"This city continues to surprise me," Santana declared.

Gyles muttered, "The question now is if this is a good or a bad surprise."

They headed down the stairs, the trees and the hum of the city fading behind them. Fluorescent lights that stung their eyes lined the stairway. After a short distance, the staircase angled ninety degrees to the left. A few more stairs and it snaked around again.

They wound their way down without speaking, their footsteps echoing around them. When they finally reached the bottom, they encountered a small foyer that looked as though it would've made a great scene in a post-apocalyptic movie. The walls were stone, cracked with moss and mushrooms thriving in the dark spaces. Somewhere, water trickled. An empty desk stood on the right, and a vending machine with a broken glass front sat in the corner, the inside devoid of any remaining treats. Two bolted-shut doors led through separate walls.

"Dead end?" Gyles asked softly, the room carrying his voice anyway.

"No." Santana strode to one of the doors and examined the hefty lock holding the chains looped around the handle. While the links were rusty and coated in a film of dust, the padlock gleamed as though many hands had handled it recently.

"There are people inside." Santana examined the rest of the room. "But they want to remain hidden."

"They're doing a great job," Gyles returned. "Why would anyone go to these lengths to remain hidden from the public eye? As long as they do their business in a private residence, wouldn't they be safe anyway?"

Santana chewed on this thought. "Who knows why so many people do the shit they do? This is Atlantica, after all."

She gripped the padlock and turned it over in her hand. After a moment, she explored the other door, finding the same situation with the chains and the lock. A few deliberating moments later, she pulled out her pistol and fired at the lock.

The report exploded around the room. She wondered how far up the staircase the sound would travel and if it would draw attention. After all, she wasn't sure if she was in public or private space right now, although she assumed it would be the former.

Gyles clapped his hands to his ears. The padlock shattered, the U-bolt springing away from the mechanism. The chain unwound like an angry snake, dropping with a clatter to the floor.

Santana waited for the sound to stop reverberating before she holstered her weapon. When quiet resumed, she gripped the handle of the door and pushed it open.

"Hold," a voice called from the darkness behind the door. Enough light filtered from the stairwell to highlight the sharp edges of a rugged jawline and dark, keen eyes. "Consider the moves you are about to make."

Santana's eyes strayed to the shotgun muzzle aiming at her chest.

CHAPTER EIGHT

"What do you want?" the man asked.

Gyles shifted beside her, raising his hands. Santana held her position, her arms by her sides. "I'd like for you to lower your weapon."

The man's gaze darted to her pistol. "Hand it over."

"You must be joking." She smiled. "Then I'd be unarmed."

"You have reason to be armed?" the man asked. Even in the dim light, she could see his rash of stubble and wavy dark hair. If she didn't know any better, she'd say this man was a younger, more attractive Dick Chambers.

"You don't?" she replied.

Quiet passed between them. Behind the man, Santana became aware of more people moving around in the darkness, feet padding on stone and hushed whispers.

"Our contact information directed us to this address," Santana explained. "A mutual friend of ours sent me. Said that Therese might be able to help."

A flicker of recognition flashed at the mention of the woman's name. "What are we talking here?"

"Where's Therese?" Santana asked.

The man shifted, adjusting his grip on the shotgun. "Look, miss. We don't want any trouble to take place here. We run a tight operation, one free from public knowledge and AJS infiltration. The minute you step across that boundary line, you're putty in our hands, and one wrong move will get you killed, do you understand that?"

"I do." Santana had to give it to the guy. At least he was honest.

The man took a step backward. "Cross the threshold."

"Cross the threshold?" Was this guy from the Middle Ages?

Santana glanced at Gyles. He shook his head. Santana took a step forward, then another. She crossed into the darkness, then awaited their next move.

"And your friend," the man instructed.

"Santana…" Gyles complained.

Santana held her ground. She addressed the man. "Give us a name first. Something to show he can trust you."

The man snickered. "I could give you any alias I choose."

"You could," Santana agreed. "But you won't."

Another stretch of silence passed.

"Mark," the man answered.

"Santana," she informed him.

Gyles sighed. "Gyles."

"Well, Gyles," Mark crooned. "Join your little friend Santana, won't you? Then we can get to talking."

Gyles swallowed dryly.

"Gyles…" Santana whispered. "You trust your brother, don't you?"

Gyles nodded, then stepped to Santana's side.

Rough hands grabbed their clothes and dragged them another few feet inside. Gyles groaned, but it was now too dark to see anything. The door slammed shut behind them and the muttering of voices raised around them.

Santana had no idea how many of them there were, but their organization was scrappy. A few of them bumped into her as they guided the pair through the dark, turning corners and ushering them until they lost all semblance of direction. Santana tried to keep a map in her head, but it was useless. She was at the mercy of these strangers now.

She hoped that Kealan was right.

"You don't need to be so rough," Santana called to the others. "Just show us the way."

A few muted chuckles met her ears. Occasionally Santana noted glimpses of dull blue and red lights leaking out of rooms they were passing, appearing to be lighting up glass cases and cages. As much as she tried to focus on the lights, she couldn't. On they marched.

Then they were sitting down. Hands pressed down on their shoulders, and soft padding met their asses.

"Santana?" Gyles asked uncertainly.

"I'm here," Santana replied. She rooted around in her pocket, letting her fingers slide over the small metal button. A soft hissing came from her pocket, barely audible to the others who were momentarily distracted from the pair. "You okay?"

"Okay is a relative term," Gyles replied softly.

Voices muttered around them, indistinguishable. Santana's eyes had adjusted to the darkness enough to make out the silhouettes of figures but still didn't have an accurate headcount.

A lamp switched on in the corner, reminding Santana of the bouncing device from the Pixar animations. Someone spun the head of the light in their direction, the sudden barrage blinding them. She flinched, bringing an arm to shield her eyes. The others remained behind the light, lost from clear view.

"State your full name," a deep, bass voice demanded.

"Santana Sokolov," Santana replied.

When Gyles didn't respond, she nudged him with her elbow.

He relinquished. "Gyles Forde."

"What is your purpose?" the voice inquired. Santana could

make out a bald dome behind the light and guessed that the voice was coming from them.

"We require information," Santana stated bluntly. While she knew they were at these strangers' mercy, a small part of her still wanted to show that she wasn't to be fucked with and wasn't a doll for them to toy with. That much was clear from the sour smell that reached her nostrils, the contraption in her pocket performing its required duties.

"What information?" the man prompted.

Santana grinned, peering through the slits of her eyes as she lowered her arm and tried to adjust to the lamplight. "Talk to us like humans, and I'll be able to tell you."

Gyles shifted uncomfortably.

"You misunderstand your position," the voice replied. "Answer our questions if you want to live."

Santana gave a small nod. "I think it's you who misunderstands *your* position. See, the moment you switched on that light, I triggered a device that is now slowly leaking a poisonous toxin into the room. First, it will affect my friend here." She turned to face her companion. "Sorry, Gyles."

Gyles' eyes widened.

"Next," Santana continued, "it will work its way toward you. Hell, it may even already be on its way. Just give it thirty seconds or so, and you'll begin to drop like…"

A thud came from beside her. Gyles dropped to the floor, eyes peeled open, head smacking the stone.

"Right on schedule," Santana announced.

The atmosphere shifted in the room. The bodies behind the light shuffled, a sudden urgency roiling unspoken across the group. The bald man stood behind the lamp, his stature not what Santana expected. He was short and thin, his head almost too big for his body. "You bullshit!" he announced, anger and panic clear in his tone.

Santana shrugged. "Test it, if you like." She glanced at her pocket, where a dark patch was growing. "Gas turns to liquid, but what leaks out will spread across the room." She stared at where she imagined the man's eyes to be, ignoring the pain cast by the intensity of the light.

"Did you know the blue-ringed octopus grows to only twenty centimeters in length, but its toxin is at least a thousand times more deadly than cyanide?" She shook her head. The panic among the group grew. "It's powerful for so little a creature, able to paralyze a human and close off all their bodily functions. Death is painful. Death comes quick. The victim remains aware of themselves as their body shuts down. It's all rather agonizing."

One person behind the lamp gave a strangled cough, then another. Before long, they were all coughing and struggling for breath.

The balding man swept aside the lamp with one hand, the light extinguishing as the glass bulb smashed. He grabbed Santana by the collar. "What did you do?"

Santana remained unfazed. "It's a medical marvel. Until last year, there was no cure for the octopus' paralysis. Once infected, the victim would die, no stopping it." She drew a long breath. The man's hands shook as they gripped her. "Now there's a cure. Imagine that, eh? I took it earlier today for such an occasion. My friend, here…no such luck."

The man's grip weakened. "Fix us."

Santana brought her hand out of her pocket, holding up a small vial that he couldn't see. "Science is amazing, isn't it? To have connections with powerful people who can concentrate the toxin into gaseous form? Well, if we can dispense the poison that way, we can with the antidote too."

She took her phone from the other pocket and activated the flashlight. Her face appeared in the dark, ghoulish and harsh. "I'll help you if you help us."

"Anything," the man gasped, slipping down her body, knees buckling. "Anything you want."

"Okay," Santana replied. "I'll hold you to that. I have more where this came from."

With a triumphant throw, she smashed the vial on the floor. The room filled with a strange mix of sweet and sour scents, honey and vinegar. She cast her flashlight around the room, bringing the others into view, delighting in turning the tables on their captors.

As the smell worked its way through the room and the others greedily inhaled its odor, Santana made her way to the wall by the door. She flicked on the overhead lights, the large fluorescent strips pulsating before finally kicking in.

The scene was chaotic. At least ten strangers huddled together in the center of the room, taking huge lungfuls of the gas, fighting each other to be the one saved from the toxin. Gyles pushed himself to his knees, drawing back from the group.

The bald man took a large inhalation, then rose to his feet. He wiped his hands down his front, straightening his clothes. He wore a navy boiler suit with frayed patches at the elbows. Mark was among the huddled group in the corner.

Santana exchanged a look with Gyles. There was a red welt on his head and a concerned look in his eyes.

The bald man glared at Santana. She offered a pleasant smile and held up a vial filled with blue smoke. "Let's try this again, shall we?"

CHAPTER NINE

When the others eventually picked themselves off the floor, the bald man directed them to take Santana and Gyles somewhere a little more hospitable.

They walked along the hallway, the overhead lights now activated to show their way. The walls around them were black stone tiles, and the overhead lights were naked bulbs on cords. They passed stairwells that led deeper beneath the ground, and only once did they come across a shaft where natural daylight was allowed to sift into the place through a long rectangular chimney capped with a thick block of glass. A glimpse gave a view of the underside of a canopy of leaves.

When they approached a large black door with a golden plaque on its front that read, "CEO," the bald man unlocked the door and entered the room. He told all the others besides Mark to stay back while he dealt with Santana and Gyles.

Mark entered after Santana and Gyles, then closed the door behind him. The tension was thick. The office was well-lit with flame-inspired sconces on the walls. A large wooden desk occupied the center of the room, although its surface was scratched and the polish faded.

"What do you want?" the bald man asked.

"Your name would be a great start," Santana offered. Gyles remained silent beside her, eyes downcast.

The man's face soured. "Adam."

Santana nodded, waiting for more, but it didn't come.

"Well, Adam, we've been sent here by a mutual contact, and we need your help." She held his gaze, his lip curled.

"You enter our quarters, try to kill my people, and you expect us to help you willingly?" Adam scoffed. "State your purpose so I can decide whether or not to let you free."

Santana rolled her eyes, then held up the vial once more.

Adam grumbled.

Santana took a chair from the other side of the desk and sat. She fished inside her pocket and took out the glass vial with the hair inside. "I have recently come into possession of this. I need to identify what it's from."

"You're a cop?" Adam asked.

"No," Santana replied. "A concerned citizen."

She rolled the hair across the table. Adam reluctantly picked it up and examined it. "You mean *who* this is from?"

"No," Santana replied. "*What* it's from. That's from a creature, and I need to identify it."

Adam shifted in his chair, leaning back and lacing his fingers across his chest. "You've gone through all this trouble to find out what animal species a hair belongs to?" He nodded at the vial. "It's obvious, isn't it? A jaguar or leopard. A spotty yellow cat. Done. You can go now."

Santana leaned forward, sensing something else behind his eyes. "You might be bitter about your circumstances, but I can tell there's more here. You deal with DNA sequencing. Your organization didn't hide this place from the public for no reason. You have an operation going on, and you can either help us on our way, or I can find a way to take what I need without you." She narrowed her eyes. "What's it going to be?"

Adam smiled, although it was uncertain. "You have no idea what you're talking about."

"As your people were guiding us in the dark, we passed several experimental laboratory rooms," Santana explained. "I noticed UV lights, terrariums, and several animal enclosures. Granted, I didn't get a look at your species." She held up her blue vial. "You understood the nature of the blue-ringed octopus venom before I explained its consequences, the fear in your eyes telling me everything I needed to know."

She looked at a nearby bookcase, the shelves overstuffed with books of all shapes and sizes. "You have dozens of books on ancient and extinct creatures, as well as medical journals on DNA, RNA, enzymes, and more. There are even trinkets and idols of prehistoric bones and fossil samples decorating this place." She laughed. "It couldn't be any more obvious."

"I'm merely a fan," Adam stated.

"And your name...Adam?" She laughed now, enjoying the curious look in Gyles' eyes as she continued. "Adam and Eve? God's first creation?"

"It's my name." Adam shuffled uncomfortably.

"No," Santana countered. "It's not." She leaned down, then tossed the item she picked off the floor onto the desk. The long, triangular object was engraved with the legend, "Toby Bastille, CEO."

"For a smart man," Santana continued, "you're shit at lying."

Toby smirked, clearly impressed. "Nice work. I didn't know you were both detective and infiltrator." He sat forward again, all pretense dropped. "So you're here to use our equipment? To sequence the creature you hold in that vial?"

"Is that a possibility?" Santana asked.

Toby considered this for a long moment. His eyes flashed to Mark in the corner, sitting silently and watching the whole exchange. "The problem I have, Miss Sokolov, is that I don't work well under threat. We brought you deeper into our base of operations after you forced your way inside, and now you expect us to help. Even with your bottles of toxins, I don't know that I can allow this. It'll send a particular message to my people."

"Okay, first off…" Santana began.

Gyles interrupted. "Where is 'here?' What is this place?"

Toby's eyebrow raised. "You force your way inside, and you don't even know what we do?"

They both remained silent.

Toby chuckled. "Wow, this is a turn up for the books." He rose from his desk and walked over to the bookshelf. After a moment, he conceded. "We are the Clone Kings. An underground operation specializing in the revival and thrival of creatures and species that deserve life but were forced into extinction by humans."

Gyles scoffed. When Toby glared at him, he put a hand over his mouth.

"Problem?" Toby asked.

Gyles removed his hand. "Clone Kings? Thrival? Sounds like a kid's anime series. You couldn't have come up with anything better than that?"

Toby wasn't impressed. Santana had to fight to hide her amusement.

"It's our mission to restore the world to its former glory," Toby continued, pushing past the interruption. "Deep in this underground base, we run an operation that costs billions, all with the sole intention of revival. Do you think it's fair that we wiped the dodo from the planet? Is it fair that the white tiger, the woolly mammoth, the quagga, all of these creatures are no longer permitted to live?"

"It depends who you ask," Santana replied. "Some believe that it's the way of nature. Old gives way to new. The woolly mammoth was born of the Ice Age and died with the end of the era."

Toby frowned. "Which side do you fall on?"

"I fall on the side of nature," Santana replied. "All of this gene sequencing and modification of the world's natural building blocks…it doesn't interest me. The world out there is beautiful. Let's enjoy it for what it is."

"And deforestation? Mining? The destruction of the world's natural habitats?" Toby pressed.

Santana straightened in her chair. "I believe that humans can do more to prevent habitat destruction. But…" She considered her response. "What we're talking about here is playing God."

Toby grinned. "We call it 'Playing Adam.'"

Gyles scoffed.

Toby glared.

"Whatever you call it," Santana continued, "that's not the point of why we're here. You have equipment we need. Can we use it?"

Toby fell into thought, struggling with the dilemma in his head.

"Still comes the question," Toby stated, "why help a pair who forced their way in intending to kill us?"

Santana rolled her eyes. "I never planned to kill you."

"You unleashed a deadly toxin among my people." Toby's voice raised. "You nearly killed one of your own."

Gyles gave Santana a "he's right" look.

"You want the truth?" Santana held up the vial with blue gas and unscrewed the top. The gas leaked out, disappearing into the air until it was undetectable. Mark, Gyles, and Toby pushed themselves back, fear in their eyes.

"What are you doing?" Toby roared.

Santana tipped the vial upside-down. "It's only animal pheromones."

The fear in Toby's eyes faded. "Animal pheromones?"

Santana nodded. "It was all a ploy, a ruse."

"How's that possible?" Gyles asked. "I passed out."

"Yeah, you passed out from fear," Santana stated. "Right on

time, might I add." She nodded at Toby. "It's amazing what the human mind will do under a perceived threat. Tell someone they're getting ill, and they'll immediately notice symptoms. All I needed to do was convince a few of your guys that they were about to seize up, and their minds did the rest of the work. Even you…" She tilted her head. "You fell for it, too."

"There was no toxin?" Mark asked.

"No." Santana slipped the vial back into her pocket. "I would never hurt an ally of mine." She looked at Gyles. "You were safe all along. If there were ever any chance of me poisoning the room, you'd be first to know."

She chuckled. "I mean, I *could* do it. I know people. I *am* equipped." She took out a separate vial that looked empty. "The blue color of the last one added extra depth, don't you think?"

The men looked at each other uncertainly. Toby walked toward Santana. He stopped beside her, looming over her, eyes dark. After a moment, he strode to the door, stopping with his hand on the knob. "Follow me, Miss Sokolov. Let's get to the sequencing."

"Boss?" Mark asked.

Toby held up a hand with a grin. He met Santana's gaze. "As fucked up as all of that was, I have to hand it to her. The bitch knows what she's doing." He opened the door. Those who were waiting outside stepped back, lining the walls. "After you, Santana."

Santana rose from her chair, taking the vial in her hand. She crossed to Toby and passed into the corridor with Gyles and Mark in tow.

CHAPTER TEN

The facility was impressive to behold. Once they'd crossed through the initial façade of darkened rooms and small laboratories, the place only grew more and more intriguing.

They went down several sets of stairs, the rooms growing bigger around them. Activity bustled, strange smells and sounds reaching their ears. People talked, machines *beeped* and blared, and on a few occasions, they heard squawks and roars and yowls.

It seemed that they'd dedicated each floor to the study of a particular type of animal. They passed through exhibits and labs dealing with lizards, then insects, before moving on to amphibians. Santana had to hold herself back from taking her time to ask questions about the multitude of creatures kept in the lab. Frogs, dragonflies, tarantulas, and Komodo dragons caught her eye.

Glass cases were stacked against the walls for some animals, while entire rooms had become makeshift exhibits for the larger ones. The next floor contained several birds, large and small. Finally, they made it to the mammalian level, where the earthy stink of creatures met their nostrils, and the atmosphere turned humid.

The expanse of rooms was alarming. There was no natural sunlight this far down, but several light setups simulated daylight. Toby nodded at workers as they passed. It wasn't until they passed a young blonde woman sitting at a computer desk, her head inches from the screen as she processed the reams of graphical data presented to her, that Santana allowed herself to stop.

A sign on the desk read, "Therese."

"*You're* Therese?" Santana asked.

The woman looked up from her examination. "I am." She turned uncertainly to Toby.

Santana pointed at Gyles. "He's Kealan's brother."

Therese looked dumbfounded. She held up a thumb. "Cool."

"Hi," Gyles offered with flushed cheeks.

"Hi," she repeated.

Santana extended her hand and shook Therese's. She mouthed, "He's single."

Toby marched them onward.

"What was that?" Gyles whispered as they snaked through more desks in the cluttered space. Somewhere in a room nearby came the whinny of a horse.

"Pretty little thing, don't you think?" Santana grinned.

Gyles didn't answer.

Soon the vast electric hum of machinery replaced the chatter of animals. Toby took them into a room that stretched out ahead of them, packed with boxy servers in neat rows. Lights blinked on each unit.

Along the edge of the room was a long desk, harshly lit by screens. Toby crossed to a large man whose muffin top spilled over his waistband and clapped a hand on his shoulder.

"Shouldn't you be working?" He grinned.

The man was a sitting stereotype. Fast-food and snack wrappers cluttered his desk. In one hand, he held a soda cup that was far too big for a modern consumer, and there were patches beneath his armpits that emitted a questionable scent.

He nudged his glasses up his nose with the tip of his finger, then spun to greet them. "I'm always working, boss. You know this."

Toby looked at the others. "I can't get this one to stop. Loyal and more intelligent than anyone should be. Dex, this is Santana Sokolov and Gyles Forde, two new friends of ours."

Dex eyed them suspiciously. "We don't make friends."

"We can make exceptions." Toby chuckled. "Plus, I think you'll like what they're putting down."

"It can't be better than this." He smashed his chubby fingers against the stained keyboard, eyes turning to the screen. The monitor was the size of a car door, angled down from the wall to face him. Dex clicked away from an application that looked way too complicated for Santana's liking before bringing up strings of code.

He tapped for a moment, talking to the computer in a language that Santana didn't understand. When he finished, he triumphantly bashed the "Enter" key.

The windows minimized, replaced instead with what appeared to be a profile screen, not all that dissimilar to how Santana had seen criminal profiles in movies. An image showed on the left, with a set of statistics and figures on the right. Only, it wasn't a human pictured on the screen.

"Son of a bitch..." Toby muttered.

The image displayed a lizard-like thing. It was small, with a splatter of red and black coloring across its skin. Yellow lids encased black eyes. The creature's skin was slimy and glistening.

"They've only gone and fucking done it," Dex announced. He gave a disbelieving laugh. "The Yunnan Lake newt. Back from the fucking dead."

Toby shook his head, a mixture of marvel and irritation in his eyes. "Damn...When was the last reported sighting?"

"1979." Dex looked at the others. "A newt from China. Driven to extinction from human overpopulation and destruction of their habitat." He shook his head. "Beautiful little thing, isn't she?"

"Incredible," Toby breathed.

Gyles stepped closer to the screen, his interest piqued. "You're telling me you guys have brought this thing back from extinction? How?"

Dex took off his glasses and polished the lenses on his shirt. "Great effort. To bring a creature back from extinction is, as I'm sure you can appreciate, a fiddly endeavor. It's like trying to complete a ten-thousand-piece jigsaw without all the pieces. You have to take what you can get. Find samples. Scrape necrotic skin tissue off taxidermied beasts. Try to find any semblance of tissue or cells that remain in the world."

"If that fails," Toby continued, "you have to go to their cousins."

"Cousins?" Gyles' brow creased. "I'm not sure I understand."

"It's pretty simple, really." Dex returned his glasses to his face and made his button eyes return to normal size. "Every living species on this planet evolved from something that is now gone. When a creature evolves, it leaves behind a signature, a ledger of its former coding that we, as bioengineers, can decode and hack. For example, did you know that humans have a tail bone?"

Santana nodded. Gyles shook his head.

"It's a remnant from our ancestors," Dex informed him. "Thousands of years ago, our primitive forebears sported a tail. As years passed and the need for the tail diminished, the tail bone tucked in on itself and no longer protruded on a human body. However, the tail *bone* remains. Legacy. It's all about what gets left behind."

"In the coding of all creatures are commonalities," Toby carried on. "To revive a creature like the Yunnan Lake newt, one simply needs enough of the original coding to start the process, then the rest of the gaps are filled in with its closest living relatives. Luckily for us, there are still a plethora of newt species living in China who derived from the same mother genus."

He laced his fingers behind his back. "It's all quite simple, really."

"Sounds it," Gyles offered sarcastically.

"Congratulations," Santana offered, reaching inside her jacket to find the unidentified hair.

"Oh, it's not ours," Dex stated. "We didn't revive it."

Santana frowned.

Toby stepped toward the monitor, pointing at a series of numbers in the bottom right-hand corner. "This is the IP address of another underground cloning group. The system that we use to decode and run the sequences sits on a shared server network."

"Meaning?" Santana asked.

Dex looked at her as though it was the simplest thing in the world. "Meaning that most, not all, groups who specialize in cloning to revive the extinct creatures of this planet all run on a shared piece of software. It's top of the line. The best of the best. None of our programmers could've created such a magnificent system."

"It does mean that it automatically shares any new findings across the network," Toby clarified. "This number can be traced back to a specific group, somewhere across the globe. That way, we're almost working together in working apart, and we can all keep abreast of the progress made around the world."

Santana ran her fingers through her hair. "I bet the ICG *loves* that."

Toby smirked. "That's the greatest thing about *this* particular piece of kit. The ICG is one of the only groups not able to access it. A security team somewhere in Atlantica is dedicated solely to ensuring that no leaks happen, and no staff or individuals affiliated with the International Cloning Group get their hands on it."

"What would happen if they did?" Gyles asked.

Dex gave Gyles another questioning look. "The whole operation dies. The ICG benefits from our *years* of research and strips all that we've worked to complete."

Gyles returned a blank look.

"International law binds the ICG," Toby informed him. "The global system has its eyes on them, and they're the public face of what we all do. Only, they have restrictions. They have rules. They have consequences for breaking those rules. They're only allowed to revive one of each species. That's not what we want to do. We want to reintroduce fleets of species back into the wild. Return them to their natural homes."

"So who brought back the newt?" Santana pressed.

Dex swiveled his chair to face the computer. He peered closely at the screen, concentrating on the numbers. After copying the digits into another portal, he announced, "The Extinction Revival Network of Intrepid Entrepreneurs."

Santana burst into laughter.

Dex and Toby gave her a strange look.

"You're kidding? You don't see it?"

Toby held her gaze.

"E.R.N.I.E.?" She laughed again. "Ernie? What's next? A group named after Bert?"

Toby raised his eyebrows, seemingly only now realizing the hilarity himself. He grinned. "I'd never considered that."

Dex rolled his eyes. "Children."

"I'm not the one who named my reviving group after a puppet on a kid's show," Santana stated.

"Who are they?" Gyles tried to hide his smile.

Toby cocked his head. "The Extinction Revival Network are… well…they're the same as us…only…"

"More guns," Dex stated sadly. "They have a reputation for sticking their noses into other people's business and claiming what isn't rightfully theirs. The organization shares the same basic values as us. Only their approach is more…"

"Explosive," Toby finished.

Santana nodded thoughtfully. "Given that your idea of a welcome is to interrogate and threaten *us* with death, if you think these guys are explosive, I'm imagining that's pretty bad news."

Toby nodded. "A few groups have disbanded or faded from existence after they've successfully brought back a new species. The Extinction…I mean, Ernie…they miraculously seem to possess the data only a few weeks later."

"Too much of a coincidence?" Santana asked.

Dex nodded.

"Well, whoever they are," Santana started, "they're probably going to like what we've found here." She offered the vial to Dex.

Dex took it, eyes narrowing on the hair inside the glass. "What's this?"

"That's what we want to find out," Santana replied.

Dex looked at Toby. Toby gave an approving nod. Dex shrugged, then turned back to the system in front of him. With a trained shove, he propelled himself along the desk on his wheeled chair until he came to a machine that looked like an instant coffee maker. He unscrewed the lid of the vial, then found a pair of tweezers. Deftly, he plucked out the hair, then placed it into the receptacle in the machine.

"Regular or decaf?" Toby quipped.

Santana didn't laugh. She moved closer to the machine, intrigue taking her. The machine's lights illuminated, a *whirring* coming from it as it took the hair inside. A small screen lit up, and a progress bar appeared. It was designed to look like a spinning strand of DNA, the full thread in black and white, slowly turning to color as the machine worked its magic.

Dex propelled himself back to the computer. He tapped several keys in a rapid sequence, then shoved himself back to the machine.

After a minute or so, the device gave a confirming *bleep*, then shut off. He opened the receptacle and carefully returned the hair to the vial. He handed it back to Santana, then returned to the computer.

Santana followed him, eyes glued to the monitor. Strings of code appeared on the screen, but not like the computer code she'd seen before. This one held millions of combinations of the same four letters—G, C, A, and T.

"The building blocks of life," Santana marveled, remembering these from her biology classes.

"Guanine, cytosine, adenine, and thymine," Dex muttered, uninterested. "All biological makeup is comprised of variations of these four letters."

"Incredible," Gyles breathed.

Dex worked the keyboard, fingers dancing manically over its clackety surface. The letters continued to scroll, millions upon millions of lines of code. After a few moments, the computer took over, with certain strings beginning to highlight themselves.

In a small window to the right, select sequences were extracted, creating a code of its own. A few more moments and the letters faded, replaced with images of several modern and domestic animals that Santana was familiar with.

Tigers, wolves, kangaroos, and rats spammed the screen. Every variation of mammal appeared in multicolor. She saw badgers, porcupines, whales, and grizzly bears.

"We have some kind of mammal," Dex announced.

Toby watched the screen with unblinking eyes.

The creatures became more refined as the process continued and certain genus species dropped. The creatures all became quadrupedal, arched backs hunching. Tails protruded, and creatures with snouts populated the screen.

Then they regressed into their more primitive forms, taking forms that surprised Santana and caught her off-guard.

"Not a cat?" Santana muttered, surprised at the evolution taking place on the screen. The creatures became more primal, moving away from the likeness of a cat and into something Santana hadn't expected.

Santana laid a hand on Dex's shoulder.

"Easy now..." Dex cooed. "We're getting there." Something flashed red on the screen. "We're beginning to zero in on data that is scarce and limited. This is the part where the computer homes in, begins to make its best guesses at what we might've found."

"What *I* found," Santana corrected, twisting the truth slightly.

"Exactly," Dex replied breathily.

The images scrolled on by, a picture of their target coalescing on the screen. A 3D model appeared, rotating and shifting shape as fur and skull shape and tail and spine became more defined. After a final moment, the animal appeared.

"Well...there you go," Toby muttered, eyes wide with amazement.

"There you go..." Santana breathed.

Dex sat back, lacing his hands behind his head.

They were silent for a moment.

Gyles looked between the others. "What the hell is it?"

"A Thylacoleo carnifex." Toby pointed at the Latin name appearing on the screen beneath the rotating model. "A marsupial lion."

The lion was a strange thing to see. It didn't look much like a cat, but more like a cross between a bear, a dog, and a monkey. Its fur was dark brown with patches of blonde spots, and its paws looked designed to grip and climb. A long tail swished behind the creature as the AI began to animate what it was processing.

"Seems a strange cat to me," Gyles announced.

Santana agreed. "It's not a cat, is it?"

Dex shook his head. "No. According to this system, the marsupial lion is in no way related to a modern lion. It's a marsupial. See this pouch here? That's where it would keep its young." A broad smile spread across his face. "This is amazing. It's believed that the last living marsupial lion died over thirty thousand years ago. Can you believe what you've stumbled across?"

Santana's breath caught. A marsupial lion? Living? In Atlantica?

Toby matched Dex's grin. "This is incredible. This might be one of the oldest species ever to have been revived." He peered closer to the screen. "Look at the biology…it's a ninety-nine percent match on the original DNA coding found in the fossilized remains of the creature. And now *we* have the source DNA."

Santana narrowed her eyes at Toby. "Excuse me?"

"With the hair's analysis in the system, we have all the information we need to create our own, should we wish." Toby's eyes were hungry. "We can bring back this genus and show the world what they've been missing out on."

"Great idea," Gyles replied sarcastically. "It's not like the first living example isn't already out there killing people as we speak."

Toby's head whirled to Gyles. "Excuse me?"

Santana met his gaze.

"Nothing," Gyles replied quickly.

Santana tried to switch gears, not thinking about how irresponsible it would be to introduce more of these creatures into the wild. "Who were the lion's original revivers?" Her eyes moved to the series of numbers at the bottom of the screen.

Dex ran a scan. "A group by the name of…Kobra."

"Kobra?" Santana asked.

"That's all I've got for you." Dex sat back, gaze returning to the lion.

"You don't know them?" Santana asked.

Toby shook his head. "Unfortunately, we don't get all the information from the network. Despite the utility of this program, we still protect each other's privacy. Well…as best we can. That doesn't mean some hackers still don't get through."

Santana examined the hair in the vial. Now that she knew

better, the notion that it could've been a cat faded from her mind. The hair was too coarse and more brown than blonde. She looked back at the creature on the screen, wondering what kind of group would unleash this monster back into the world, and also…

How did they train it?

CHAPTER ELEVEN

The smell of smoke hit them the moment they walked through the door.

"That's going to be a bitch to get rid of." Gyles acknowledged the smell before Santana could comment. "I'll get it sorted."

Santana sat on the sofa and pinched her eyes. The scent was unpleasant, but she knew he was right. That kind of thing couldn't last forever.

She let her mind process all that she'd learned over the past twenty-four hours as Gyles busied himself with spraying enough air freshener to choke a rhino. He opened the windows and sprayed and sprayed until they could taste the smell of lavender on their tongues.

When he was finally satisfied, he crossed to the kitchen. "Coffee?"

Santana looked up at him. "Not going to set it on fire this time?"

"That was bacon."

Santana grinned.

"I promise." He rolled his eyes.

He busied himself in the kitchen, clattering around with mugs

80

and coffee grinds. "They were some interesting people, don't you think?"

"They were."

"I'll be honest," he offered without turning. "I didn't think we were going to get out of there in one piece. They did a real U-turn once you pulled that stunt with the toxin." He glanced over his shoulder. "That was genius, by the way." He rubbed his head. "Hurt, though."

"Sorry," Santana replied. "You have to know that I would never intentionally hurt you."

"I know." He put on the second cup, then handed the first one to Santana. "A marsupial lion." He shook his head. "Can you believe it?"

Santana took out her phone and browsed the Internet, opening several tabs containing information on the creature. "Last known to exist thirty thousand years ago…carnivorous marsupial…retractable, cat-like claws…existed in Australia…"

"Sounds like a beast," Gyles offered.

Santana nodded. "Considering the amount of damage it did to the victim, I would've expected it to be larger. This says it was barely over a meter long."

"Victim?" Gyles asked. "You saw the body?"

"I saw the crime scene," Santana replied. "And images of the carnage."

"Damn." Gyles sat beside Santana. "Sounds brutal."

"You have no idea." They drank in silence, Santana scrolling on her phone while Gyles' nose kept twitching, searching for a hint of the smell of smoke.

"Thank you," Gyles offered at last.

"What for?" Santana put the phone down, images of marsupial beasts burned into her mind.

"My first full day out," Gyles offered shyly.

Santana couldn't help but laugh. "It wasn't all as smooth-sailing as I'd hoped."

"Still." Gyles smiled. "It was good to be out again. Despite the interaction with the Clone Kings—by the way, what the hell is that for a name?—it was good. So, thank you."

"You're welcome." Santana sipped her coffee as Gyles' phone vibrated on the table.

Gyles glanced at the phone, confusion on his face. "Unknown caller? Who could that be?"

"One way to find out."

Gyles uncertainly picked the phone up and placed it to his ear. "Hello?"

A woman's voice came from the other end, although Santana couldn't make out what she said. Gyles nodded and gave cautious answers to questions that Santana couldn't hear. His cheeks flushed.

"I mean…maybe Friday?" he replied. "Okay then. Sounds good. See you then."

He put the phone down, casting a furtive glance at Santana. "What did you do?"

Santana drank her coffee, looking around nonchalantly. "Who was that?"

"Therese," Gyles replied. "Looks like someone gave her my number as they passed her in the offices earlier. She wants to meet up for a drink this Friday."

"How strange. I wonder who did that."

Gyles grinned. "Thank you…again."

"Don't thank me yet," Santana shot back. "She might be a psychotic loon. Still, only one way to find out."

Gyles gave a goofy grin, then turned on the PlayStation.

That night, Santana tossed and turned in her bed.

Her dreams were restless, each dream-like vision haunted by primitive creatures who no longer roamed the land. Growing up in a city like Atlantica, Santana had known that cloning and revival groups were springing up across the island, but she'd never given it much notice. There had always been experiments to clone sheep and rabbits and domestic creatures, but to bring about beings like this…

In her head, she was strolling along the pristine pathways of a wildlife park, pink bricks lining the way beneath her feet. Gift shops lined the way, and the smell of hot dogs and sugary snacks filled the air. She roamed around the enclosures, witnessing the impossible born to life, a *Jurassic Park* for prehistoric, non-dino creatures.

She stared at the woolly mammoths, the creatures given a large plain of ice and snow to roam. She stopped at the Smilodon's exhibit, witnessed dodos and primitive hyenas and Tasmanian tigers and more. She wandered through the insect house, surrounded by butterflies and moths and beetles that once littered the land but hadn't for thousands of years.

It was extraordinary. It was humbling. It was *real*.

In her dream she flashed between exhibits, looking through the glass of fish tanks, standing on balconies and overseeing replicas of tundra and Serengeti and more.

Then she was at an enclosure that stood empty.

Trees populated the inside, barring a good view of whatever lived behind the bars. The trunks were scratched with huge gory scars, sap bleeding down its length. On the floor were bones littered with scraps of meat still clinging to them.

A howl erupted, prickling her skin. Sweat clung to her back. She looked around, finding that she was the only one looking into the exhibit. The park around her was empty. The wind dropped. All was quiet.

She looked back to the trees to find large yellow eyes staring at her through the leaves. They were trained on her from a distance, a gap of twenty feet enough to deter any creature from leaping at her and attacking.

But it didn't. The branch bowed as the creature sprang off. It soared toward her, exposing its packed, muscular body. Santana stepped back, reaching for her bullwhip, but it wasn't there.

The creature fell short by inches. Santana only had a moment of relief before its claws gripped the bars and it continued its ascent. Paws gripped the top bars like hands, and the creature drew itself up, poised on the metal rail, saliva pooling on its lips.

The creature's musty smell caused her nose to wrinkle. She stepped back, slowly becoming aware that this was all a dream, that it couldn't be real.

Then the creature jumped at her, paws pressing against her chest. She felt the weight of it in her sleep as it pushed her back and rested atop her.

Her eyelids fluttered.

She opened her eyes to a darkened bedroom.

And a weighty pressure on her chest.

The weight bore down on her. A foul reek stung her nostrils.

Santana looked down into the glinting eyes of a beast on her chest. A low rumbling growl emitted from its throat, four paws pressing on her.

"Fuck…" she whispered, mind already working on her attack.

The creature sniffed her face, coarse whiskers tickling her cheek. She slowly fanned her arms out on either side, careful not to make any sudden movements. The beast was playing, biding its time, assessing its prey.

It hadn't met Santana Sokolov before.

"Easy now, friend…" Santana cooed, arms spread wide. She opened her fingers, then flexed them on her bedsheets. "You don't want to do something you'll regret now."

The beast drew its head back, a snarl escaping its throat. Santana drew a long breath, then counted to three.

One.

Two.

Three!

In one fluid movement, she clapped her hands together, dragging the bedsheet with her. The creature flinched, claws puncturing the material as Santana enshrouded it in cloth. She pulled tight, knowing that her best bet in this situation was to restrict its movement before it could do any damage.

She pulled her arms and the sheet toward her, dragging the beast into a strange embrace. The creature protested, fighting against her. It was strong. Loud claps accompanied its snapping jaws as it wriggled and writhed like a dog trying to escape a tunnel it had found itself stuck in.

Santana squeezed for dear life, muscles like knotted rope as she brought her legs into the fray, holding the creature firmly still. It chomped at her, teeth sinking into her shoulder. She let out a pained cry as the beast rocked her across the bed and onto the floor.

She *thumped* down onto the hardwood, still holding tight. Her bedroom door swung open, and the main light switched on. Gyles appeared, his expression aghast as he tried to process what he was seeing.

"A little help," Santana cried, spotting the splotches of blood on her white sheets.

Gyles nodded, running toward her. He threw himself on the beast, squishing Santana beneath his stomach and eliciting a pained yowl from the creature. Together they held it tight, managing to reduce its movements.

Still, the creature fought. It pulled its teeth from Santana's shoulder, then turned its head to Gyles, trying to snap at the being who was crushing its back.

"My tranq gun!" Santana shouted. "Get my tranq gun."

"From where?" Gyles asked.

"Under my pillow," Santana replied, voice strained. "Next to my pistol."

"You have *two* guns in bed with you?" Gyles asked.

"Just get it!" Santana returned.

For a moment, Gyles remained holding the beast, debating whether it would be a good idea to let go. When Santana barked at him again, he jumped up and fished the two guns from beneath her pillow. He threw the pistol on the sheets, then turned the tranq gun on the creature.

A muted report accompanied the dart's expulsion. He fired twice, then three times before Santana called for him to stop. He waited, chest rising and falling with exertion, both of them holding their position as the creature first increased its fervor, then slowly began to quiet.

After a few weak flails of its paws, it finally stilled, coming to rest against Santana's chest like a baby drawn to its mother's bosom.

For a moment they were still. Santana groaned as blood trickled from her shoulder. Gyles offered her a hand. Santana ensured the beast was unconscious before rolling it off her and getting to her feet.

"You okay?" Gyles looked concerned as he stared at her shoulder.

"I've had better wake-ups. I've also had worse."

They both looked down at the creature, neither one ready to announce the reality of what they faced. It was there now, in full color, the being from the computer monitor lying asleep on Santana's bedroom floor.

"It's a thyloneum carnivore," Gyles stated.

Santana chuckled, the laughter quickly turning to a hiss as a throb of pain shot from her shoulder. "Thylacoleo carnifex."

"That's what I said," Gyles offered. "How do you think it got in?"

The question hit Santana hard. How had the creature got in? True, she always left the living room balcony doors wide open.

Still, any entrance through there should've triggered her booby traps. Plus, her bedroom door had been closed.

She crossed to the balcony and looked down toward the city. She couldn't see the ground level—a steady mist barred her view —but a thought hit her. At the crime scene she'd visited, hadn't the creature been taken back in by its owners?

She barked an instruction for Gyles to keep an eye on the lion, telling him to shoot it in the head with the pistol if necessary as she tore from the apartment and sprinted downstairs.

She took the stairs two at a time, her footsteps echoing down the stairwell. As she reached the ground level, she raced out the front of her apartment building.

A car idled at the end of her street with its headlights dimmed. The moment she appeared, the headlights sprang to full beam. The engine revved and wheels skidded as the vehicle pulled out from its parking spot and sped up the street.

Santana looked for a license plate number, but the space was blank.

CHAPTER TWELVE

Santana couldn't help but smile at the situation she returned to.

The lion was still asleep, curled up in its makeshift bedsheet cocoon. Gyles stood against the far wall with as much distance as he could put between the two, pistol extended in both hands and pointing directly at the creature's head.

"No sign of movement?" Santana asked.

Gyles shook his head. "Did you find anything outside?"

Santana told him about the car.

"Quick to take off?" He shifted his shoulders and grimaced. "Sounds like guilt to me."

Santana walked toward the beast and crouched beside it. Its chest rose and fell slowly, more slowly than she imagined it should. "You might've gone overboard with the tranquilizers."

"I'd rather that than the motherfucking thing still chomping on your shoulder." He took a step forward, relaxing slightly. "How is it?"

"Painful," Santana admitted. "Let's take care of this thing before we take care of me." She glanced around the room. "We need to bind it, ensure it doesn't attack again. Then we need to call in some authorities to take care of it."

"Bind it with what?" Gyles asked. "That maw looks like it could chomp through steel."

Santana nodded. "I wouldn't doubt that. One of the websites I read said it has the strongest bite of any mammalian species, comparable to that of a two-hundred-and-fifty-kilo African lion. That's one hell of a chomp."

"So what do we do?" Gyles asked.

Santana left Gyles to watch the creature as she headed to her store cupboard at the back of the living room. Inside was a mass of coils and ropes and various bottles and tankards she used for her expeditions. She found the strongest rope she had—towing rope that could pull a semi-truck along the road—and brought it back to the bedroom.

Working quickly but remaining careful of the creature's limbs, she snaked the rope around the lion's body, ensuring that she also worked the bonds around its jaws. After several loops and knots, she sat back and examined her work.

It looked ridiculous, the bright yellow rope holding the creature in place. It would stop the lion from walking and running, but she doubted it would do much for its mouth. If it could use its mouth, it could also bark and screech and howl.

"I need to make a call." Santana left the room once more.

She called in a favor from an old friend, skipping past the pleasantries and getting straight to the point. She needed this animal gone from her apartment. She needed it protected and looked after. She needed someone who wouldn't prioritize profit over decency, and that left her with limited options.

After the fourth ring, Sandra Reynolds picked up the phone. Santana confirmed that her team would come to Santana's apartment for collection. Then she hung up.

She returned to the bedroom.

Gyles met her with a pitiful expression. "Can we clean you up now?"

Santana glanced down at her shoulder. The blood was already clotting, although her sleeping vest was a mess. "Sure."

The mess was easy enough to clean up. Santana hissed as Gyles applied antiseptic and dabbed at the worst of it. She knew she needed stitches, and after some convincing, Gyles pulled the needle and thread across the worst wounds.

When the knock came on her door, Santana was relieved to allow strangers into her apartment.

"We're here for the animal," a tall man with a crop of blond hair declared in a monotonous voice.

"This way," Santana stated.

They dragged in a cage with bars so thick that she doubted even the lion could escape. When they fixed their eyes on the beast, they looked among each other, impressed with the find they were about to take back to their boss. They closed the lion in the cage. Before they set off, Santana allowed herself one last look at the creature.

It slept soundly, eyes fluttering as it dreamed. Now that the threat of danger was over and her shoulder attended to, Santana allowed herself a moment to appreciate what sat before her. A creature that had long since died out on Earth, here, in her apartment. She was among the first humans to witness this majestic beast from this close in thirty thousand years.

The weight of it all fell on her shoulders. She was humbled, awed, and amazed by the wonders of science.

Then the lion was gone. She waved the team off at the door and shut it behind her. With that done, she pressed her back to the door, then slid down onto her ass as a spike of pain shot through her shoulder.

Gyles handed her some water and painkillers before attending to her room and stripping the blood-soaked sheets from her bed.

Light poured into the apartment as Santana slept on the couch.

There was no dreaming this time around, only a deep, uninterrupted slumber. Gyles sat with his back to the arm of the couch, head lolled back, mouth open and catching flies. His head shifted to the side before dropping and startling him into consciousness.

"Hmmm?" he asked the room. He turned and smiled at Santana. Her eyes fluttered as she drifted to wakefulness.

She sat up sharply. A small string of dribble had pooled at the side of her mouth. She wiped it off, then turned to the balcony doors. "Morning?" she said uncertainly. "What time is it?"

"No idea," Gyles replied. He glanced at his phone. "A little after eleven."

"Holy shit…" Santana stretched out her arms. "I had the craziest dream last night." As her muscles drew taut, a hot spike flashed from her shoulder. She looked down at the bandages. "Okay, maybe not a dream."

Gyles gave a hollow chuckle. "Kinda seems impossible thinking back on it, doesn't it?"

Santana shook her head. "Nothing is impossible in Atlantica."

They slowly got ready for the day. Santana cleaned up in the shower while being careful with her wound. Gyles made another attempt at breakfast, and this time didn't burn the place down.

They ate together on the sofa, lost in thoughts of lions and extinct creatures. When they finished, Santana set the plates aside and shrugged on her jacket.

"Where are you going?" Gyles asked.

Santana checked her pockets, ensuring she had everything she needed. "I need to find out who the fuck those guys were last night."

"How are you going to do that?" Gyles asked. "You said the car didn't have a license plate."

Santana considered this. "Honestly, it's a long shot. I have a friend who might be able to help me zero in on the perpetrators."

"Of course you do." Gyles grinned. "Go get them, tiger."

"*Lion,*" Santana corrected with a smile. "You be careful today. Don't do anything I wouldn't do."

"That leaves me with a *lot* of options," Gyles shot back.

Santana stepped out of the cab and looked across the long green to the AJS station.

The place was a hive of activity. Officers in blue uniforms strolled in and out of the open front doors, the hexagonal shimmer on their high-tech all-in-ones winking at her. Men and women from all walks of life populated the space, some more distressed than others.

She made the long walk down the neat path and entered a large reception area, ignoring the stares from some of the officers as she went. Santana knew she stuck out like a sore thumb, but she didn't care. Not only was she comfortable dressed for adventuring in the jungle, but the practical benefits alone outweighed any reason to dress more like a standard civilian of Atlantica.

She stopped at the reception desk where a young woman sat focused on her computer screen. She tapped away, lazily chewing a piece of gum. A thick sheet of bulletproof glass separated them.

"Hi," Santana offered.

The woman waited a moment before slowly pulling her gaze from the screen. "Hi. Can I help you?"

"I'm looking for Terra Kris," Santana replied. "Is she available today?"

At the mention of Terra's name, the woman grew more alert. "I'm sorry, miss, but you can't request a visit with one of our officers unless you already have an existing appointment."

"I need to speak to her real quick," Santana pressed. "I'm an old friend."

"If you have a problem, miss," the woman insisted. "You'll have to go through our regular channels. I'm sure you can appreciate that our officers are busy people. There's a lot that needs attending to out there."

"Honestly," Santana stated, "It's only a small—"

"Sokolov!" a familiar voice called.

Santana turned to find Terra standing at the mouth of a nearby corridor. She wore a big grin. Her electric blue uniform hugged her figure. "To what do I owe this pleasure?"

Santana gave the reception clerk a triumphant look then strolled over to Terra. The clerk narrowed her eyes, then returned her attention to the screen.

"Bit of an icy welcome," Santana offered.

Terra waved a hand. "Ignore Melissa. She's new. And working under my instructions." She reconsidered her words. "Well, mine and Corporal Black's. Come, let me show you around the place."

Terra led Santana down the hall, providing nuggets of information about the AJS precinct as she went. There were walls covered in scrap pieces of paper with notes on that Santana didn't get time to read. Several doors led off into smaller offices. After a small stretch, they came to a large, open, square room sunk into the floor. The corridor bordered it, its walls glass to allow a clear view inside.

"Welcome to the bullpen." Terra smirked, opened a door, and brought Santana inside.

"The bullpen?" Santana asked.

Terra nodded. "Not my favorite name in the place. A bit of a legacy thing that derives from how some civilians still refer to law enforcement. Think it was supposed to be an empowering thing in the beginning, then it just sorta stuck."

Desks arranged in no particular order filled the area. Coats hung from the backs of empty chairs. Computers stood with blank screens. Each workspace held personal trinkets from the families of the officers. Whether because of the hour or another reason entirely, only one lone woman occupied her desk.

Terra beelined for an empty desk at the far end of the room. On it was a single framed photograph. The picture showed an older man and woman beaming as they stared at the camera with a younger Terra wedged between them. In her hands, Terra held a wriggling dog, its picture blurry from it being unable to remain still.

"How is Skooch?" Santana remembered the last time she'd seen the pooch. It had been years ago. Santana happened to pass through Terra's neighborhood, and the pair bumped into each other. The Papillon had enthusiastically showered her with kisses. Terra was impressed that she'd taken such a liking to a stranger.

"Great." Terra threw her jacket over her shoulders and collected her bag from beneath the desk. "Still as lively as ever. Keeps Mom and Dad company when they're home. Not that it's all that much these days."

"Still nose to the grindstone?" Santana asked.

"You have no idea." Terra grinned. "Come on. Let's get out of here."

"Where are we going?"

"Somewhere more private." Terra's eyes darted to the tall, dark woman sitting across the bullpen. She raised her voice. "Some people around here aren't to be trusted. Ain't that right, Slim?"

Slim glanced at Terra, shook her head, and returned to her work.

"What did I tell you?" Terra whispered conspiratorially to Santana. "Nothing but trouble."

CHAPTER THIRTEEN

"Linoleum complex?" Terra asked, hands in her jacket pockets as she looked over the long green.

"Thylacoleo carnifex," Santana corrected. "A marsupial lion."

"Sounds horrendous," Terra replied. Santana could see her picturing the beast in her head. "Like a kangaroo with a mane? Wait…Kangaroos *are* marsupials, aren't they?"

Santana laughed. "Yes. Yes, they are."

The park spread out before them, a mixture of clusters of trees with open spaces of grass and ponds. Scattered around them was a mix of families and individuals, some picnicking on the lawn, others jogging along the numerous paths that wound around the place.

Santana had never visited New York's Central Park before, but she could see its influence on this place from a mile off. The only real difference between the two was that Atlantica's version of the landmark wore rougher edges, the place more of an afterthought by the city's mayor. Central Park's boundaries were clean and defined.

Santana took her cell phone from her pocket and showed Terra an image of the creature. In the madness of the night before, she hadn't thought of taking a picture of the living beast, but luckily the Internet was filled with semi-accurate depictions of the lost animal.

"Oh…" Terra replied in surprise. "It's nothing like I imagined."

"Me neither. It's quite cute to look at. I mean, if you strip away its menace and try not to think about its snarling jaws as it attempts to rip out your throat."

Terra turned her gaze to Santana's shoulder as Santana peeled off enough of her jacket to show the mass of bandages beneath.

"Shit…" Terra breathed. "They're on to you."

Santana nodded. "Someone is. Seems way too coincidental to have discovered the source of the hair, then have someone unleash the beast on me that same night."

She stared out at the park, the trees all shades of green. A flock of colorful birds swam on a nearby pond's surface. "It's certainly a wonder to behold…the lion, that is. But if there are people in this city bringing back killing machines from the dead, that's a real problem for you guys."

"I'll say." Terra crossed her legs beneath her. "And to have someone capable enough of training something so primitive. That's an impressive skill, indeed."

Santana nodded.

"What did you do with the lion?" Terra asked.

Santana told Terra about her contact and her collection team. "She's a good one. Probably one of the few in the city. She'll house the beast, ensure that it's looked after without exploiting its presence on this Earth for profit or gain."

Terra scoffed.

"What?" Santana asked.

"Remains to be proven," Terra replied. When she caught Santana's gaze, she added, "I've yet to meet an Atlantican who doesn't turn corrupt in some capacity in the end."

Santana chewed this over, then muttered beneath her breath. "John Chambers?"

Terra frowned. "Why is that name so familiar?"

Santana sighed. "Don't make me say it."

"Say what?" Terra asked, genuine confusion in her eyes.

"*Dick*," Santana conceded, hating herself a little for having to call the private investigator by that nickname.

"Oh!" At the realization, Terra burst into laughter. "Him."

"Wait…" Santana turned to face Terra. "You know him?"

"Yeah." Terra chuckled. "One of my biggest pains in the ass over the last few years. Dick has a heart of gold, but he pushes the boundaries." She stopped laughing and turned contemplative. "Although you might be right. He could be one of the few." A thought struck her. "Wait, how do *you* know him?"

Santana considered how much to tell Terra. Not all that long ago, Santana had been visited by a stranger and given a relic of her mother's. The pendant, the man informed her, had been left in safekeeping, waiting for the right moment to hand down to Santana. Inside the jewelry had been a picture of Santana with her mother and father, as well as a couple of loose leaves of paper with maps, markings, and instructions that didn't make any sense to her.

It had only been the next day that Santana discovered someone had murdered the man, her pendant stolen, too.

She'd hired Dick to assist her, having heard his reputation as a man who got things done. Dick had stayed true to his word and reclaimed the pendant for Santana, the piece of gold jewelry now safely tucked away in the floorboards beneath her bed. To this day, she still didn't know the trinket's significance.

All of this turned over in Santana's mind, a mixture of a late-night visit to an older woman's apartment, the name Sadie Turnberry appearing in her thoughts. Couple that with her most recent visit to the jungle in search of the Temple of the Sun, and she started to consider that she knew John "Dick" Chambers pretty well.

Though, how well did she *actually* know him?

"We've done small scraps of work together," Santana settled with, trying not to let Terra see the true extent of her thoughts.

Terra smiled. "Interesting."

"Interesting?" Santana parroted.

"Yeah…" Terra narrowed her eyes at a group of youths who wandered along the tree line, hoodies raised high, glancing around as if they were up to no good. "Dick certainly gets around."

Santana waited for Terra to continue, noticing the soft blinking light behind her eye. "Are you scanning those kids right now?"

Terra turned to Santana as if suddenly realizing she was there. "Sorry, it's become a bit of a habit. Hard not to when you've got an APRIL fixed inside your skull." She glanced back at the kids. "Not the cleanest of records, but they're not up to anything that I can detect. APRIL, keep an eye on them, please."

Santana looked at the kids, then back at Terra. "John…" she prodded.

"John?" Terra asked.

"Dick," Santana conceded once more.

Terra grinned. "You hate that, don't you?"

"That's not his name," Santana protested.

Terra shrugged. "Your name is what you call yourself. 'What's in a name?'"

"Is that Shakespeare?" Santana asked.

"Probably." Terra turned to the kids who were disappearing into the trees.

"Terra?" Santana nudged.

"Right." Terra shook her head and turned her full attention to Santana. "Dick has something of a notorious reputation among the AJS force. He's someone working on the outside. Able to get into the private quarters of others and complete a lot of the jobs that the AJS simply can't do, thanks to the island's rules. We've crossed paths *many* times over the years…"

She chuckled, thoughts turning inward. "In more ways than one."

Santana raised her eyebrows. "Have you two…"

"What?" Terra asked.

"You know…" Santana's eyes darted to Terra's crotch.

"No!" Terra protested, a disgusted look on her face. She retched dramatically. "Hell, no. Me and Dick? No thanks. The guy is a sleazeball."

Santana couldn't argue there. During her first encounter with Dick Chambers, she had to peel away his eyes from her ass. Even back then, she got the impression that the man knew of his rugged looks.

"Then what happened?" Santana's curiosity got the better of her.

Terra smirked, although she also looked somewhat abashed. "I shot him in the ass."

"Terra!"

Terra held up her hands. "A genuine error, okay! We were involved in a bit of a scrap—a shootout between some bad folks. We were forced to get each other's six but got separated. As I was turning to find where he'd gone, I saw a guy over his shoulder about to shoot him. I fired my pistol as someone wrestled me from behind. My aim slipped, but the report and the impact were enough to get Dick out of the way of the attack."

Her gaze turned inward, and a nostalgic smile tugged on her lips. "Straight in the ass. Dead center in one of the cheeks. When I say he's a pain in my ass, I really mean that I'm the pain in his."

They laughed together. Santana wiped a tear with her finger. "Well, that is a story for the books. He didn't mention that when we met."

"I'm sure he wouldn't…" Terra trailed off. "Have you two…ever…?"

"No!" Santana quickly returned, seeing where the line of questioning was heading. "Definitely not. No. No, thank you. I wouldn't put myself into that position with anyone who insists on people calling him by a phallic synonym."

"Dick?" Terra asked.

Santana nodded.

"Fair." Terra tried to bring them back on track. "So, Sandra…"

"Yes," Santana replied, correcting course, cheeks still hurting from laughing. "Sandra has a compound on the borders of the city, a huge place filled with exotic animals. She'll do well with the beast, and at least we know that while it's locked away, no one else will get hurt. All we have to do is track down the group behind it all."

Terra lowered her gaze.

"Terra?" Santana asked. "I get the feeling you're holding something back from me."

Terra considered her response. "There have been developments on my side, though considerably slower than yours, it seems."

"Oh?"

Terra nodded. "You have to understand that this isn't my primary case. As one of the leading officers in the precinct, now, I have a lot on my plate to manage. I've been squeezing in moments between jobs, and it's been a grind, but I've managed to get something…"

She relaxed back onto the bench, scanning around the park as she spoke. "Those four guys who threatened us the other night…I thought I spotted something strange on their case files when I scanned them, but it wasn't until I was home that I was able to research more deeply, take more time."

"Must be hard to stop working with that thing inside your head. Gives a whole new meaning to 'switching off.'"

Terra grinned. "Those men… They seemed to share several crimes and injustices throughout the years, and in cross-examining these incidents in their case files, I came across something interesting. Their registered addresses are all within one block of each other. They committed all their crimes within a half-mile radius of those addresses."

"So they're nesting birds?" Santana asked. "They don't want to fly too far from the tree?"

"Exactly. Here's where it gets more interesting." Terra shuffled closer to Santana. "The head honcho, Darius Letterman, came into a substantial amount of money last year. His three stooges have all inflated their bank accounts recently, too."

"You're able to sift through their accounts?" Santana was amazed. "How?"

Terra held up a hand. "The point is that all of this money has been considerable donations from a single user reference: Kelly Osmond Braxton."

"Okay?" Santana asked. "I don't see what…"

"Furthermore," Terra continued, undeterred, "since becoming pretty damn wealthy, Darius' expenses have crept up. A *lot* of his money has been invested into equipment to store wild animals. Cages and glassware and treats, tranqs, you name it, they've purchased it."

"So you're saying that guy the other night has been keeping dangerous animals somewhere in the city?" Santana asked. "It was right under our noses that night?"

"That may well be." Terra was deep in thought. "The big questions that remain for me are these. Number one, what does this all have to do with the victims of the animal attacks? Number two, where does Kobra fit into all of this? Number three, what's it all for? There are many easier ways to kill someone in this city than to recreate an extinct wild animal and set it free ."

Santana weighed Terra's words, considering all the options. None of it made sense. It was all a lot of effort to train a wild creature to attack, let alone having to prepare a beast that had been gone for thirty thousand years. Her nose filled with memories of the lion's stink, and her expression soured.

She turned to Terra, able to read something in her gaze that made her uncomfortable. "What is it? What aren't you telling me?"

Terra looked out above the canopy and to the skyscrapers beyond. "We're not out of the woods, Santana. That creature you bagged last night. It won't stop the attacks."

"Why not?" Santana didn't need Terra to fill in the blanks as realization dawned on her. "Oh no…"

Terra nodded. "Victim was reported late last night, three blocks from your place." She turned to face Santana. "They have more than one of the damned things."

CHAPTER FOURTEEN

Terra's AJS bike zipped through the city.

Santana clung to the back, head filled with images and information that Terra had shared with her. Another victim had been clawed to shreds by the marsupial lions, another fallen body to a creature that shouldn't have existed.

Fuck... Santana wondered what they were going to discover next.

The victim had been a twenty-three-year-old girl by the name of Lindsay Dayton. Once again, the connection between Lindsay and Darius and his men was unclear. There was nothing on file to tie the two, but then again, that wouldn't be unusual. Atlanticans often went a long way to hide their secrets.

They drew up into the sleepy suburb around early afternoon. The streets were wide, and the houses were huge. Mansions and manors lined the roads, with walls and fences creating perimeters the length of soccer pitches.

The two women dismounted and made their way to a set of large golden gates. An intercom was attached to the brickwork pillars, and Santana buzzed to alert Sandra of their arrival.

A tinny voice announced, "Hey stranger! Straight in through the gates, jiggle the side door, you know the drill."

The golden gates swung open as a buzz of electricity ran through them. Santana nodded at the bike, and the pair of them rode along the long road toward the impressive estate.

They parked the bike by a large water fountain, then made their way through a series of wooden arches decorated in vines, ivy, and blooming purple flowers. When they reached the side door, Santana crouched to remove a key from beneath a rock. She held it up to Terra with a headshake, knowing that Terra would get a kick out of the stupidity of leaving a key so close to the house, then twisted the key in the lock. She jiggled the handle roughly until the door swung open.

The kitchen was twice the size of Santana's apartment and smelled of cookies. Yet, while the delicious smell could've relaxed her some, the cold emptiness of the cavernous space was less than homey.

"Sandra keeps staff to a minimum," Santana explained. "She lives with only a small group of people who care for the animals and help her manage the estate. Doesn't trust too many people."

"Living alone in a space like this..." Terra shook her head. "More money than sense."

Santana chuckled. "Come on, if I know Sandra, she'll be this way."

She took Terra through the kitchen and into a large hallway. The walls were rich oak, with posters and art pieces hanging at perfect angles on them. The canvases showed flowers and creatures, all brightly colored interpretations of real-life flora and fauna.

"More money than sense," Terra repeated softly. Santana hoped she wouldn't repeat this in front of Sandra.

Once through a door from the hallway, things began to get interesting. They moved toward the back of the house where a large conservatory opened, providing a sunroom extension to the back of the building. Flowers bloomed, light spilled inside, heat wafted toward them, and there, sitting on a plush couch, was Sandra Reynolds.

Sandra was the very depiction of a lady of leisure. Santana wasn't sure how Sandra had acquired her wealth, but from as far back as she could remember, Sandra had been able to live the life she chose.

Santana remembered visits to Sandra's estate as a child, running around and studying all the animals while her mother and father spoke about grown-up business with Sandra. Over the years, the variety and species of animals had changed and shifted, but Sandra remained the same.

Sandra lounged on the couch with her feet up, an open book to her side. She was stout with a healthy glow to her skin. A bob of dyed blonde hair curled neatly toward her chin. She wore a white blouse with tan pants, her feet bare.

"Santana," she declared, a smile brimming. "Good to see you, darling. How long has it been?"

"Too long," Santana replied.

Sandra rose to her feet, holding out her arms for Santana. She had a motherly charm, which might explain why Santana's visits had lessened over the years. Sandra often reminded Santana of her mother in many ways, those maternal mannerisms coming naturally to a woman who never had children of her own.

"You're looking well." Sandra held Santana by the shoulders and examined her. "Keeping fit, I see? You look just like your mother when she was your age."

Santana took a step back, motioning to Terra. "This is Terra Kris, Atlantica Officer for Justice."

Terra extended a hand. "Pleased to meet you, ma'am."

"Oh, pish-posh," Sandra declared, nudging Terra's hand away. "Any friend of Santana's is family of mine." She embraced Terra, who awkwardly stood there, unsure what to do.

Sandra released her and waved them on into the conservatory. "Tea, dears? Coffee? Come, it's high time for a drink, don't you think?" She stopped herself, chuckling. "Drink...think. I'm a poet; I didn't know it."

Clearly pleased with her joke, she resumed her place on her couch. A small table sat an arm's distance from her, a silver pot with steam ribboning from the spout. Without waiting for an answer, she poured three cups.

Terra and Santana exchanged a glance. Terra shrugged, amused by the interaction. They sat in nearby chairs.

Through the glass windows, Santana could see the back of the estate. A small stretch of movie-crisp grass stretched between the home and the outlying buildings. From here, it looked like one large building, but Santana knew that it was an amalgamation of many. Over the years, Sandra had extended and upgraded the original structures, keen to ensure only the best quality for her animals.

"So, tell me." Sandra nudged the tray toward the women. "What's new with you?"

Santana proceeded to tell Sandra nothing much. She mentioned that she was still working out in the jungle for her mysterious benefactor, and other than discovering a few trinkets, not much exciting was happening. She preferred to keep it that way to stop Sandra from putting herself in awkward situations.

"Your mother would be so proud." Sandra followed that with a sip of her drink. "How's your father doing these days? I don't hear from him anymore. Shame, really. We used to get on so well."

"Do you ever phone him?" Santana asked.

Sandra scoffed. "God, no. I tried when you both first moved away from Atlantica after...well...you know. But he never answered. It was like when your mother passed—Lord rest her soul—he wanted to erase any connection with this place."

"He does that," Santana admitted. Although she loved her father dearly, it was rare that she heard from him. He busied himself in Russia, attending to things that were out of Santana's realm of knowledge, spending much of his time drinking vodka in the evenings at his local tavern. "Things haven't been easy for him."

Sandra gave Santana a pitying look. Santana didn't like it, the look making her feel like a naïve child again. "But if you want excitement and stories," Santana stated, trying to direct Sandra's attention away from her, "You should hear all about the AJS. Terra has stories that could keep you glued to the edge of your seat for days."

"Oh, yes," Sandra announced as if remembering she had another visitor. "It must be an exciting job working for the Atlantica Justice System. I'll admit, I was hesitant to accept you through the doorway, dear. It's been some time since the AJS has graced these halls."

"Understandable," Terra agreed. "Given the nature of this city, am I right in presuming that much of your activity out there," she nodded at the doors, "would be considered illegal in other countries?"

"Got it in one."

"So why would you ever feel comfortable with law enforcement in your house?" Terra didn't expect an answer. "The good news is that while I can't register anything happening on your property in an official capacity, you can help us with a case by proxy." She leaned forward, resting her elbows on her knees. "How is the beast?"

Sandra's eyes lit up. "Oh, she's a beauty—a stunning creature. Santana, thank you so much for bringing her to me. I can't tell you how fascinating it is to see her at play."

"Play?" Santana asked. "You understand she's a wild creature? Not a pet."

"Oh, pish-posh." Sandra waved again. She set her teacup down. "Come on. I'll show you how she's getting on. I can't wait for you to see what I've done with the place."

The smell of animals hit Santana when they opened the reinforced steel doors, taking Santana back to the dark rooms of the Clone Kings beneath the city. If there was one thing that Santana appreciated about Sandra, she cared for her animals and their safety. The reinforced doors were six inches thick, state-of-the-art, with sensors to ensure that only humans came and went as they pleased.

They entered a humid butterfly conservatory filled with lush, tropical greenery. Running water from simulated streams circled the room, and Santana spied several lizards running along the stems of the greenery.

Terra glanced around, visibly uncomfortable and out of her comfort zone. Santana offered a friendly smile as they passed through rubber strip doorways and made their way into the main house.

Fish tanks lined the walls as the natural light faded behind them. There were no windows in here. The only lights were the artificial heaters to warm the tropical tanks.

There were red-belly piranhas, mantis shrimp, and several colorful fish that even Santana couldn't name. They hadn't been here the last time she'd visited. Despite Sandra's non-stop chattering as they walked, she didn't fill them in on every creature.

The next two rooms were for wolves and dragons. The wolves moved as a pack in a room that looked like a dense, dark forest. The dragons bathed in a desert-like climate with a light so bright that it emulated the desert sun. Dotted along the sands were insects and critters that grew curious about the giant Komodos but kept a safe distance.

"Through here," Sandra stated at last, turning a key in the lock of yet another door. When she opened it, a series of short, sharp barks erupted.

They entered a viewing area that looked down into a large pit. The bottom lay deeper than the ground level, and glass bordered the entire enclosure. Trees dotted the space with several toys for the animal's amusement. A tire swing hung from a thick branch. Scattered chew toys lay around, most already torn to shreds.

Santana's heart rate quickened as flashes of her dream jumped to mind. The only differences between her dream and this place were the sparse trees, and the enclosure was glass instead of iron bars.

"She's a feisty one." Sandra chuckled. "Only woke up a few hours ago and already tore most of this place to pieces." She rested her arms on a rail, looking at the marsupial lion as though looking at a pet chihuahua. "Got a hell of a personality, too."

The marsupial lion stared at them and reared back on its haunches. It barked and yapped, angrily warning them of its power. After a few utterances, it sprinted toward the viewing platform, leveraging the lower branches of a tree as a spring-board. Santana was taken aback by its acrobatic prowess as the creature launched toward them.

Terra took a cautious step back. Santana kept her gaze on the creature. Sandra remained where she was, unfazed.

The lion closed in on them, its eyes blazing until it hit the glass.

The *thud* was loud. Santana expected a crack to appear where the creature had hit. But there was no mark, only a strange shape created by the string of saliva where its mouth hit the barrier.

The lion fell fifteen feet to the ground where it grumbled, shook its head, then continued its barking.

"The power…" Sandra marveled. "Impressive, isn't it?"

"It is," Santana whispered. She unconsciously rested a hand on her shoulder. "Although I much prefer when there's a barrier between me and it."

Sandra nodded.

"How is this even possible?" Wonder filled Terra's eyes. "Now there's more than one of them out there? This is a dangerous position to put the city in."

"More than one?" Sandra turned to Terra. "What are you saying?"

Santana answered. "That's why we're here. I wanted to see the lion now that it was awake for this reason. Well, two reasons."

"You wanted to check I had it safely in my keeping." Sandra smirked.

Santana raised an eyebrow.

"I get it," Sandra stated. "Of course. Due diligence. Your mother used to be the same."

Santana smiled.

"Reason number two?" Sandra prompted.

Santana nodded. "Right. Reason number two is to see how the creature behaves. If it has any signature moves or anything that can inform how we go about catching the next one."

"There's only one other?" Sandra questioned.

Terra cocked her head. "We can only assume."

"Well…" Sandra stroked her chin thoughtfully. "Lucky for you, I might be able to help with that. Follow me."

They left the marsupial lion behind, the creature pacing back and forth by the glass, eyes fixed on them until they were gone. Sandra took them through a series of rooms until they could hear barking.

"You've never taken an interest in dogs," Santana stated as the barks increased in fervor.

Sandra offered a warm smile. "I know. Doesn't mean a woman can't change." She opened the door, and half a dozen German Shepherds sprang at her, eagerly gathering around and sniffing her feet, jumping at her chest, and barking loudly.

"Easy, now. Down, girls. Come on…" She laughed, then whistled a clear, sharp note. The moment the sound cut through the barking, the dogs stopped, each one sitting dutifully.

"They're beautiful." Terra crouched and smiled at the dogs.

"Ex-sniffers," Sandra informed them. "An old gentleman in the city passed, and they no longer had anyone to care for them."

"What's an old guy needing sniffers for in the city?" Santana asked.

Sandra offered a small shrug. "From what I can gather, he was one of the few out there offering vigilante justice. They also found the guy dead in his room with a stash of cocaine hidden beneath his floorboards."

"Old-school," Terra offered.

Sandra clapped. Santana expected the dogs to flinch, but they remained rock-solid. "They're yours if you need them. Pick one. Hell, maybe even two if it helps. Their noses are as tuned as anything, and they might go some way to helping you with your cause."

Santana crouched, her eyes drawn to one dog in particular. She was the fluffiest of the lot, with a patch of black around one eye. "I think this girl will do just fine."

Sandra smiled. "Consider it done."

"What's her name?" Terra asked.

Santana reached forward and examined the tag on her collar. "Duchess."

CHAPTER FIFTEEN

They left Sandra's house with two more things than they originally came with.

"Now, it's simple," Sandra offered as she had handed over Duchess' leash. "She's a clever girl and will listen to your commands. Just take the item you want her to sniff, and give her the command, 'Track.' She'll do the rest for you."

"Track..." Santana muttered. The dogs' ears raised, heads cocking to the side.

After a proper introduction with Duchess, one-on-one, in another room, they returned to the marsupial lion's exhibit. The creature was as feisty as ever, tracking them relentlessly as they strode to the viewing platform. Terra and Santana waited up top while Sandra disappeared through another door.

"It's got a thing for you," Terra stated.

"It's got a thing for *us*," Santana corrected.

Terra chuckled. "No. You. That thing won't take its eyes off you. Watch."

Terra stepped away from Santana, moving to the opposite side of the viewing platform. The lion made no effort to track Terra, its eyes glued to Santana's.

Terra returned. "See?"

"Shit." Santana sighed. It was sad to see the creature so angry, so fixed in its motive. "It wants to finish what it started."

"Obedience…" Terra shook her head. Beside them, Duchess sat with its eyes pinned on the lion. "I wonder what they did to make it so determined on its mission."

"Usually a form of starvation," Santana replied. "Any creature can be manipulated and trained with the withdrawal of basic needs. Water, food, sex. Take those three things away, beat them until they're husks, then give them a thing to hate."

They waited in silence for Sandra to appear. Santana's hairs stood on end when she saw the door at the side of the exhibit shift, and a shadow appeared behind it. The lion's ears twitched, but its focus was undeterred.

The door opened a crack. Sandra appeared, dressed in what Santana could describe as medieval chainmail, only with a little more attention to modern fashion. She stuck her head inside the enclosure, then sidled in. She carefully closed the door behind her.

A scattering of plastic and bone toys spread out before her. A few feet away was the desecrated beef knuckle Sandra had given the lion to chew on and play with. It was one of the only pieces in there that was in some way still intact.

She eased toward it, crouching as she did until her hands closed on the item.

The lion's ears twitched again. A growl came from its throat.

Sandra eased back, clutching the knuckle in one hand. She reached back for the door, hand finding the knob. She twisted it, then opened it slightly.

The lion turned its glare on her.

Sandra froze.

Santana clutched the rail.

The world was still for a moment. Santana knew from experience how fast the beast could be. In a flash, the lion would be on

Sandra, wrapping its jaws around her limbs, its muscular body too much for Sandra to bear.

Sandra took a step back.

The lion watched her.

Sandra took another step.

Duchess barked.

The lion turned its body to her.

Sandra slipped through the door…

The lion turned its gaze to Santana, seemingly uninterested in the easy option presented to her. Santana breathed a sigh of relief.

Sandra joined them on the balcony a few moments later. Santana's throat was still dry. Sandra handed her the paper bag, its outside stained with the grease and saliva from the bone. "Your source scent," Sandra explained. "To help with your tracking."

Ten minutes later, Santana and Terra were back outside the manor with the golden gates closing behind them.

"Well, she's an interesting character," Terra offered. "I hope there aren't too many women like that in Atlantica."

"You'll be surprised," Santana replied. "She's one of the good ones. Looks after what she has."

Terra looked back at the manor and shook her head. "How many are *you* aware of?"

"How many what?"

"Vigilante zookeepers."

Santana laughed. "That's one word for them. Honestly, I know of at least two dozen. Some better than others. I'm not friendly with them all. I prefer my animals out in the wild."

"Not caged up as some rich person's pet?"

"Exactly," Santana confirmed. "Although, with the marsupial lion, I'll make a rare exception."

"Yeah." Terra turned toward the city. "Somewhere in there, we've got to find the bastards. Somewhere in there are a group of assholes playing God." She put her hands on her hips. "We've got what we need to find those pricks now. So let's get on it." She crossed to her bike and mounted the seat.

"Er…Terra?" Santana called.

Terra glanced at Santana, who was pointing at the dog beside her. "I'm no expert, but I don't think she can ride that thing."

Terra grinned. "Call yourself a cab. I'll meet you at the address. APRIL, send Santana a text with the information for our meetup." Satisfied, Terra nodded. "See you soon, sport." She twisted the accelerator, and the bike silently slipped out onto the street. In seconds, she was gone.

Santana took her cell phone and called a driverless cab. That was one great thing about removing the driver from the equation. Not only did you not have to put up with small talk, but there was no problem with taking pets on journeys.

With the cab called, she sat on the curb beside Duchess. The dog was a little confused, occasionally glancing back at the manor. Santana called her over, and Duchess slipped to her side. She nuzzled her wet nose into Santana's ear and offered a few affectionate licks. "You have no idea the amount of trouble we're about to unlock, do you?"

Duchess looked at her with intelligent eyes. Santana ran her fingers through the dog's thick hair. When the cab pulled up, Santana offered a quick, "Come on," and Duchess hopped inside.

The journey across town was long, and traffic was heavy at this late hour. More than once, Santana considered walking the rest of the way, wondering if it would be easier than sitting in an endless stream of red lights. The sky had darkened, and the first drops of rain splattered on the windscreen as Johnny Cash played over the cab's speakers.

Santana watched the outside world, staring at groups of people heading home after a long day's work. An endless stream of suits rolled by the windows, their black umbrellas protecting those beneath. Lights were milky and blurry through the rain-slicked glass, and by the time Santana neared the address Terra had sent, the downpour had increased dramatically.

Duchess lay on the seat beside Santana, head resting on her paws. Her ears were down, and Santana did her best to soothe the creature. "It's okay. We'll be there soon."

Santana's phone vibrated in her pocket. She checked the message, surprised to find it was from Terra.

Rain check. I got called into the station. Urgent.

Santana sighed. "Well, there goes that." She ruffled Duchess' hair and offered a warm smile. "Probably for the best, anyway. Means I can rest this damn shoulder and stock up on equipment for the job ahead." She glanced outside. "What do you reckon? Fancy a walk in the rain?"

Duchess picked her head up, gaze turned to the window.

"I'll take that as a yes."

The rain was cold, but it was refreshing. After the driverless cab's stuffy interior, each drop was like a jolt of electricity to Santana's system. She hopped to the sidewalk, Duchess in tow, and the pair of them strolled down the block. Droplets beat hard against them.

Santana's clothes soon grew sodden. She wiped the worst of the downpour from her eyes, a smile on her face as she passed through the blurry city around her. Duchess' thickness vanished as her hair clung to her body, her size shrinking rapidly and making the dog considerably less threatening to look at than before.

Santana started running. Duchess joined her. Their feet splashed and stomped in puddles. Judgmental eyes turned on them as they passed, but they didn't pay attention. Soon, Santana stood outside her apartment block, dripping from head to toe.

She stepped under the awning that stretched from the entrance and caught her breath. She doubled over, hands on her knees. For the first time since the previous night, the pain in her shoulder was nonexistent. She laughed and looked down at the dog beside her. "It's raining cats and dogs out there."

Duchess barked in response.

With a grin, Santana entered her building's foyer. She moved quickly, already at the stairs before the clerk could comment on Santana's appearance or the dog's arrival beside her. She took the stairs carefully, each footstep accompanied by a wet squelch. Duchess stopped at each landing and shook her fur. By the time they were at the top, Santana was breathless, and Duchess' hair had puffed out so much that the dog had doubled in size.

When Santana opened the door to her apartment, she froze. Something was different, and it took a moment for her to realize what it was.

The lights were off. The balcony doors were closed.

She stepped inside, closing the door behind her. Her wet clothes were chafing her body, but it was the two cups on the coffee table that brought her the most alarm.

"Holy…" Santana breathed, the smile returning to her face. "I have the apartment to myself again."

She checked her phone, the words in the top right corner confirming her suspicion. "It's Friday." Gyles was on his date with Therese.

Santana laughed, feeling weightless for the first time in weeks. She removed Duchess' leash and let the dog introduce herself to the room. The German Shepherd sniffed the floor, then worked around the place, familiarizing herself with the smells and the layout. Santana, meanwhile, worked on removing her clothing.

She peeled off each layer, dropping her shirt and pants onto the floor with little care. It wasn't until that moment that she truly appreciated what it had been like living alone, and she missed it—God did she miss it—more than she cared to admit. Before Gyles and their exploration of the temples, Santana's apartment had been her one safe space to just be, to live and breathe and eat and not worry about anyone. Even out in the jungle, she cared about others since they funded most of her missions. Here… This was her little slice of heaven.

Santana kicked off the last of her garments, then strode over to Duchess, who'd taken a seat on the couch. Her tongue was out, the dog panting as her tail wagged. Santana stroked her head and offered a "Good girl" before heading into her bedroom and starting the shower.

Warm water soothed her chilled skin. She hissed as it splashed against her wound, and she allowed herself a moment to examine the site. Small marks pocked the skin, indicative of where the lion's teeth had penetrated.

It didn't look infected, which was a good sign. Gyles' work with the iodine had seen to that. The stitches were a little crooked, and there would likely be a scar when it had healed, but Santana didn't mind. What was one more to add to the collection?

She switched off the shower, then stepped out onto the bath mat. She dabbed the worst of the moisture with a towel, then wrapped up her hair. She stepped out toward the living room and rested against the door jamb. Duchess was fast asleep, curled on the couch. The place was dark, the evening quiet. She drew a deep breath and allowed herself a moment to soak in the peace of it all.

Santana strode over to the kitchenette in the darkness. She turned on the coffee maker and leaned against the counter.

A key turned in the door.

Soft voices spoke to each other.

The door opened.

Santana ran, leaving the coffee maker to drip behind her. She aimed for her bedroom the moment the lights flooded on and two people entered the apartment.

She closed the door, almost certain they'd seen her bare ass.

She leaned against the cold surface of the door. Duchess

barked and growled, riled by the strangers. Santana held a hand to her mouth as Gyles' voice rose, protesting to the woman he'd entered the apartment with. There was a brief bout of shouting before the apartment door slammed shut.

Duchess' barks grew louder. Santana closed her eyes as she masked the mirth on her lips. Gyles called through the door, "Santana! A word, please!"

Santana composed herself, then peeked around the door.

CHAPTER SIXTEEN

Gyles was flustered. His eyes stayed fixed on the dog. Duchess reared back on her haunches with her teeth bared as she kept Gyles pinned to the front door, growls rumbling from her throat.

"Is there a problem?" Santana asked as if nothing had happened at all.

"Yes, there's a problem! A *big* problem," Gyles shouted. "Who the fuck is this dog? Why is it here? Can you tell it to leave me the fuck alone?"

Santana clicked her teeth. "Duchess, down."

"Duchess?" Gyles breathed.

Duchess dropped her ass to the floor, eyes still locked on Gyles.

Santana snapped her fingers and pointed beside her. "Here, Duchess."

Duchess turned and ran to Santana, taking a seat by her side. Gyles relaxed a little but kept his eyes on the dog. "Thank you."

"You're welcome." She waited for Gyles to say more. When he didn't, she raised a finger. "Would you excuse me for a moment? I need to get dressed."

She closed the door as Gyles bellowed, "*Now* she gets dressed!"

Santana chuckled as she went around her room and found suitable clothes. She chose shorts and a white t-shirt that was a size too big before returning to the living room.

Gyles stood by the kitchen counter, fingers combing through his hair. He turned uncertainly to the dog as the door to Santana's bedroom opened. "Is she going to be friendly?"

"Of course," Santana replied. "She's a trained hound. Only attacks intruders, strangers, and invaders. Here, hold out your hand and let her know you're safe."

Gyles narrowed his eyes, then held out a hand. With a little encouragement from Santana, she padded over to Gyles, then nuzzled her nose into his palm.

"Introductions complete." Santana sat on the couch and folded her legs beneath her. "You can relax now."

Gyles straightened, hands resting against the counter. He glowered at the floor, something troubling him behind his eyes.

Santana sighed. "I'm sorry."

Gyles was silent.

"I'm *sorry*," Santana repeated, not remembering the last time she'd apologized twice in such quick succession. "I lost track of time."

Gyles gave a small nod, unable to meet her gaze.

"I didn't know you'd be bringing her back home," Santana continued. "Must have been a great date. How was it? Tell me *everything*." She grinned, trying to remain chirpy to cut through Gyles' annoyance.

After a few seconds, he softened. "It was amazing. *She's* amazing."

Santana crossed to the coffee pot and poured them both a drink.

Gyles continued, "We had such an amazing time. We met up outside her apartment, walked around the block for a bit. We took a stroll through King's Park under the streetlights and sat by the fountain—there were these two hilarious ducks with red crests on their head that we laughed at for ages. Then we grabbed some food at this little Italian place on Rover's Boulevard. Drank some wine. Ate dessert. Then… Yeah…"

"Thought you'd head back here for a nightcap?" Santana winked as she handed Gyles his coffee.

"I didn't know you'd be here," Gyles protested. "I didn't know how long you'd be."

"All the more reason to maybe not bring a stranger back to canoodle on my couch." Santana smirked.

Gyles looked away guiltily.

"No…" Santana stated. "You were *not* going to use my bed?"

Gyles rubbed the back of his neck. "No… Well… Not really. No. No, we weren't."

Santana shook her head, unable to hold back her laughter. "Look at you, terrified of leaving the apartment for two weeks, now out on the lam and playing Casanova with some stranger. What a difference twenty-four hours makes."

"I'm sorry," Gyles commented.

"Me, too." Santana returned to the couch. Duchess hopped on beside her.

"In all seriousness, if you're looking at entertaining your lady friends, you're going to have to find a place. I realized tonight that this was the first time in too long that I could call this place my own. I haven't minded accommodating you while you were on your…whatever you call it…recovery? But it might be time you start looking for a new place."

Gyles nodded slowly. "I think you're right." He chewed his lip. "What is it?"

"I don't know that I can afford it." Gyles dug one hand into his pocket.

Santana cocked her head. "Don't worry about that. Find yourself a place that works for you, something that isn't too flashy, and I'll front you for the first two months while you sort yourself out."

Gyles' brow creased. "You'd do that?"

"Of course," Santana replied, surprised by her words. It had been some time since she'd allowed herself to grow close to anyone in this city. Life as an adventurer dictated a solitary existence with little attachment.

Gyles glanced around her apartment, scrutinizing her setup.

"What now?" Santana nudged.

"Well..." Gyles considered his words. "Don't take this the wrong way, but how can you afford to front that cost? This place isn't exactly lavish. It doesn't scream, 'I've got money to burn.'"

Santana raised her eyebrows.

"No offense," Gyles quickly added.

"None taken," Santana replied unconvincingly. "Don't take this the wrong way, but what did Therese see in you? Your shirt doesn't fit properly, there are scuffs on your knees, and your five o'clock shadow has turned into three-day darkness."

Gyles grinned.

Santana quickly added, "No offense."

"None taken." Gyles laughed.

Santana took a swig of her coffee. "I have money. That job we did out in the jungle? I didn't do it for free. I have what's needed to set you up, so don't worry about that." She looked at the balcony, staring out into the wispy darkness. "It's quite nice to have someone to help. A lot of my work has me looking for relics left by dead people to give to rich people who, by all moral and ethical rights, should be dead themselves."

"Sounds lonely," Gyles commented.

Santana remained quiet. A nostalgic smile played on her lips before she turned her gaze back to Gyles. "So what's going to happen with you and Therese?"

Gyles sighed. "I have *no* idea. I've never brought a girl back to my place on the first date. Much less had her walk in on another woman naked in my apartment."

"Whose apartment?" Santana interrupted.

"Yours."

"That's right." Santana stroked Duchess' back. "Maybe you can call her tomorrow."

"I don't know… What would you think if you were in that situation?"

Santana cast her gaze to the floor. "I couldn't tell you. I've never found myself in that situation."

"Invited back to a guy's house to find a naked woman walking around his apartment?" Gyles laughed. "That's sitcom-level comedy there."

Santana shook her head. "No. I've never been on a date. Like a *real* date." When Gyles' mirth melted to pity, she added, "My life doesn't allow it. I don't need it. My love is the wild, and that's where my heart sits."

She drew a deep breath. "Ever since I was a little girl, that's all that I've cared about. My parents took me on adventures, showed me the ways of the wild. I could make a campfire with no tools by the time I was five years old. At six, I knew how to siphon juice from trees and fight off a grizzly bear."

Santana's eyes grew glassy. "It's what has always excited me— visiting new places with my parents. Finding things that were formerly undiscovered. The thrill of stumbling across a segment of time and memory…

"You sit on the PlayStation and play Tomb Raider, but I *live* it. Out there, in the wild…that's my home. That's my love. I don't have anything more to give."

Gyles joined Santana on the couch. "That's beautiful." He wiped away an imaginary tear.

"Oh, shut up." Santana shoved Gyles playfully. He steadied himself, barely catching the drops of coffee that threatened to spill from his mug.

"Really though, Santana…" Gyles continued. "Are you sure you're not lonely?"

Santana frowned. "No. Why would I be?"

"Even your parents had each other," Gyles replied.

His words made her freeze. She considered her response, gaze falling once more to the floor. "That was their choice. That was their life. In the end, it all amounted to the same. My father is still alone." Santana drained her coffee, fingers locked in Duchess' fur.

Gyles sensed the line he'd overstepped. He turned his attention instead to the German Shepherd. "You never did tell me who this adorable creature is."

"Adorable? You weren't saying that a short while ago."

"Things change."

Santana guessed that he wasn't only talking about the dog.

She introduced him officially to Duchess, informing Gyles about the new home of the marsupial lion and her rental of the dog. She told him about their revelation that there were more lions out there, and they needed to track them down.

"The only problem is that I'm working with a partner who has other commitments to attend to," Santana stated.

Gyles grinned. "Whoa, you sound a little bitter."

Santana chewed this over. "No. Not bitter. Terra does amazing work and is involved in some high-level shit right now. She's already told me that this is a side-project for her, so I can't be mad."

"But you want to solve it, right?"

Santana nodded. "Of course. The mystery is killing me."

"Do you know where you need to go?"

"I know the rough location," Santana replied. "Duchess is our keen little sniffer."

Gyles sat up straight. "Then why don't we get going? Tonight. You wanted to find out the truth, right? Let's go now. Get it done."

Santana leveled her gaze on Gyles. "You're sure? You're happy to go back out into the world and piss more people off?"

"Why not?" he stated. "After the way things have gone tonight, what have I got to lose?"

Santana laughed. "You could get yourself killed out there."

"Well, then you won't need to worry about fronting me for an apartment for two months, will you?" Gyles grinned.

CHAPTER SEVENTEEN

The city was dark.

Santana, Gyles, and Duchess rode in the driverless cab in silence as the city blurred by them. Santana's heart raced. The last time she'd been in this part of the city was to enter the victim's apartment and see the damage left behind.

A spate of attacks from a marsupial lion in the heart of Atlantica... All conducted within a half-mile radius... Victims who were in their early twenties...Darius Letterman...Clone Kings...Kobra... A late-night visitor with razor-sharp claws and teeth...

Santana pondered it all under the gentle hum of the engine. When Tyler had given her the week off to find something interesting to do with her time, she'd never envisioned this: crossing the city to search for a killer who utilized extinct creatures as their weapons.

He probably wanted me to try jet-skiing or archery.

Santana grinned. She was an excellent archer.

The cab pulled up one block from the victim's building. Santana and Gyles stepped out onto a quiet street. A smattering of lights showed inside the surrounding apartments, but there was little disturbance. The rain fell around them, less intense, but enough to darken their clothes. Santana led them beneath a canopy that covered the doors to one of the nearby buildings.

"Here you go, girl," Santana offered, crouching to Duchess' level and presenting the bone knuckle. It was the size of her fist, the lion's teeth marks still evident on its surface. "Duchess, track."

Duchess' ears pricked up. She leaned closer, nose wriggling as the scent activated her senses. She stuck her nose onto the bone, sniffing as much as she could before giving a confirmation bark.

Santana put a finger to her lips and shushed Duchess, but she was already on her way. Nose to the ground, she sniffed the surrounding sidewalk. She turned in circles. She trailed along to the streetlights. Her head disappeared into bushes.

"What is it, girl?" Santana asked. "Anything?"

Duchess ignored her, continuing to examine the surrounding area. After a minute or two, it became clear that there was nothing to pick up.

"Damn," Gyles offered.

"I expected as much," Santana replied. "Duchess, come."

She slapped her hand against her thigh, and Duchess followed. She jogged across the road, the three of them splashing through puddles as they approached the curb. They rounded the corner, Santana's gaze falling on the apartment building she'd entered a few days ago.

She scanned the surrounding streets, checking for anyone watching. The place was deserted.

"I'm not sure that's a good sign," she muttered.

"What?" Gyles asked.

Santana didn't elaborate. She cautiously approached the apartment building, then tucked herself against the brickwork. Here they had shelter from the rain, and she offered the knuckle to Duchess again. "Track."

This time the dog didn't bark but instead put her head down and went straight to searching.

Santana's throat was dry as Duchess sniffed around the space.

Across the road, a lone silhouetted figure appeared through the rain, walking along the sidewalk.

Santana kept her gaze on the man, dressed in a dark jacket and slacks. He continued on his way, not turning his head, oblivious to the three of them on the other side of the road.

Duchess sniffed in front of the apartment. Her body stiffened as she stood straight and pointed her nose in a singular direction.

"What is it, girl?" Santana asked, checking where the man had gone.

He was nowhere in sight.

Duchess waited for Santana and Gyles to stand by her, then she continued on her way. Her wet hair clung to her skin. Her nose stayed fixed to the sidewalk as she snaked around, following the scent trail.

Santana knew about canines' incredible sense of smell, but still, it somehow seemed impossible. The marsupial lion had attacked several nights ago. It had rained since then. A thousand different pairs of shoes must've graced this sidewalk, and still the dog could pick up the smell.

What else was there in the world that humans didn't know about?

They rounded the corner, and the dog looked up. Santana recognized the exterior of the apartment, the window still slightly ajar. She bent down to the dog and scratched behind her ears. "Good job. Now, lead us in the other direction."

The dog turned to her and cocked her head.

Santana pointed back the way they'd come. "Duchess, track."

The dog yipped, then sped into action. Sprinting through the curtain of rain, the German Shepherd led them back to the front of the apartment block. She stuck her nose to the concrete, then sprinted off in the other direction.

Santana pumped her arms, racing after the dog as she bounded ahead. Gyles panted behind her, doing his best to catch up with the pair.

"Can you tell her to slow down?" Gyles complained.

Santana called Duchess, but she didn't slow. Every few meters she stuck her nose to the ground, then sprang off following the scent.

She was fast—impressively so. After a couple of blocks, Duchess hovered on the edge of Santana's vision, the dog ghostly under the sheet of rain. If she ran any farther away, they'd be in danger of losing her.

"Duchess!" Santana called, pinching two fingers between her lips and whistling.

Duchess gave a delighted bark, then sprinted out of sight.

"Fuck..." Santana glanced over her shoulder. Gyles was on the edges of her vision back there. Her blood turned cold, knowing that it would be an awful idea to lose the dog, not least because she might be the key to unlocking this whole thing, but because she couldn't return to Sandra and tell her that she'd lost one of her animals. That's something she'd never do.

She doubled down, adrenaline fueling her as she sprinted in Duchess' direction. The roads had been quiet to this point, but as she turned onto the next street, twin headlights blinded her.

She stopped and shielded her eyes. The rain fragmented the light, filling her vision with twinkling rainbows. Gyles huffed behind her, a moan escaping his lips as he stopped. The lights caught him, too.

The car screeched as the driver applied the brakes. The wheels skidded along the slick blacktop. The silver hood of a Mercedes barreled at them, its headlights blinding them. Santana had enough foresight to grab Gyles' shoulders and throw him out of the way before the car could hit them.

The Mercedes slalomed across the road, passing the spot where they'd stood seconds before. Santana and Gyles crashed to the ground, watching the car's progress as the driver fought with the steering. The car stopped. An angry voice bellowed at them before the driver kicked the engine back into gear and rolled away.

"Thank you," Gyles muttered from beneath Santana's body.

"Don't mention it." She rose to her feet and offered Gyles a hand. "Don't tell your new girlfriend about this. She'll start suspecting that there's something between us."

Gyles chuckled. "Understood."

They stood at the side of the road, looking around in all directions. There was no sign of Duchess, and whichever way Santana had been heading, she was now unconvinced it was the right direction.

"So much for using a sniffer dog to guide us," Gyles commented.

Santana nodded. "Sandra's going to kill me."

"Was she expensive?" Gyles asked.

Santana sighed. "Not financially…" She cupped her hands to her mouth. "Duchess!"

"Duchess!" Gyles called, joining Santana.

"Duchess!" Santana hated calling for the dog, considering that their mission was supposed to be stealth-based, but what was she to do? "Duchess!"

A bark sounded in the distance.

"Which way was that?" Gyles asked.

Santana headed toward the sound. Another yap came, and Santana quickened her pace, adjusting her position to the right slightly to close in on the dog.

One final bark and Santana could see her. She stood thirty feet ahead, coiled back, shoulders low to the ground. She'd bared her teeth, and her growl rumbled above the *hiss* of the rain.

"Duchess, there you are," Santana called.

Gyles pulled up beside Santana, clutching his hips and gasping for air. "Thank God…"

Something was wrong. Duchess didn't turn to them on their arrival, nor was she sniffing the ground anymore. Her determination to follow the scent had waned, and it only took Santana a few more steps forward to realize why.

The creature stalked out of the haze of rain, appearing like a ghoul before them. As it neared the three of them, its shape solidified to a compact mass of coiled muscle and predatory aggression.

"Shit," Santana muttered as she reached for her pistol. "Gyles, stay back…"

Gyles drew his gun, both of them aiming at the creature.

The lion mirrored Duchess' posture, teeth exposed and shoulders low. Santana had seen that position before, earlier that day in a glass enclosure, a beast preparing to spring at its prey. It was an almost identical clone of the first lion, with only a few minor differences. Santana couldn't help but notice that one of its ears was missing, the other one tucked back tight to its head.

"Easy now…" Santana warned, the tension pregnant in the air as the rain beat down on them.

Duchess barked.

The lion growled.

Santana took a step forward.

The lion sprang.

CHAPTER EIGHTEEN

Duchess broke rank, sprinting toward the lion. The lion sprang from the ground, jumping off to the side where a rail lined the nearby apartment building. Duchess' attack missed by inches as the creature used its environment to its advantage and came for Santana.

"Santana, duck!" Gyles cried.

Santana dove to the side as Gyles shot at the beast. The lion balanced flawlessly on the rail before arcing in the air to where Santana had been.

It yowled, the bullet scraping its side and leaving a deep trench in its flank. Santana rolled to her feet and spun as the lion turned its head to her and flashed its teeth.

Santana's eyes stung from the rain. She blinked at the creature, turning her aim at its head. Duchess streamed past her, launching herself at the lion. She dug her teeth into its neck, and the two of them tumbled along the road.

"I can't get a clear shot," Santana complained.

Gunshots rang out from behind her. She glanced over her shoulder, barely able to make out someone on the sidewalk, crouched behind a car. She ran toward the scrapping pair, taking cover behind a nearby SUV.

Another shot rang. Gyles cried out in surprise, then ran to join her. Duchess yelped as the lion swatted her away with its meaty paw. She rolled across the blacktop, scrambling to get back to her feet.

The lion searched for Santana, spotting her a short distance away. Several trees lined the sidewalk, and the lion made for the nearest trunk before scaling effortlessly into its canopy and out of sight.

Santana pointed her pistol at the tree and let off a barrage of shots. The lion growled, but there was no confirming drop of the creature's body.

"Where is it?" Gyles shouted.

"I don't know!" Santana replied as another mess of shots broke out from behind her. The SUV's windows smashed. The car alarm wailed. One of the tires burst, and the SUV tilted drunkenly to one side. "Fuck, who is that?"

Gyles glanced through the broken glass. "I can't see."

"Cover me," Santana ordered as something shifted in the tree above.

She ran out from cover. Gyles shot into the rain, more glass breaking. Santana wondered if it was from the cars or the apartment windows. There was no way to tell.

She stood directly beneath the tree, looking for the shifting mass of the lion. Something glinted, and for a fleeting moment, the lion's eyes stared at her.

"I'm sorry…" Santana apologized, gun aimed at the creature.

She fired, but the lion was too quick. It zig-zagged, launching itself from branch to branch before throwing itself at Santana. Its weight bore down on her, knocking her to the ground. Its hot, stale breath soured her nose, and as she reached for the gun that had fallen from her hand, a report sounded, and Gyles grunted in pain.

"Get off!" Santana roared at the beast as it lifted its paw and readied for a swipe.

She shoved the creature, the attack missing her by millimeters. Before the lion could recover, Duchess sprang into sight, once again throwing herself in harm's way.

Her teeth clamped into the lion's neck as she clung to the creature's back. The lion yelped, its eyes flashing, taking its attention from Santana as it turned its head to try and bite the dog. It failed since its muscles were too tightly packed, and that range of motion wouldn't evolve for another fifteen thousand years at least.

"Gyles?" Santana asked, turning on her stomach on the soaked ground and finding him slouched against the side of the car. Footsteps sounded as the others ran toward them.

Santana reached into her pocket, then twisted toward the scrapping animals. She aimed the tranquilizer at the lion, waiting for a moment when she would get a clear shot without blurs of browns and blacks getting in her way. She narrowed her eyes and blinked against the rain, her vision fuzzy.

She fired once, then twice, then three more times.

She didn't know if she'd found her target, but voices now accompanied the footsteps, and she didn't plan to wait around to find out what these people wanted. She slowly drew herself to her feet as she holstered the dart gun and reclaimed her pistol. Her chest rose and fell, and her clothes clung to her skin. Her hair was heavy, falling in wet strings across her face.

Two figures stood in the middle of the road, cloaked with black hoods. Santana couldn't make out any distinguishing features between that and the rainfall. They aimed their pistols at Santana. Santana aimed hers at them.

"Lower your weapon," a feminine voice called.

Santana remained still. In the distance, they heard the faint blare of AJS sirens. Santana and the lion had earned the law's attention.

"Now!" the voice commanded.

Santana knew that she had no choice. With Gyles down and Duchess incapacitated or dead, she was alone. With a sour curl of her lips, she let the pistol slip from her hand.

She felt the tug at her hip as the gun caught on her bullwhip.

"Hands where we can see them," the voice instructed.

Santana held up her hands, glancing toward Gyles. She couldn't get a good look at him from where she stood since the car blocked him from view. The two figures approached Santana cautiously as the sirens grew louder. They grew clearer, their faces still shadowed by their hoods as they each took one of Santana's arms.

"Come with us. Now." This time it was the second figure, a feminine voice with a deeper timbre.

"Do I have a choice?" Santana asked.

They didn't respond as they guided her forward. Santana allowed them to lead her as they hurried her across the road. One of her captors glanced behind them as they went. They directed her toward a nearby storm shelter built into one of the apartment bases. A set of stone steps led down to a steel door, water running down toward it like a river.

Before they could take a step, one of the figures groaned in pain. Something knocked into the side of them, and soon the snarls of a creature told Santana what she needed to know.

Duchess was alive.

The grip on one side lessened. Santana pulled herself free as the figure wrestled with the dog. The grip from the other person tightened, although Santana was free enough to turn and throw a punch into the person's nose. Bone *crunched* beneath her fist. The person's hood slid back, revealing a head of braided hair. The woman grimaced, once more training her weapon on Santana as Santana reached for hers.

She didn't need to worry. A third figure leaped out from the curtain of rain, body slamming into the woman. Gyles and the woman tumbled down the stairs, stopping against the door with a *thud*.

AJS sirens blared. Through the fog of rain came a haze of red and blue flashing lights.

"Okay! Okay!" the nearest person declared, panic in their voice. "We're not the enemy. We're *not* your enemy."

Santana whirled her weapon on the figure in the grip of Duchess' teeth.

"Who are you?" Santana barked.

"Probably your best shot at not spending tonight either in the morgue or a jail cell," the figure returned. Below them, the woman had won the upper hand and smashed her pistol into the side of Gyles' head. He lay back, out cold.

"Sure seems like it," Santana declared, finger ready on the trigger.

Car tires screeched. The faint shape of AJS cruisers sped into view.

"Fuck..." Santana muttered. She went down the stairs. At least down there, they would be out of direct sight.

"Trust us," the person asked. Santana detected the notes of sincerity in her voice, yet she hated herself for it. Hadn't these assholes been firing at them moments ago?

"Open the door," Santana commanded.

The woman's hand was on the handle. "Already on it." The door screeched open. Santana lowered her pistol and took Gyles' arms. Duchess clung to the figure's leg as they all stepped inside the darkness of the storm shelter.

The sound of distant thunder rumbled in the skies.

CHAPTER NINETEEN

The moment the doors closed, the others strode away, disappearing through a nearby doorway.

Santana was alone with the unconscious Gyles and the sodden dog. She looked down at Duchess and frowned. "Cover me, okay?"

Duchess stared up at her with intelligent eyes. She didn't look good. Her hair was soaking wet and disheveled. There was a long scratch on her rump, and as she walked closer to Santana, a limp accompanied every other step.

Santana sighed. "We'll get you patched up, too. Let's figure out the situation first." She motioned at Gyles. "Will you be able to help me drag him?"

Duchess' ears lowered.

"I didn't think so." Santana grabbed Gyles' wrists and dragged him along the floor. She maneuvered him through the doorway, finding the other two wandering around the space as they worked to light several candles. The room was basic stone walls, with two tattered couches in the middle and a stack of cardboard boxes stacked on metal shelves lining the edges.

Santana kept her awareness on the others as she scooped Gyles beneath his arms and attempted to settle him on one of the couches. She imagined it would be much more comfortable than the stone floor. Gyles was a big man, and it took some effort. The nearest woman spotted her attempts and came over to help. "Here…"

Santana wanted to protest. It was their fault that they were in this predicament, wasn't it? Gyles wouldn't have fallen down the stairs if it hadn't had been for their attack. Still, that note of sincerity was back in her voice.

The woman took Gyles' legs. Together they placed him gently on the couch where Gyles shifted, lips smacking before a long snore escaped his nose.

Santana couldn't help but chuckle.

"He's a deep sleeper," the woman offered.

Santana glared at her. "He is after he nearly loses his life."

The woman bowed her head, then returned to her duties around the room. Santana watched them for a few moments as they busied themselves with dragging boxes and moving tables. Outside, Santana heard another rumble of thunder, but if the AJS were being noisy, there was no sign of that.

"Who are you?" Santana's eyes narrowed. The second woman had taken down her hood, revealing a dome of shorn hair. Her eye makeup was dark, creating panda patches around her eyes. She was scrawny, considerably thinner than the other woman whose face and lips were healthily plump.

They glanced over their shoulders at Santana. The thin woman replied, "Erika."

The other woman followed, "Cyrus."

"You?" Erika asked.

"Santana."

"Okay." Cyrus nodded, providing no other explanation as they worked on something that Santana couldn't see. They gathered closely, speaking in hushed whispers. Santana glanced back at the door, keeping her awareness raised in case anyone else was in this part of the building.

Duchess yipped.

Santana turned her attention to the dog and crouched with her back to the wall as she removed her pack. She rifled inside for her first aid kit, pulling out a small green canvas bag a moment later. Duchess lay at her feet, head resting on her paws.

The dog's gaze remained fixed on the two women, and Santana settled a touch, knowing that if anyone else was to arrive, she could use Duchess' sensitive hearing to raise the alarm.

"Look at you, girl…" Santana cooed. "You're a mess."

The dog's blood was clotting on her rump. Santana drew out a scrap piece of cloth and patted her until she was dry in that area. Blood oozed lazily to the surface, and Santana applied pressure to the wound. Duchess was brave but still complained by baring her teeth. Occasionally she turned her gaze to Santana with pain in her eyes.

By the time the bleeding stopped, the two women had taken a stand behind the back of the bare sofa. Cyrus leaned her hands on the back. Erika folded her arms. "Is she going to be okay?"

"You better hope so," Santana shot back.

Cyrus shifted uneasily. "We're not the enemy."

"Funny, you keep saying that, but the last I checked it was you two who were firing volleys of bullets at us and knocking my friend unconscious." Santana's voice echoed around the room as the anger she'd been holding in unleashed itself.

Cyrus moved around the sofa and sat on its edge. "We were protecting our street. We heard gunshots and animal growls. We went into the rain and found a strange man and woman with a dog and…whatever that thing was. What did you expect us to do?"

Erika took over, face harshly lit by the candlelight. "There have been several animal attacks reported in this district for the last few weeks. The victims are mostly younger, in their twenties. You think we're going to sit inside when we can do something about it? Take out the people who are turning this side of town into an inner city jungle?"

"You saw the creature?" Santana asked.

"We saw *something*," Cyrus replied. She played with a bracelet on her wrist, a brown band decorated in seashells. "Now you explain what you two were doing out there. Because, from where I'm sitting, I've got a man and a woman accompanied by a dog and another animal. It doesn't look good for you."

"If you believed I was the bad guy, you wouldn't have allowed us to come inside," Santana stated.

Cyrus smiled. "True."

Erika leaned forward, her gaze intense. There was a tribal look about her that Santana didn't like. Still, she answered. "We're on the same mission as you, it seems. We're hunting down the assholes who feel like it's a smart idea to use a wild animal to do their dirty work."

She looked up toward street level. "I've seen the apartment of one of the nearby victims. It wasn't pretty. Not only do I want to stop the humans dying due to this fucked up scheme, but I'm not going to sit back and allow people to exploit animals for the sake of targeted murder."

Erika glared at Santana, although it was less antagonistic than before. "Now, what the hell was that thing out there?"

"I told you, a cat," Cyrus offered.

"Ain't like no cat I've ever seen," Erika replied.

"It wasn't a cat," Santana stated. "It was a marsupial lion."

They stared at her blankly.

"A lion is a cat," Erika stated flatly. "A jungle cat." She looked at Cyrus. "Right?"

"Marsupial lions aren't cats," Santana clarified. "They're marsupials, more closely related to kangaroos and wallabies than lions. Their appearance is mongrelized, more like a cross between a bear and a dog than a lion or big cat."

Erika frowned. "Did you hear yourself?"

"What kind of bullshit is this?" Cyrus added.

"It's not bullshit," Santana looked exasperated. "It's the truth. It was a marsupial lion. I know because it's the second one I've encountered in the last few days." She peeled away her clothes to show her shoulder, exposing the sodden bandages beneath.

The women exchanged a look. Erika crooned, "As far as I'm concerned, you know way too much about this beastie not to be somehow involved." She drew her pistol and aimed it at Santana's chest. "Where is the creature, and how do we kill it?"

Cyrus rolled her eyes, laid a hand atop Erika's pistol, and lowered it to the floor. "Will you calm down? She's not a part of this."

"How can you know for certain?" Erika argued. "Weren't you listening to her?"

"I was. Looks like *you* weren't." She rounded the sofa, approaching Santana. There was a curious look in her eye. Santana stiffened. Duchess growled. Cyrus offered a hand. "You're on the good team, right?"

"I am," Santana replied. "As much as there's good and bad in this morally gray city."

Cyrus laughed. "It sounds like we all want the same thing, right? So why don't we sit down and tell each other what we know." She looked back at Erika. "We can be civil. Ride out the storm. Wait for the AJS to clear. Maybe there's a way we can help each other out here? Win-win."

Santana locked eyes with Erika. Her gaze burned deep into her, but it didn't faze Santana. "I'm game if your friend is."

"Erika?" Cyrus asked.

"Fine," Erika conceded. "I'm keeping hold of my gun."

"Fine," Santana replied. Gyles gave a loud snore, then rolled toward the back of the couch. "He's going to have one hell of a hangover when he wakes up."

"He shouldn't have jumped me, then," Cyrus stated.

Santana nodded. "I don't blame him."

"Me neither," Cyrus replied as they all took their places on the couches.

CHAPTER TWENTY

Santana awoke to darkness.

She lay on the couch, nestled into the crooks and gaps. Her shoulder ached, her back hurt, and there was a dull throb in her temple.

Nothing compared to Gyles' when he wakes up.

Gyles slept quietly on the other couch, his breathing deep. They had spoken for a couple of hours, the group of them, exchanging their war stories and telling the other as much as they dared to tell. Santana told them all about the marsupial lion and her interactions with the one she'd put to sleep the previous night.

When they asked if the lion was dead, Santana hadn't bothered to tell them the truth, wanting to keep Sandra and her menagerie as far out of the equation as possible. When questioned about her experience with the lion that night, Santana had colored in as much as she could remember.

They all wondered about the state of the creature outside. Santana had flooded its veins with tranquilizers and assumed the animal was either catatonic or dead. The AJS would have found it lying in the street and would hopefully remove its body. Santana wondered if Terra would be a part of that operation or if she would later find the creature in evidence, laid out on a steel gurney with blank eyes and tongue lolled out of its mouth.

Flashes of the creature's attack plagued Santana. It was ferocious and determined. Once more she got the impression that the target of its attack was her. In the same way they'd set Duchess on the hunt for the lion, Santana was the scent for the beast. How many more of these would she have to deal with before all was said and done? How many more cuts and scratches and bites and bruises would her body withstand?

She had looked at Gyles and Duchess, then. Under the flickering candles, there was a somber air to the room. Both of them had come to harm because of Santana. She'd dragged both of them into this mess, and as a result, they'd put their lives in harm's way and could've died.

Duchess had boldly scrapped with the beast, managing to gain an advantage to jump on it and cling on with her teeth, but it could easily have gone the other way. If the lion hadn't been so set on attacking Santana, Duchess wouldn't have stood a chance.

Then there was Gyles, who Santana had been sure was down and out. Glass had shattered, pain had struck, bullets had fired, and Gyles had slumped against the car. She still awaited an explanation but couldn't be more thankful that he was alive and had the energy to launch himself at the person he believed to be the attacker. A stupid move, but a bold move, nonetheless.

Cyrus and Erika had gone on to tell Santana of their position in the city. The storm shelter basement of the apartment building was their permanent home. Both Erika and Cyrus had fallen on hard times, and when they could no longer afford their former places, they'd roamed around the city as Atlantica's homeless.

"I hardly see any homeless citizens on the streets these days," Santana commented.

Cyrus had explained that Atlantica did a great job of hiding its homeless. In the dark alleys and spaces around the edges and beneath the city, homeless citizens congregated out of sight. City Hall worked its hardest to keep Atlantica looking spotless and appealing to outside tourism, so the AJS were often put on guard to enforce curfews and keep vagrants moving on.

"Given that much of the rest of the world's law enforcement spend their time in private residences dealing with domestic disputes," Erika detailed, "Atlantica's officers find themselves with extra time on their hands to enforce the rule."

The pair of them had shuffled on to temporary shelters for weeks until they met each other in a chance encounter in a convenience store. The man who owned the place took pity on both of them and offered them the basement.

"It's basic, and it's cold," Cyrus stated. "But at least it's something. We pay what we can, and we eat whatever's left of the fresh produce from the store. Or, at least, we used to."

When pressed what she meant by that, Erika added, "Brian died last week."

It took Santana a few moments to scour her brain for why the name sounded so familiar. Her eyes narrowed as she located it. "Brian Felkins?"

Erika and Cyrus gave her a strange look. "Yes. How do you know that?"

Santana explained, "His was the apartment I visited. He's the reason I learned about the lion."

"Shit…" Cyrus breathed.

They told Santana what they knew of Brian Felkins. That he was a happy-go-lucky guy who happened to stumble across a large amount of money. He fronted at the convenience store on the corner, but he'd tied up most of his assets in investments and stocks.

"He was huge on crypto," Cyrus commented. "He kept his cards close to his chest, but you could always tell when he was having a good day."

Erika chuckled. "We'd eat well those days."

"We would," Cyrus agreed.

"So your landlord was savaged by a strange creature, and now you're playing vigilantes on the block?" Santana asked. "That doesn't put you two in a great situation, does it?"

The women looked at each other.

Cyrus replied, "That's exactly why we're doing it. I mean, Brian was the first domino in the equation. We *live* here, Santana. This is our home. We don't have jobs. We don't have money. The minute this building is listed, and someone else takes over, what happens to us then? Where do we go? What do we have to do to survive?"

Santana nodded sadly. "What's the second domino?"

This time Erika replied. "The other victims are all women in their twenties." Her face darkened. "That doesn't give us great odds."

Santana sighed. "If it's any consolation, you don't have to do this alone, and I might have some leads that will interest you."

Santana outlined what she knew about Darius Letterman and the activity which had happened in the surrounding blocks. She answered Erika's and Cyrus' questions as best she could but admitted that her information was limited. She didn't tell them about Terra Kris and the AJS aid she was receiving along the way.

"We need to go to the source. Find the bad guys," Erika stated.

"Duh..." Cyrus added.

"When the storm dies, we set out," Santana commented. "Day or night, we go. The five of us. We put a stop to this shit."

"Five?" Erika asked.

Cyrus rolled her eyes. "The dog."

"Oh." Erika cast a judgmental glance at Duchess.

After that, they had chatted for a short while longer about their lives before their fall. Erika and Cyrus lamented on their riches and the lavish lifestyle they'd led but managed to find some good in their humble living now.

"You don't understand the true value of life until everything has been stripped away, y'know?" Cyrus stated.

Erika nodded solemnly.

A short while later, Erika and Cyrus blew out the candles and left Santana to her slumber. Santana had fallen asleep easily, her body exhausted from the recent attack and the day's events.

Now she was awake, and in the darkness, her mind whirled and raced. She sat up. Duchess shifted on the floor, alert to Santana's movements. "It's okay, girl," she offered, reaching down and gently stroking the dog's head.

The place was quiet, and it was impossible to see anything with no windows leading to street level. She activated her phone screen, and a milky light lit the immediate vicinity.

Santana clamped a hand to her mouth to stifle a laugh. Gyles lay facing her, mouth open, strings of saliva darkening the side of the couch. He was still out cold. Santana couldn't decide between waking him to check that he was okay and no permanent brain damage had occurred and letting him rest and recover.

She rose to her feet, bare skin on the cold stone floor. Duchess delicately rose to her feet, but Santana commanded her to stay. Her head cocked, then she lay once more on the floor.

Santana made her way silently to the open doorway. To her right was the exit to the storm shelter. To her left, the corridor stretched into darkness. She was tempted to activate her flashlight but didn't want to alert anyone to her presence. Stealth was the key to safety.

A nervous feeling roiled in her gut. Gooseflesh erupted on her skin. She wasn't exactly sure what she was searching for, but her feet led her onward. She passed several doors that were all stripped of paint, many crooked and on their side. More boxes lined the corridor, and naked bulbs hung above her.

Someone coughed.

Santana froze. A soft voice reached her ears, menace in the words. "Die, you motherfucker."

Santana's brow creased. She patted her side, looking for her pistol, but discovered it was missing. Her bullwhip was with her, however, and she readied it in her hand, the long end of the coil trailing behind her.

She snaked around a corner and saw a soft light at the end of the hallway. The light was blue and flickering. It reminded Santana of the Atlanticore fragments and their strange alien light. The voice grew louder, and Santana now recognized Erika speaking. "You goddamn son of a bitch. I'll destroy you if it's the last thing I do."

A sudden burst of gunfire had Santana throwing herself against the wall. She pocketed her phone, removing the light that might draw Erika's attention as someone howled in pain. Santana glanced back the way she'd come. Then, with a determined look, she rushed to the doorway.

She drew her hand back, readying the whip. As the room came into sight, Santana snapped the whip, its end speeding toward the woman sitting by a desk in the center of the room. Erika had enough time to spin in her chair with shocked horror as the whip *cracked* and found its target.

A shower of glass erupted from the computer monitor, and the screen turned black.

Erika threw her hands over her head. "What the fuck are you doing?"

She scowled at Santana. A pair of glasses rested on the bridge of her nose. Santana drew the whip back, readying another strike as she took in the scene before her.

There were no bodies. There were no bullet holes. There was no blood.

There was only Erika sitting at a computer, speakers on, the desk littered with glass.

Erika looked around her in disgust. "You bitch. Do you have any idea how much that monitor cost?"

Santana lowered her hand, cheeks flushing. "I...I didn't..."

"Three thousand dollars," Erika expanded. "Just for the monitor alone, let alone the rest of the setup." She shook her head angrily. "You better hope that everything else is okay."

She busied herself hurrying around the space, checking that all the equipment was working. Satisfied, she turned back to Santana, her face of thunder. "What the hell were you thinking?"

Santana held her stare. "It sounded like someone was in trouble. I saw the light, heard the scream."

"It's Grand Theft Auto VII," Erika returned. "It's a video game. Jesus, not every gunshot in Atlantica is a cry for justice." She sighed. "I'm going to have to clean all this shit up now."

"Here, let me," Santana offered. She worked with Erika to clear all the shards of glass from the desk. They scooped the worst of it into a rusting wastepaper bin, then Santana helped Erika take a box from the side of the room and unpack its contents.

They set the backup monitor on the desk. Erika busied herself with the cables, tutting and making noises as she did. A minute later, the monitor illuminated, showcasing a logo on its screen. Another few seconds, and the word "Wasted" appeared on the screen in calligraphic font.

"And now I've lost the fucking mission." Erika poked her head out from beneath the desk, examining the monitor. She pushed herself into her chair. "At least I don't have to read those words in high definition, right? It would be *horrible* to have to experience the game on a luxury screen that lets you see what you're playing."

"I'm sorry," Santana offered.

"You said that already," Erika stated. "Not going to help me get my monitor back, is it?"

Santana rolled her eyes, then plucked her phone from her pocket. She tapped on the screen, then placed her phone above Erika's, which lay inactive on the desk. A chime confirmed the transfer.

"What was that?" Erika was confused.

"Your new monitor. I always pay my debts." She sat on a nearby wheeled chair. "Once again, I'm sorry."

Erika eyed her curiously. "You're a strange one."

"I've heard," Santana replied. "Though why do you think that, in this instance?"

Erika shrugged. "Most people wouldn't so willingly part with their cash like that." She glanced back at the monitor. It was half the size of the original, with cracks in two of the corners. A long scratch lined the center, with pixels of all colors distorted along its length. "Thank you."

"Don't mention it," Santana replied.

They sat a moment in quiet.

Santana glanced around the room. There was nothing much of note in there aside from the desk and the computer. It was a strange setup, not quite an office, not quite storage, not quite anything. "I thought you guys were broke?" Santana asked.

Erika raised an eyebrow.

"The computer," Santana clarified. "Doesn't look cheap."

"It's not," Erika admitted. "It's all I was able to salvage from my old life. I'd never much considered myself a 'gamer' until an ex introduced me to World of Warcraft." She scoffed with a nostalgic smile. "I lost hours to that thing—days, even. We'd sit side-by-side in our high-rise apartment, watching over the city as we slew orcs and adventured in mountains. Over time I upgraded to the best equipment moncy could buy..."

"Then he left you?" Santana asked.

Erika narrowed her eyes at Santana. "You're good at reading people."

"That's the first time anyone's said that to me."

Erika cast her gaze to the floor. "He took everything from me. Claimed that I wouldn't have had it if it wasn't for him. Over time I invested again, but never that much." She drew a long breath. "When I lost all my money, this was one of the only things

I managed to smuggle. Brian allowed me to plug it in, set me up with the Internet password. It's my only connection with my former life…and damn, I'm good."

"Must give you a real sense of control."

"It does," Erika admitted.

"Makes sense why you and Cyrus are all about vigilante justice." Santana nodded at the GTA screen. "Guns and bitches and drugs, right?"

Erika laughed, which took Santana off-balance. Was this the first time she'd heard Erika laugh? The first time she'd seen her relax?

"It's more than that," Erika replied. "That's a common misconception." Her gaze turned to the door. Santana looked over her shoulder, expecting someone would be standing there, but the place was empty. "Cyrus disagrees with me, of course. She says I waste too much time at night in the land of make-believe…but…"

"It's yours," Santana finished.

"It's mine," Erika agreed.

"Oh, cool. GTA," Gyles announced, standing at the door and blearily rubbing his eyes with the heel of his hand. "Which is that?"

His eyes were barely open, and he swayed a little where he stood.

"Are you okay?" Santana asked. "Here, take a seat."

She helped Gyles over to the chair she'd been sitting on. She fussed over him, checking the dilation of his pupils and examining the bump on his head.

"You took a hell of a tumble," Erika stated.

Gyles looked at her blankly. "A tumble?"

Erika looked at Santana for help. "Do you want to tell him, or should I?"

"You don't remember the attack with the lion?" Santana asked,

Gyles searched his memory, a pained look on his face. "Oh…

yeah. In the rain. We were on the trail of the lion, then…" He glared at Erika. "Someone shot at us."

"*Someones.*" Cyrus leaned against the doorjamb. "It's good to see you awake, friend."

"Friend?" Gyles turned to Santana. She relayed all that had happened, taking into account the perspective of the two women. He sat silent while they spoke, each chipping in a part of the tale.

"I remember…" Gyles replied at last. "I remember seeing them with you through the rain. The fear that they were going to hurt you. Then…"

"You jumped," Santana finished.

"I jumped." Gyles looked around guiltily, refusing to meet the women's eyes. "Although I clearly did more damage to myself than to you guys."

"I don't know." Cyrus rubbed her neck. "Those stairs weren't too friendly to me, either. You just got the raw end of the deal."

Gyles offered a weak smile.

Santana turned to Cyrus. "Sorry if we woke you."

"Don't mention it." She looked over the top of Santana to her companion, eyes fixing on the screen again. "Should've known I'd find you here."

"I figured one last game before we…y'know…" Erika explained.

"Don't talk like that," Cyrus scolded. "We're not going to die."

Santana looked between the two, confused. "What's going on?"

Erika sighed.

Cyrus spoke for her. "Erika believes that this mission we're about to set out on will be her last."

"Could be," Erika commented.

"You don't know that," Cyrus returned.

"This is Atlantica!" Erika cried, voice raised and cutting through the room. "The moment we track them and step into their boundaries, we're fair game. Who knows what will happen?"

Santana met Cyrus' gaze, the woman looking for backup. Santana could offer none. She was right.

Santana sighed. "As long as we have a game plan going in, we have as much chance of survival as we do of death."

"What's the game plan?" Gyles asked, seemingly joining Erika's side. "They've sent two lions after you. I hate to use an overtired cliche, but if we manage to find them, aren't we entering the lion's den?"

Santana considered this, allowing her mind a moment to think. Gyles was right. Twice now they'd set a lion upon her. She still didn't have a clear reason why, although she believed she knew.

The lions were a cleanup crew, taking out those who knew too much about their operation. If the enemy had researched Santana, they knew that she was probably the best person in Atlantica to take out if they wanted to continue their endeavors.

An idea came to her then, as her mind filled with visions of marsupial lions leaping and jagged teeth snapping in her face. An idea so simple, it was a wonder she hadn't thought of it already.

"Has the AJS cleared the area?" Santana asked.

Cyrus shrugged. "Haven't checked."

"Find out if they're gone," Santana replied. "We need to know when we can move out."

Cyrus nodded, then left.

"In the meantime," Santana continued, "I might have to make a quick pitstop. Will you three be safe down here?"

"Four," Erika corrected. "The dog."

Santana smirked. "Right."

Cyrus returned a moment later. "A few of them are still up there, but there's room to leave without being noticed."

"Gotcha," Santana replied. "I'll be back *real* soon."

Gyles looked as if he was about to protest but remained quiet.

Santana moved through the corridors, only stopping when she reached the room where Duchess obediently waited.

"I'll be back soon, girl. Okay?" Santana cooed as she sat to pull on her boots.

Duchess' tail wagged weakly. Cyrus appeared behind Santana. "Don't worry. I've got her."

Santana smiled, then carefully opened the front doors. She looked up the steps and into the misty darkness. The rain had stopped, and in its wake, the fog fell thick—perfect conditions for Santana.

She checked her cell phone and found four missed calls and twelve messages from Terra. A glance at the preview made Santana's heart sink.

They had set a lion on her last night, too. Of course, they had. Erika was right—anything could happen.

This was Atlantica, after all.

CHAPTER TWENTY-ONE

Santana hammered her fist on the glass door.

The sign read "Closed," but she knew that Emily wouldn't be asleep. Even with the running of the Emporium, Emily was a night owl. It was something Santana had marveled at over the years, how a British woman could be so averse to sleep but still get so much done.

The animals inside were rattled. They barked and squawked and shrilled at Santana's disturbance. Soon, a voice called out, muffled through the glass.

"I've got a gun," Emily declared.

Santana couldn't see her in the darkness.

"I've got a problem," Santana replied, cupping her hands to the glass to get a better view. A shadow shifted down one of the aisles, and Emily's head poked into sight, accompanied by the long barrel of a shotgun. "Santana?"

"Hey." Santana offered an apologetic smile and stepped back.

Emily worked through the series of protective locks, then opened the door. Santana checked over her shoulder before entering the building.

"I could've killed you," Emily stated. "What were you doing out there?"

"First off, no you couldn't have," Santana replied. She rapped on the glass with her knuckles. "Bulletproof. I'm not an idiot."

Emily offered a warm smile.

"Second of all, I need your help," Santana stated.

Emily nodded, curiosity lighting her features. She worked her way around the store, settling the animals down before waving Santana to the back. "Come on, then. Let's see what I can do for you."

Emily led Santana through the back of the store. The cats were asleep at the side of the halls, but there had been no attempt at any kind of tidying. Seed and boxes remained strewn across the floor, and Santana had to watch where she stepped to follow Emily.

Emily unlocked the security door, and Santana entered the familiar mist of Emily's private stores. In the center of the room sat a glass tank with a snake coiled at the bottom. It appeared to be dead, to begin with, but as the door closed, the snake's head raised, its eyes fixed on Emily.

Emily followed Santana's gaze. "An inland taipan," she explained. "The world's most venomous snake. Not only does it have the highest levels of toxicity of any of its brethren, it injects the *most* out of them all. You get bitten by this sucker, and you'll know it. Well...maybe you won't. Depends on how much you remember in the moments before you die."

"Looks cute." Santana crouched to eye level with the reptile. The taipan turned its gaze to her, rearing its head back. It flashed its teeth, then lunged at the glass.

Santana held her resolve.

"I'd be careful." Emily chuckled. "Don't get her too riled up. I have to milk her in the morning." She crouched beside Santana. "One bite is capable of killing a hundred men. Can you imagine what it's like to harness that power in weaponry? Toxic gas... darts...solvents for poisoning drinks... You name it."

"I thought you meant you'd be working on an anti-venom." Santana smiled.

Emily raised an eyebrow. "Have you met me?" She stood. "A small portion of it will, of course. You don't want to work in a lab where you create poisonous weapons without having an anti-venom to hand. Though, truth be told, there'd be little point in producing one. Once that shit gets inside you, it's practically game over. You'd have to be a real Speedy Gonzales to get the antidote into your veins."

She eyed Santana curiously. "So, once again I ask, to what do I owe this pleasure? Do you need me to outline the three types of toxins again?"

Santana rose to her full height. "No, that won't be necessary. I'm in the market for something a little different today."

"Oh? Do tell."

Santana considered her response, her gaze catching the metal lockers behind Emily. "Tell me. What do you know about animal scents?"

Santana left the Emporium a half-hour later, her pack laden with clattering vials. The sun was beginning to show, the night yielding to the first patches of pink and purple in the sky.

Cars lazily drove by, only a fraction of what the later traffic would become. Santana waved goodbye to Emily, then took a right and strolled down the street. She stopped at the corner, then drew out her phone. She hailed a driverless cab, and three minutes later she was speeding through the city.

She rested her head and closed her eyes, allowing herself a moment of calm. Somewhere in the city, AJS sirens blared, a sound she'd become used to. Avoiding the constant alarm of sirens was one of the main reasons Santana felt so at home in the wilds. Out there, apart from the chirp of insects and the occasional rustle of an animal through the brush, all was relatively quiet.

Something *beeped* on the cab's dashboard. Santana opened her eyes and found a blinking red light on the panel. "What's going on?"

There was no response. Santana looked around the cab, hunting for a source of disruption. There was nothing that she could see. The radio still played softly, and the cab continued along its way.

She looked over her shoulder out the back window. Several cars were following her, all shades and colors and shapes. She was about to turn back when she spotted something that raised the hairs on the back of her neck.

She couldn't put her finger on what it was, but she sat up straight, studying the fleet behind her. As they turned onto a new road, some of the cars veered off, heading in different directions.

One car in particular—*the black car*—held her gaze.

Santana narrowed her eyes, head tilting to the side as she tried to see through the darkened windows. She could make out the shape of two figures inside, but there were no distinguishing features.

"Move faster," Santana ordered the cab.

The cab remained silent.

Santana's heart rate quickened. She reached for her bag and secured her pistol in her hand. The car behind drew closer, following them like a silent shadow.

They were only a few blocks away from her destination now, and Santana grew nervous. She wondered if she was overreacting until a memory surfaced: sprinting down her apartment building stairs, emerging into the night, the screech of tires as a car sped into the distance.

This car?

Santana considered the fact that she was maybe being paranoid until the car window rolled down and a hand emerged.

She ducked as the first shot fired.

"Shit!" She squeezed herself into the footwell. The glass on the back window held firm but with a large spiderweb crack in the center. Santana thanked her lucky stars that the city had invested in bulletproof glass for many—unfortunately not all—businesses.

The cab rounded another corner. Another shot fired. The glass cracked more but held firm. Santana watched out the side windows, only able to determine her location by the façades of the large buildings that blurred past.

"How long until we get there?" Santana asked.

"One minute until destination," the cab announced. "Calling the Atlantica Justice System."

"Double shit." That was all she needed—a group of asshole bad guys and the friggin' justice team.

She tapped through her address book and found Terra's number. She dialed and was delightedly surprised when Terra answered. "Santana? I've been trying to get hold of you."

A shot fired.

"What was that?" Terra asked.

Santana chuckled, but there was no humor in it. "You'd have thought that all your years on the force might've trained you to detect a gunshot when you heard one."

Terra replied, "Santana, where are you?"

"No idea," Santana answered. "I'm in the footwell of a cab speeding toward somewhere near Brian Felkins' place."

"Oh, damn," Terra replied. "You're the call we received on the system. Hold right there. I'll be with you guys as soon as I can."

"I'm not sure how long I have to play with," Santana stated.

Terra had already hung up.

Tires screeched on the blacktop. Santana pushed herself up, raising her head enough to peer through the shattered window. Through the cracks and chips, she could now see the black car right behind them. A man leaned out the side window as he lined up his shot and fired again.

Santana ducked. This time the window caved in, covering her in glass. The cab sped up, a sudden burst of speed throwing Santana against the footrest.

Shouts rang from behind her. Another shot fired and embedded itself in a front headrest.

Santana's lip curled. She pushed herself up on her elbows, ignoring the irritating pain that accompanied the movement, then shot back.

The man tucked himself inside the car. Santana's shot clipped his side mirror. The driver poked his head around and shot back. Santana moved just in time, the bullet hitting the windshield now.

"Pull over," Santana declared.

The cab sped up.

"I said pull over, dammit!" Santana bellowed.

"Security protocol dictates public service vehicles cannot allow customers to put themselves in the way of harm," an electronic voice announced.

Santana turned to the dash panel, catching her first glimpse of the road for a few minutes. All of the driverless cabs—and there were many—had slowed and moved out of the way. It seemed that the network talked and knew when to allow another to pass to preserve its passenger's safety.

"Holy... It's Asimov's laws of robotics. A robot may not injure a human being, or through inaction, allow a human being to come to harm." Santana paused then ordered, "I am commanding you to pull over. Let me out, now."

The cab drove on, its speed unaltered. Behind them, tires screeched and more shots fired.

Santana's ears pricked at the sound of an AJS siren. She peeked through the front window, expecting a series of AJS cruisers to speed around the corner. Instead, a lone motorcycle raced into view.

The bike careened toward them. The shots from behind redirected toward Terra, who kept low behind her bike's frame. She zigzagged until she was closer, then raised her Glock and shot at the assholes.

One of the tires burst. The car passed Santana, and now she was pissed. She wasn't going to let this cab carry her away from the action like some damsel in distress.

She pressed her back to the side of the cab and kicked the opposite door. When it wouldn't budge, she shot at the glass several times before aiming a final bullet at the lock.

"Updating damage report," the cab announced. "Please be aware that we will add damages to your account."

With a final kick, the door swung open. Santana leaned forward as if preparing to jump out of a plane. "Send me the bill."

She launched from the cab, straightening her body to allow her to roll like a pencil and dispel the impact. Her skin grazed along the rough blacktop. She grunted, feeling nauseous as her body whirled.

When she stopped, she stood, shaking her head. Terra had veered behind a nearby Land Rover and was engaged in a shootout with the people from the car. Something *pinged* off the ground near Santana, and she saw then that one of them had peeled off and was snaking toward her.

Santana shot back, catching the guy in his forearm. She ducked behind the nearest parked car, then turned to find several civilians watching from the safety of the windows above.

Everyone loves a good show in Atlantica.

She leaned around the corner, gun at the ready, but the man was nowhere in sight.

Movement in the window above caught her eye. Someone pointed angrily to a place behind her. Santana grasped her bullwhip and closed her eyes, listening for any sound that might alert her to their presence.

A *crunch* sounded.

A *scrape* met her ears.

She whirled, flicking out the whip. A great crack accompanied the lash as the man groaned in pain. A red streak appeared on his shoulder, the material of his shirt parting at the whip's touch. Santana lashed out again, this time leaving a glowing welt on his hand. The man dropped the gun.

Santana wasn't done.

Her body ached. Glass prickled her skin. She cracked the whip, then aimed it toward the man's neck. The coil looped around the thick fat connecting the man's chin to his collarbone, creating a stranglehold that he couldn't undo.

Santana tugged toward her, and the man's feet scrambled to keep up with him, his body almost hurtling to the ground. When he was within reach, Santana loosed the whip from his neck, then launched a fist at his cheek.

The man spat blood as his eyes rolled. He drunkenly fought to steady himself, throwing a lazy punch in Santana's direction, but she stepped around it, landing a foot on the small of his back.

The man went down. His eyes were closed. Santana retrieved his gun, then headed over to where the main action was.

Terra had made quite a mess of the car, the outer shell riddled with bullet holes. She'd blown out the two tires on this side, and it looked as if the two remaining gentlemen would be going nowhere.

Santana worked her way to Terra, stopping at a car adjacent to the one the officer ducked behind. She crouched and called, "You took your sweet time."

Terra smirked. "Some call it fashionably late."

"Don't talk to me about fashion," Santana returned.

Terra laughed, then flinched as a bullet tore over her. "You wanna talk clothes, or you want to end this?"

"End this, please." Santana grinned.

She dropped the man's pistol, then retrieved her tranquilizer gun. Terra gave her a long, analyzing stare, that green light flickering behind her eye. "Tranqs?"

"We want them alive, don't we?" Santana called.

Terra considered this.

"Terra!" Santana shot back.

"Fine," Terra acquiesced with a hint of playfulness. "I'll draw them out. You do your thing."

Terra loaded a fresh magazine, then blasted the car with a barrage of bullets. The two men groaned, shrinking out of sight. Santana curved around the side of her parked car, then dashed across the road toward the pair.

The moment they came into sight, she was ready. She pulled the trigger, a dart flying straight into the thick flesh of the first man's shoulder.

He stood, firing at her. Santana dove to reach a car on their side of the road. She rolled, using her momentum to carry her forward. When she was upright once more, she leaned around the back of the car and found her final shot.

The second man yelled in surprise, then ripped the dart from his skin. It was already too late. The tranquilizer was working its magic in his bloodstream.

The first man shot at Santana, eyelids closing. His bullet ran stray, arm raising as he fought for balance. The shot found its way into the upper windows above, the class cracking as several gasps and cries rang out.

There were no casualties.

The second man shouted something that caught Santana by surprise.

"Beg. Zapustit'!"

Russian? Santana thought.

Then the man was down, fast asleep on the sidewalk. His head *thumped* loudly against the stone, and the world fell quiet.

Santana made her way to the two men. Terra crossed the road with eyes fixed on the pair, gun still ready in her hands. There was a determined look on her face that Santana admired, a look that spoke of justice and the law.

"They're secure?" Terra asked.

"Not until they're in cuffs," Santana replied.

Terra crouched and bound the pair's wrists.

"We make a good team," Santana offered, brushing off the worst of the glass from her forearms. Most of it was superficial damage, although a few shards had worked their way beneath the skin.

"Are you saying you want to join the AJS?" Terra replied without looking. "Because I've told you before…I can make that happen. It's about time you came over to the blue side."

Santana scoffed. "I meant you should join me in the jungle. Me and you out there in the trees… We'd be unstoppable. Full freedom. The stars above you at night."

Terra laughed. "In Atlantica? With this perm fog? I'd *love* to see that."

"You've still not seen the stars?" Santana asked.

Terra stood, still distracted. "I've seen stars, Sokolov. Just maybe not with the crystal clarity that you have."

"We have to get you off this island one day," Santana offered.

A sad look haunted Terra's face. "Yeah. One day." She glanced around, looking for something. When Santana followed her gaze, she realized what she was looking for.

The third man had vanished.

"Where is he?" Santana asked.

Terra remained quiet, eyes narrowing. She held up a finger to Santana, then touched one to her ear. She slowly scanned the place. Santana got a distinct impression that Terra could see things that Santana couldn't.

"There," Terra announced softly, eyes boring into a red postal van on the other side of the road. "He's poised, ready to run."

"How can you—" Santana asked, still not quite able to believe what Terra had told her about APRIL's abilities.

Terra had already broken into a sprint. She tore across the road, aiming for the hood of the van. Santana heard scuffles as the third man took off. She ran after Terra, ready to provide backup, but she needn't have bothered.

Terra jumped onto the hood of the vehicle, then raised herself to her full height. She drew her pistol, closed one eye, and tracked the man.

He broke toward a nearby green, head down, one shoulder dropped lower than the other. Terra lined up the shot. Then, as the man neared the safety of a brick wall, she shot.

The man went down, a cry of pain accompanying his descent. Terra lowered her gun slowly, waiting a moment before confirming, "He's down. Let's bring them in."

Santana drew up beside her, taking in the impressiveness of the shot Terra had made.

Terra hopped from the hood of the car. "I'll grab this one. You make sure the others stay exactly where they are."

Santana nodded, then returned to the two sleeping attackers.

CHAPTER TWENTY-TWO

Terra called for backup to help them handle the three perps they'd cuffed. While the two women were strong, two of the men were fast asleep, and one wouldn't walk for some time. Terra's bullet had ripped through his ankle.

"We'll get them in the cruisers, then back to the station for questioning," Terra announced.

The two officers nodded dutifully, then turned to grab the sleeping perps' arms.

"No," Santana protested.

"What?" Terra asked, surprised.

"I've got a place nearby where we can find out what's going on. It'll be quicker, and you won't have to abide by the city's shitty rules," Santana informed them. "Let's get them private so we can extract the information we need."

"Are you suggesting torture?" Terra's gaze drifted to the two officers who'd paused near their cruiser.

Santana shook her head. "I'm talking about *a more convenient place to ask questions.*"

Terra chuckled. "Sokolov, it's a nice notion, but it's rare that anyone will allow an officer of the law to come into private quarters with permission. There's too much at stake for the—"

"Trust me," Santana replied. When the officers glanced at each other again, she added, "I'll direct you. Just… Come on."

She confidently strode to the other officers and helped them put the men in the back. She sat with them, pressed against the glass as the three lolled around on the back seat. She directed the officers around the corner toward the storm shelter beneath the apartment building.

"Wait there," she told the officers.

Terra dismounted her bike with an amused grin. "You heard her," she told the other officers.

Santana led Terra down the stairs, then knocked loudly. A series of bolts slid before Erika's head appeared behind the door.

Santana stopped her from closing it with a steady hand. "Erika, wait."

Erika didn't reappear. Instead, it was Cyrus' head that poked around the door. "Santana? What's going on? I thought you were getting something."

"I got more than what I asked for." Santana displayed her forearms to demonstrate. "I have three assholes out here who Terra has kindly offered to allow us to bring into private quarters to question."

Confusion painted Cyrus' face. "Can't you just take them to the AJS…"

"*Private*," Terra emphasized.

Realization dawned on Cyrus' face. "Where are they?"

"In the cruiser," Santana replied. "The officers are ready to bring them in at our command."

"*My* command," Terra corrected.

"No," Erika announced boldly, reappearing around the door. "We're not letting the fuzz in here."

"Erika…" Santana began.

"No!" Erika repeated. "They're like fucking vampires. The

moment they step through the threshold, they can do whatever the fuck they like. No. I won't allow it. No."

"We're not doing anything wrong," Cyrus argued.

"We're homeless!" Erika argued. "You remember our predicament, don't you? We're stowaways."

"*Private* stowaways." Cyrus turned to Erika. "They can't do anything inside our place." Her brow creased. "Wait…Can they?"

Santana held up her hands. "Ladies, ladies… Look. She's a friend of mine. We can trust her. I wouldn't bring a cop inside unless I knew they were good people."

Cyrus and Erika exchanged a glance.

"Trust me," Santana added. "I'm on your side, remember?"

A small bark emitted from behind the women, followed by another set of footsteps. Duchess appeared through the crack in the door, Gyles calling after her. "Duchess!"

Duchess saw Terra and slipped between the two women. She sniffed Terra's ankles, then licked her leg. Terra crouched and gently stroked the mane of hair around her neck. "Hey girl, how you doing?" She noticed the areas where the hair had parted, and blood had clotted. "What happened to you?"

"Long story," Santana replied. Judging by Terra's look, she already guessed the truth. Santana returned her attention to the women. "See? Duchess knows good from bad."

Cyrus sighed. "Fine. Come on in."

Erika looked like she wanted to argue but thought better of it.

The officers at the top of the stairs started down.

"Just you," Cyrus clarified.

Terra gave the others instructions to bring the three men down. They obeyed, then returned to their cruiser. Terra told them to head back to the station. She would contact them when she needed further assistance.

They muttered to each other as they turned. Terra glared at them. "I'd keep your words to yourself until you return to the station, friends. Bad mouthing a senior officer won't do well for your career prospects, will it?"

They shut their mouths, and soon Santana heard the cruiser doors close. Terra shook her head. "They still don't realize that I can hear them now."

She passed inside with Santana, leaving Cyrus and Erika perplexed.

They lugged the men to the same couches where Santana and Gyles had slept the night before. Once they were seated, they examined their bonds and ensured they were stripped of any items that might cause harm. Erika lit candles while Cyrus brought in additional chairs.

Duchess stood by Santana's side, eyes locked on the three men.

"What happened to you?" Gyles asked Santana softly enough that the others couldn't hear.

"Long story."

Gyles chuckled. "Always is with you."

They took their seats facing the three men. Erika and Cyrus lingered near the door, arms folded like two security guards at a night club.

"You might want to start talking," Terra instructed the only man who was conscious right now. He was older than the others, his hair silver, combed in a severe part that had been ruffled from the morning's events. His lip curled, eyes boring into the two women as he sat awkwardly, every tiny movement increasing the pain in his ankle.

Santana glanced down at the mess Terra had created. There was a red chunk missing, some of the bone visible and pink. It hung crooked, and Santana found herself feeling sorry for the guy who had, only a short time ago, been trying to kill her.

"Talk," Terra repeated, this time drawing her weapon and holding it on the man.

The man grumbled and spat on the couch.

Duchess bristled.

"You won't get shit from me," the man informed them. "You want us dead? Just do it. Put that bullet through. You won't make us talk."

Terra nodded, then rose from her chair. She approached the two sleeping men and crouched in front of them. "I believe that *you* won't," Terra stated. "But these two…maybe they're smarter than you."

She drew a cartridge from her pocket with two small prongs on one side. With force, she pressed the cartridge into the stomach of one man, then the other. At its touch, an electric hum and crackle sounded in the room, and the men jolted awake.

Their bonds held them tightly. They shouted, surprised to find they weren't where they'd been. They took in the room, drinking in the people around them, before one of them cried, "Gde my? Kto ty?"

The other locked eyes with Terra, then Santana. "Tishe. Nichego ne govoryat. Derzhi guby zakrytymi."

Terra moved back a touch as the second man to wake attempted to kick her, only realizing then that he was bound by the ankles to the couch.

"APRIL," Terra announced, "care to translate?"

"No need," Santana replied. She pointed at the first man to wake, who looked like a real-life version of Mr. Potato Head. His face was round and speckled with dark spots, three chins wrinkled at his lower jaw. "This guy wants to know where they are," she turned her finger to the other, "and this gentleman is telling everyone to keep quiet. Ain't that about right?"

The third man was the youngest, but seemed to be the one who had the most of his faculties. His eyes were dark and keen, blond hair short and spiked at the front. "You speak the mother tongue?"

Santana nodded. "Da. Rossiya tozhe moy dom."

Yes. Russia is my home, too.

Terra chuckled. "If you don't mind, I'd rather we did this in English. It makes it easier for all those involved, y'know?"

"Poshel ty," the younger man crowed.

"What did he say?" Terra asked.

"Fuck you," Santana replied.

Terra placed a hand on her chest. "I was only asking."

Santana smirked. Behind them, Gyles chuckled.

Duchess grew a touch braver, her nose twitching as she sniffed toward the men.

Terra turned her chair, straddling the seat and leaning on the back. "So? Who's going to squeal first? We've got all day to play games down here, in private, away from the public eye. What's it going to take to make the parrots squawk?"

"You stupid Atlantican," Silver replied. "You are of the law. You have nothing inside these quarters. The law doesn't protect you here."

"Nor does it protect you." Terra looked over her shoulder. "These lovely ladies have invited me into their home. So while I might not entirely be representing the AJS in this...whatever this place is...I'm going to make damn sure I do whatever it takes to get the information from you to hold you to account."

She leaned closer to Silver. "No matter what it takes."

Potato Head opened his mouth to respond, but cut short as Santana stood and cracked the whip at his side. The cushion bounced, a split appearing on its surface as stuffing sprouted from the wound.

"I recommend you try listening, to start with," Santana commanded.

Potato Head glared at her.

Terra shot Santana a satisfied smile. "Okay, then. Here we go. What were you three doing tailing Ms. Sokolov through the city today?"

They remained silent, gazes boring into Terra. "It's a simple question. One that Ms. Sokolov deserves answers to, don't you think?"

Duchess' nose worked against the floor, the dog sniffing around the men before turning and heading toward Erika and Cyrus.

"No?" Terra stood, shaking her head. "You're going to make us do this the hard way, are you?"

She crossed to the men and crouched before them. She drew the cartridge from her pocket once more and held it in front of them. She thumbed the button, and hot white sparks crossed between the two prongs.

"Who first?" She turned to Silver. "You, I think."

Before he could protest, Terra dug the prongs into the meat of his thigh. Silver's body grew rigid, his ankle hitting the floor. He jerked, mouth foaming as she held the taser to his leg.

Finally, she released the trigger, and Silver howled in pain, maneuvering his ankle into a position that would be less painful, but finding none that would soften the hot agony.

Terra raised her voice. "Now. Are we ready to talk?"

The two Russians on the other couch looked at each other nervously. The younger, blond one whispered the same instruction again. "Tishe."

Hush.

"You?" Terra dug the taser into his leg. Blondie performed an exact mimicry of Silver, his jerks stopping at the withdrawal of the Taser's prongs.

"Anything?" Terra asked.

Blondie bit his lips, chest heaving.

Terra shrugged. "How about you? Fancy a go on the electro wheel?" She flashed the sparks, and this time Potato Head protested, desperately trying to avoid going through what his comrades had. "Fine! Fine…"

Blondie barked at him. "No. Tishe!"

Potato Head avoided his gaze. "I'll talk. Spare me. Please. I'll talk…"

Terra smirked, then pocketed the taser. "Good lad. Ms. Sokolov, over to you."

Santana moved closer to the chubby man. "Why were you following me?"

As he opened his mouth to talk, Blondie unleashed a barrage of shouts in Russian, angrily toppling toward Potato Head as he attempted to cover and muffle any sound that might leave his mouth. Terra stepped forward and punched Blondie in the jaw so hard that the *crack* bounced around the room. Blondie's eyes rolled back into his head as he flopped facedown onto Potato Head's lap.

"We were sent, okay?" Potato Head stated. "You have worked yourself into the line of sight of very bad people, Ms. Sokolov. People who are determined to see you…" He turned his gaze to Terra. "…and your friend destroyed."

"Destroyed," Terra mused. "How poetic."

"Who?" Santana asked. "Who set their sights on us?"

Potato Head didn't reply, instead he fought with an internal dialogue Santana couldn't decipher.

Santana cracked the whip.

"Fine!" Potato Head gasped. "Fine… You are in the eyes of the snake. Their venom is channeling toward you. There's only so long you can go until it strikes."

"Kobra?" Santana asked.

Silver shifted at the name.

"Kobra," Potato Head repeated. "Kobra wants you dead. Kobra gets you dead. It is the way of things."

"Who is Kobra?" Terra asked. "Did Kobra send you?"

Potato Head shook his head. "No."

"Then why did you say that?" Cyrus demanded, unable to hold back.

Duchess sniffed around her feet.

"Our employer is a puppet for Kobra." Potato Head gazed down at his lap, staring at the back of Blondie's head.

"Who is your employer?" Santana pressed. She *cracked* the whip again. Blondie woke with a grunt. "Who?"

"His name is Darius…" Potato Head began.

"Letterman?" Terra finished.

Blondie's eyes widened as his consciousness returned.

"We've encountered him before," Santana stated. "Where can we find him?"

Duchess barked.

"He is hidden," Potato Head replied. "Surrounded by security measures unparalleled by any you might've encountered."

A nostalgic grin appeared on Terra's face. "I highly doubt that."

"You'll never be able to enter—" Potato Head continued.

"Zatknis'!" Blondie shouted.

Shut your mouth.

"Let him speak," Santana warned, holding the whip high.

Blondie debated speaking but chose to remain quiet.

Duchess barked again, growing in fervor. Erika tried to soothe her, but she snapped at the woman's hand.

"Where is he?" Santana shouted.

Potato Head's shoulders softened. "Beneath the abbey. Two blocks from here."

"No!" Blondie called.

The whip *cracked*. A red line appeared on Blondie's cheek.

"There's an entrance beneath the pulpit," Potato Head finished. "That's all I know."

Santana gave a satisfied nod, meeting Terra's gaze. Duchess continued her barrage of barks. Santana turned to find Gyles trying to calm her, but Duchess' nose pointed straight at the bundle of items they'd confiscated from the men.

"What is it, girl?" Santana asked. She moved to Duchess' side. The dog whined and barked, the sounds bursting against

Santana's eardrums. She drew out a discarded handkerchief that had come from Silver's pocket. Duchess stuck her nose in it, and Santana spotted several hairs against the white cloth.

She opened her pack and drew out the knuckle they'd taken from the lion's enclosure. Duchess sniffed the knuckle, then the handkerchief before exploding into a series of confirming barks.

Santana looked over her shoulder at the three Russians. "You motherfuckers…"

CHAPTER TWENTY-THREE

"The lion is below the abbey," Santana stated. "I'm certain of it."

They'd left the Russians in the room, guarded by Erika. Out of the group, she was the one who seemed to have the most intimidating effect on the three.

"They're keeping lions below a church?" Terra asked. "This city never ceases to amaze me."

Santana stood in Erika's computer room, unloading her backpack to check that she had everything she needed. Her gaze lingered on the vials Emily had provided, and she ensured that they went into her pocket instead of in her pack.

"How are we supposed to get in?" Gyles asked. "If the entrance is beneath the pulpit, what if that's the only way in and out? That'll mean they'll be onto us straight away."

Terra checked her weapons and ammunition, ensuring she was stocked and ready. "Leave that to me."

Gyles stared at her blankly. "Why? Because you have super X-ray vision that can see through walls?"

Santana and Terra exchanged a glance.

"Not X-ray," Terra replied, leaving Gyles flummoxed.

"I'm staying here," Cyrus replied. Before the others could

protest, she added, "I'll keep Duchess safe. I might want to help you guys, but the best way I can do it is to stay here with your hostages and the dog. I'll keep them watered and fed. Keep them tied up. Erika is the better shot. You'll want her, not me."

They studied her in silence for a moment before Gyles asked, "They're not hostages, are they?"

"Technically," Terra replied.

"Fine," Santana added with a wave. "Whatever works. Can we get moving, please, before they realize their stooges are gone, and they set another fucking lion on my ass?"

Terra holstered her Glock. "I thought it was your shoulder they got?"

Santana glared at her.

Terra laughed.

Ten minutes later they were out the door with Erika in tow. Duchess didn't appreciate staying behind with Cyrus and the others, but she'd done her job and dutifully remained. When they were on street level, several civilians looked their way. Some of them clearly recognize the group from the showdown in the street.

"Let's move," Terra commanded. She cast a wanting stare back at her bike, then strolled down the street toward the abbey.

Richmond Abbey was two blocks away. It was a large, traditional building made from stone, with stained glass windows that towered high on all sides. Scaffolding surrounded the spire, which had famously been struck by lightning only a few weeks ago, and repairs were underway by the construction team as the building came into view.

Surrounding the abbey was a grass common, devoid of the typical smattering of tombstones and graves that decorated the borders of religious spaces. Instead, it held a series of ponds, benches, and flowerbeds, the abbey making a conscious effort during its build to become a place of beauty and community.

They stood a short distance away on the sidewalk, taking in

the space before them. There was no sign that anything untoward was happening below the ground. Couples walked around the flowerbeds. The hum of drilling and power tools came from the platforms by the spire. Had they not known any better, it would be easy to assume that this was merely a place of peace.

"There are people inside," Terra stated, eyes narrowed on the building's façade.

Gyles frowned. "Seriously, how are you doing this?"

Santana shot him a "don't ask" look.

Erika pointed ahead. "I see two entrances. The big doors at the front, which are already open for the public to enter." She swung her arm around. "Or that door at the side. That must be for the abbot or the monks."

"I say we go in the front," Terra stated. "Stay in plain sight. We might have to disperse to remain anonymous."

"Anonymous?" Santana glanced at Terra's AJS uniform. "You might've thought of that before you came out sporting the blues."

"Good point." Terra looked around and spotted a nearby fashion store. "Wait one moment."

She vanished inside, then reappeared a few minutes later wearing a pair of sleek black slacks and a t-shirt with camouflage patterns.

"I thought you didn't want to get into jungle work," Santana muttered as the other woman reached her side.

"It was all they had," Terra replied. "Okay, here's the plan. Gyles and I will enter the abbey and search for the entrance. Erika and Santana, you stalk the grounds for a minute or two, then enter after us. Play it cool. Examine the architecture. Hell, pray at the altar for all I care. Just don't draw attention to yourself."

"You might want to avoid saying 'hell,'" Erika added with a grin.

They watched as Gyles and Terra crossed the road. When

they reached the other side, Terra placed her hand into Gyles'. Even from this distance, Santana could see his blush.

"Our turn." Santana offered a hand for Erika to hold.

Erika glanced down. "You must be kidding."

Santana laughed. "Lighten up. You're too easy. Come on."

They crossed the road, spending a few moments walking around the grounds of the abbey. They were well-maintained, the grass neatly kept, the flowers in various colors that looked almost fake with how vibrant they were. They examined the pond, spotting several soft-shelled turtles floating beneath the surface.

Santana shuddered.

"What is it?" Erika asked.

Santana shook her head. "Don't worry about it."

They turned to the abbey and made their way inside. General chatter flowed in the groups that strolled around, admiring the architecture and the narratives of the stained glass. A deep reverence settled over Santana, and she wondered how a building such as this could hold such weight, even to one who didn't believe.

"It's beautiful," she muttered.

Erika reluctantly nodded, also taken aback.

Santana monitored Terra and Gyles, who loitered around the pulpit. She strolled around the outside of the pews alongside Erika, keeping an eye on the others around her. From what she could see, only civilians filled the place, but in Atlantica, even that could be folly to assume.

"What's taking them so long?" Erika asked.

Santana motioned at the long rows of benches. "Take a pew."

"What's that mean?" Erika questioned.

Santana motioned again. "Take a seat."

"Well, just say that then." Erika sat and slid along the wooden bench to allow Santana some room.

"Clasp your hands and pray," Santana instructed.

"I'm not religious," Erika argued.

"You might need to be for the next few minutes. Because it looks like things are about to get a little rowdy."

Terra left Gyles at the pulpit as she took center stage in the abbey. She raised her hands, a gleaming badge in one palm. "Ladies and gentlemen, may I have your attention for a moment, please."

The chattering stopped as faces turned to look at Terra. A deep silence took over.

Terra continued, "I am an Officer for Justice with the Atlantica Justice System, and I would please ask that you momentarily vacate the building while we investigate an incident on these premises."

Faces stared blankly at her.

A door opened at the back of the building.

"This is not a drill," Terra added, moving forward to usher out those that were nearest. They turned, walking to the door. Slowly the others started to follow.

"Excuse me?" A man appeared through the door, his voice soft yet commanding. He wore all black robes with a gold chain and a cross emblem hanging from his neck. "Is there a problem here, Officer?"

"I have reason to believe that this is a site of interest for an ongoing investigation," Terra announced, eyes meeting Santana's. "It's best that your patrons vacate the premises while we explore further. This won't take long."

The abbot held an unnerving calm. "I don't believe the AJS has authority within the house of God, my child." He cast a forced smile. "Unless I am otherwise mistaken."

"Atlantica rule fourteen-point-three," Terra replied. "Houses of worship, unless otherwise funded by private benefactors, are to fall within the jurisdiction of Atlantican law. According to our system, this building was bought and paid for, with no private benefactors, only public donations."

The abbot nodded. He swept his smile around the room. "You heard the officer, my children. Please forgive the intrusion."

"That means you, too," Terra added.

The abbot cocked his head. "Surely you wouldn't usher an old man from his home."

"God made the Earth our home," Terra shot back. "Not a single mound of bricks and mortar."

They stared at each other a long moment before the abbot caved. "Very well." He shuffled down the center aisle and closed the doors behind them, leaving the four of them in peace.

"What are you doing?" Santana asked as she and Erika made their way toward the pulpit. "You're drawing far too much attention to us."

"There's no one down there," Terra replied. "The entrance is vacant."

"What entrance?" Gyles asked. "I couldn't see anything."

"You weren't looking hard enough," Terra replied.

She crouched, looking at the underside of the bulbous stone that topped the pulpit. There were a few cracks in it next to a plate that looked as though it held the top to the base.

"Here." Terra touched a finger to the plate. Something mechanical *clicked*. A beep sounded. She stood back, grasping the top of the pulpit as though she were a captain about to turn a ship.

She twisted the pulpit, a loud *clicking* sounding as the floor opened at her feet. A panel slid back, revealing a long tunnel with a ladder fixed to one wall.

"Oh, the many surprises of Atlantica." She dangled her legs over the edge before climbing down.

CHAPTER TWENTY-FOUR

They followed Terra down into the darkness.

Santana was the last to file in. She closed the panel over her head, almost sure that she felt a pair of eyes on her as the light cut off. She followed suit with Gyles and Erika, turning on the flashlights of their cell phones to guide their way.

Santana had a funny feeling that Terra didn't need hers.

The ladder led down thirty feet below the ground before they stopped. They piled in together, standing side-by-side as they flashed their lights around the space.

They were in a set of catacombs, the walls carved stone, and the entryways arced in the style of the abbey's front doors. The tunnels stretched out in all directions, the air cold and damp and filled with the scent of earth.

"What is this place?" Gyles asked.

"It's where they store their dead," Terra replied. "Old habits die hard, and while cemeteries and graveyards are limited to the city's outer reaches on the surface level, that doesn't mean they haven't found ways around these rules." She moved to a nearby wall where a life-size stone carving of an angel loomed over them, hands held together, blank eyes staring.

"Creepy," Erika offered.

"Yep," Santana agreed.

"Why the charade?" Gyles asked. "Why a secret entrance to hide the dead?"

"Because they're not only hiding the dead," Terra replied. "With every hidden crime uncovered, another hides around the corner. Remember that. It'll serve you well."

Santana drew up alongside Terra. "Do you know the way?"

Terra stared ahead, eyes unfocused as the light blinked behind one. "Our best guess is that way. It's where the air is warmest. Warm air equals warm bodies."

"Grim," Gyles stated.

As they started walking forward, Santana heard a snatch of Erika's passing comment to Gyles. "What does she mean 'our' best guess? Who's she talking to?"

Gyles shrugged.

They made their way through the dark, their breaths fogging up in front of them. Coffins stacked like Cub Scouts in bunk beds lined the walls, their tombs of stone immortalizing the dead within. Strange Latin scripture decorated the surfaces, and Santana found herself fascinated by their messages. She'd learned some Latin with her parents growing up and recognized the words "immortal," "Heaven," and "rapture" among the gaggle of characters.

They entered a larger octagonal chamber. Doors led off from all the walls, and in the center was a large statue of Jesus Christ, arms spread wide on the cross. Contrary to many of the fluffier images of Christ above ground, this one was brutal, with Jesus grimacing in pain as blood poured from the wounds in his palms and feet. Snaking around his body was a winding set of stairs leading down farther into the ground.

The flickering of light was visible in its depths.

Terra drew her Glock. "Arm yourselves," she commanded. "They're down below."

"How do we get to them without rousing the lot?" Gyles asked. "They'll have the advantage."

Terra stared through the floor, seeing something they clearly couldn't. "The first room only has three people there. I think we can take them if we press our element of surprise. Erika, you're going to lead the way. Okay?"

Erika steeled herself. "Of course."

"What have you got in mind?" Santana asked.

"Well…" Terra replied. "It's like this…"

They were at it again.

Mia stared at the two burly men with annoyance sketched on her face. They were impossible. Hardy and Rick were meatheads who, despite several decades of progress in the rights and respect of female empowerment, still decided to look at Mia through the lens of a Victorian husband.

"Women should be seen, not heard," Hardy had spat at her on more than one occasion, his hand hovering threateningly over his Winchester rifle.

Mia locked her lips, having learned long ago that the male opinion was a stubborn one to change. She knew who she was. She knew what she was capable of.

What did she care if these juggernaut lug-heads didn't understand her utility in their purpose? It wasn't up to them to decide her use. Darius knew better. Darius had put the three together and told them to watch the entrance.

Not that it was an exciting job. If anything, it was miserably boring. If anyone managed to make their way through the sealed entrance up top, it was doubtful they'd make their way through the labyrinth of catacombs.

Mia had remained on guard duty for the last four months. The most action she'd seen was when the slamming of stone doors later accompanied the dragging of large cages on wheels. She wasn't sure what was inside the cages since large black cloths covered their tops, but by the sounds of the raging roars that came from within, she knew it wouldn't be good news to whoever they set their animals on.

Mia sighed as Rob burst into laughter, some commercial on the TV drawing his attention and tickling his funny bone. Hardy slapped his arm, something chewy and warm spraying as his laughter joined the chorus.

Mia rubbed her eyes. The light from the TV was harsh in the gloom. She wanted the candles lit, but the men had blown them out. She was surprised the TV received a signal this far beneath the earth, but if the trailing wire that ran up through the ceiling was anything to judge by, maybe it wasn't such a shock after all.

Her ears cocked as something sounded on the steps. Mia sat up straight, eyes peeled to the winding stairs. Beside her lay a bag filled with empty food wrappers and drink bottles. She reached down, rustling the bag as she hunted for her pistol.

"Keep it down," Hardy warned over his shoulder.

Mia's lip curled. She was double their size, could lift twice what they could lift, and still, she couldn't command their respect. Give her a chance, put her in a one-on-one with either of them, and she knew she'd emerge the victor.

Maybe another time.

A shadow appeared on the stairs. She saw the feet of two individuals before she could glance at who they were. How many had left earlier today? Three? Four? Maybe they'd lost one of their number on their voyage.

A face appeared in the doorway, one that she recognized from the messages handed around their group, a target that the boss was keen to eliminate.

"Santana Sokolov," Mia muttered, getting to her feet.

Santana stood in the doorway, a surly expression on her face.

Her hands were clamped behind her back, the woman behind her out of sight but clearly in control.

"You got her?" Mia held up the pistol.

Hardy and Rob looked over their shoulders, then quickly got to their feet. They grabbed their weapons, and together the three of them stared at the newcomers.

"Move aside," an unfamiliar voice called from behind Santana. "This one needs delivering to the boss."

Mia narrowed her eyes.

"Under whose command?" Rob called, adjusting his grip on his shotgun.

Silence lingered in the air. Santana shuffled awkwardly.

"Speak," Hardy commanded.

Mia took a step forward. Hardy shot her a look. She ignored it. "Who goes there?" she asked uncertainly, able to make out a crop of dark hair behind Santana.

"Terra Kris," Terra announced. "Atlantica Justice Officer."

Before Mia could respond, Santana's arms whipped out from behind her. A loud *crack* accompanied a hot pain as the coil of a whip looped around Mia's hand.

Santana tugged and pulled Mia forward and onto her stomach.

The other woman, Terra, drew a small silver pistol and turned it on Rob and Hardy. She fired two shots in quick succession before booting Santana in the back and sending her sprawling near to where Mia was lying.

Rob made to fire the shotgun, but it dropped from his hands. He clasped the dart protruding from his neck, tearing it free with a grunt. Beside him, Hardy choked, his dart buried deep into the tissue of his Adam's apple.

"Fuck…" Mia complained.

Terra broke toward the two men, working quickly to keep them quiet. She drew two balls of cloth from her pocket and shoved them in their mouths, muting the cries of pain and protestations.

Santana low-crawled toward Mia with a determined look. Mia turned to the side, clawing for her weapon, but Santana got there first. She held the pistol and aimed it between Mia's eyes. "We're not here to kill you. Don't be a hero. You don't have to die tonight."

Mia grimaced, her hand throbbing with warm pain. "You…"

"*I* may be your saving grace tonight. Your choice. Dead or alive?"

"Alive." Mia glanced toward the two men on the far side of the room.

"Good choice." Before she knew it, Santana straddled her back, gagged her, and bound her hands. She was dragged upright and placed against the wall in a seated position, ankles and wrists bound. Santana crouched before her. "Stay still, make no fuss, don't attempt to escape, and when we finish here, we'll set you free. How about that?"

Mia met her gaze. Muffled words came from behind the cloth.

Santana pulled down the gag. "Say your piece."

Mia shuffled uncomfortably. "What are you going to do?"

Santana grinned. "Kill Darius. Maybe rescue some animals, too."

She pulled the cloth back up. A moment later, Terra returned to the stairs and called down more of their number. A man and another woman appeared. Mia couldn't help but let a soft smile play on her lips. For the first time in as long as she could remember, she was looking at a team comprised of mostly females.

CHAPTER TWENTY-FIVE

"Why can't we kill them?" Erika asked as they set the two men against the wall.

Santana gave her an amused look. Terra narrowed her eyes. "Because an officer of the law unnecessarily killing people just because she can, doesn't set the best impression, does it?"

"Oh, I don't know," Santana offered. "I'm sure you've found yourself in positions before where you needed to take a life."

"*Needed* being the operative word," Terra returned.

They secured the area, Santana working the knots and bonds on a large woman on the other side of the room. When they were all tied up and muted, Terra confiscated their weaponry, throwing the larger firearms to Gyles and Erika. "These might come in handy."

"What now?" Erika asked.

Gyles studied the Winchester.

Terra turned her gaze to the doorway. "There's a hive of people ahead. And…something else, too."

"What?" Santana asked.

Terra sighed. "You might want to see this one for yourself."

She led the way, poking her head around the door and

sneaking through a small corridor. There was a strange smell in the air that raised Santana's awareness, her stomach unsettled as they tiptoed toward the first door they'd seen since the surface.

They entered the room, and Terra quickly dispatched the woman inside before she realized what was going on. A series of half-open boxes spilled packing peanuts from within. Another two doors opened off this room, and Terra confidently led the way ahead, bringing them into a kitchen of sorts.

Two chefs stirred the contents of metal pots that were the height of small children. Steam billowed out from the top, along with the salty scent of cooked meats in a broth. Terra motioned for Santana to follow her.

Together they swept into the room behind the chefs. Terra covered her target's mouth with her hand before bringing him to his knees and tying her gag around his mouth. Santana went straight for the gag, and soon the pair were lying on the floor, cuffed to the metal table legs.

"Mmmmhhmmpphmm," one of the chefs protested. He looked imploringly at the pots.

Terra got the hint. She removed one from the heat, then the next. When she finished, she dipped a spoon into the hot liquid. Scooping some out, she tasted.

Her nose wrinkled. She spat out the broth. "You might want to add something to that. That's barely fit for animals."

The chefs exchanged a look.

"Shit." Terra turned to the door at the far end of the room, alert. "More are coming."

"How many more?" Santana asked.

Terra narrowed her eyes. Gyles and Erika studied her closely, beginning to relax and trust her although they didn't understand what was going on. "Four." She turned to the chefs. "Help me move these guys out of sight."

They worked quickly. Erika had discovered a nearby walk-in freezer where they could easily hide the chefs. Gyles helped cover

Santana and Terra as they dragged the men into the area, an intense chill hitting them when they stepped inside.

"It won't be for long. I promise," Santana stated as they closed the doors on the wide-eyed pair.

They ducked for cover, taking positions behind long metal tables. The door opened, and two of the four that Terra had mentioned stepped inside. One of them—a man, by his sound—was laughing, although the laughter faded when they saw the kitchen was empty. "Hey… Where are the cooks? They're getting hungry."

"Fuck *them*," another voice added, this one feminine. "*I'm* starving. They feed them better than they do us."

"They have to," the man replied with a note of sarcasm. "They're the stars of the show, remember?"

"Fuck them," the woman repeated as her footsteps came closer. "Unlike the cooks to leave the food unattended, though."

Santana peeked through a gap beneath the table. She saw two pairs of legs in black combat trousers, as well as two pistols holstered by their sides. She met Terra's eyes. Terra held up three fingers and began their countdown.

Three.

Two.

One.

The four of them jumped up with weapons pointed at the pair. The duo flinched, looking as though they were going to reach for their weapons until Terra stopped them. "Freeze. I wouldn't recommend that if I were you."

"You're not them," Erika added. "Let them go for their weapons. I feel like making their heads pop like dropped pumpkins."

Santana smirked.

The pair raised their hands in the air, the woman's gaze lingering on Santana. "It's you."

"Depends who you think I am," Santana replied.

"Sokolov." A strange smile appeared on the woman's lips. "Oh, they're looking forward to finding you. They're hungry for you. All of them. They've been well trained, just for you and your interfering nose."

Santana frowned. "Who? Who has?"

The man smirked. "You've gained quite the reputation among our people," he added. "The jungle girl. The only one who has escaped death under the hands of our captain."

"Kobra?" Santana asked.

A look of fear swept over the two.

"No," the woman returned. "Kobra does not concern themselves with us. We serve another power."

"Letterman," Terra stated. "We know. We're here to kill him."

The woman turned to Terra as if noticing her for the first time. "And Officer Terra Kris? I didn't recognize you out of your fatigues. What a team the pair of you make."

Terra's gaze bore into the woman. "To what do we owe your fountain of knowledge of us?"

The man shifted his weight. "You think you can do what you do without becoming the target of our organization? The moment you stuck your interfering noses into Letterman's business, he informed all of us of who you are." He chuckled. "You'll never make it farther into this place without being recognized. We're all onto you. *They're* onto you."

"Who's they?" Santana asked.

"You'll see," the woman replied.

"Enough of this," Terra declared, advancing on the pair. "Bind them, too."

The pair didn't protest, which set Santana's hackles on edge. Soon they had two more to add to their trail of captives, and they set them against the back wall. They dragged the chefs from the freezer, Santana feeling a pang of guilt for the loss of color in their faces and their chattering teeth, before huddling them with the others. "Share your body heat. We'll be back soon, and if you behave, we might consider untying you."

"Do we have to?" Erika complained.

"Come on," Terra urged, already at the far door. "We have an opening."

They broke toward Terra. She opened the door, and they sprinted along the next corridor toward an opening up ahead. They slowed as they neared it, a railing stopping their progression forward. Terra remained a meter or so back, motioning for Santana to look.

Santana gripped the railing and looked down into a large chamber.

The first thing to overwhelm her senses was the smell—animal dung, pheromones, and rotting carcasses. In the pit below were dozens of large steel animal cages, each one filled with a different beast. She spotted panthers and eagles, hogs and lions, all of them pacing restlessly within their confines. There was no care for the enclosure—no straw, hay, or grass, only metal, metal, and more metal.

Wandering around the cages were a dozen or so men and women, some dressed in black combat fatigues, others in white coats. Stationed intermittently in the room were desks with computers, most with several screens displaying graphs and charts and blinking images. The floor was hard-packed dirt—whoever had been in charge of building this place had given up on the balcony—and the only light sources were standing lamps powered by Atlanticore generators.

"Jesus," Santana muttered. Gyles and Erika joined her. "This is barbaric."

Her gaze fixed to the lion—not a marsupial lion, but instead an African lion. Its mane was shaggy and knotted. There was a sadness in its eyes as it paced back and forth, great muscles flexing but with nowhere to disperse its energy. A roar escaped its throat, a maw filled with large, yellowed teeth revealed.

Another cage contained a lone jackal. At first, Santana didn't see the creature since it was lying huddled up on the cage floor. She wondered if it was still alive until its ears pricked up and its nose started working at the new smell in the room.

"Santana, look," Terra whispered.

They were all at it. Every creature contained in that room began to sniff the air, the atmosphere growing thick with change. The guards remained unaware, simply strolling around the space, but the scientists didn't miss the shift in behavior.

"What is it, girl?" an older man working near the panther asked. "What do you detect?"

It was only when the first roar came that Santana realized what was happening. The creatures turned their collective gazes to the balcony. A raucous eruption of roars, shrills, and cries sounded as the creatures pressed against their cages in agitation. Santana took a step back, moving away from the sight of the guards, but it was already too late.

The animals had smelled their scent, and now they were hungry.

CHAPTER TWENTY-SIX

Santana pressed back against the wall. Chaos had broken out below, and now they heard the guards making their way to the stairs.

"Shit," Santana muttered. She dipped her hand into her pocket and drew out the four vials she'd received from Emily. Each had a spray pump fitted to the top. "Everyone, take one of these and apply it to yourselves, now."

"What?" Gyles asked. "What is it?"

"They've trained the animals to identify our scent," Santana replied. "Well, mine and Terra's scents, but let's be extra cautious, shall we?" Santana thought back to her encounters with the marsupial lions, how their gaze wouldn't shift from her, no matter what was happening around them.

"It's the same way they taught the creatures to come for us in the night. They somehow got our scents, and they used them for the creatures to track us to kill us. They must've done it with their other victims, too."

"Why?" Erika asked.

"I don't know," Santana replied. "Because we know too much?"

Santana sprayed a thick cloud of the clear liquid, covering as much of her body as the container would allow. Gyles covered his nose, face souring at the sudden smell. "God, that's awful."

Even Terra couldn't hide her disgust.

"It might be awful," Santana replied. "It might also be your best shot at removing yourselves as targets for these creatures."

It was working, too. Already the fuss from the animals was beginning to die down. As Terra sprayed herself and walked through the cloud of mist, a rumble of confusion swept across the cages. The cries and roars still sounded, but they were less furious.

"Now you two," Santana ordered, ducking back into the hallway as the guards reached the top of the stairs.

Erika frowned. "*We're* not the target."

"Just do it," Santana ordered.

Gyles sighed, then sprayed himself all over. He flashed Erika a resigned look and shrugged. "I'm not being funny, but I'd rather not have anything they've cooked in that lab attack me. Did you not see the marsupial lion?"

Erika grumbled, then sprayed herself.

The guards reached the top of the stairs. They walked along the balcony's walkway, footsteps ringing out on the metal. Terra ducked at the corner of the corridor, ready for combat. She held up five fingers on one hand, then flashed another one.

Six guards? How were they going to keep the element of surprise with this one?

Terra answered that for Santana by springing out from cover and raining fire on the guards. Santana couldn't believe how quickly she worked, finger flexing on the trigger and unleashing a torrent of bullets. Men and women groaned.

Terra ducked from the line of fire as bullets tore past the corridor's opening. She stepped out again, finishing the last of the guards as the scientists below cried out and grew manic, some looking for cover, others reaching inside their jacket pockets for their weapons.

"Thanks for the warning," Erika complained.

Terra raised an eyebrow while ducking into cover once more. "I'm the captain of this mission."

Erika smirked. "I'd say Santana was."

Terra grinned. "Why don't we figure this out after we've secured the area, huh?"

They all raced to the balcony, weapons ready. Working as a unit, they ran along the metal walkways, making their way toward the stairs as they aimed and fired. Bullets *pinged* off the walls and the metal. Their shots smashed computer screens and alerted the animals, riling them up and returning their cries to the din.

Santana darted ahead, diving behind the cover of the nearest desk. Nearby the panther yowled. She poked her head up and fired at a female scientist two desks over who was violently shooting in her direction.

One bullet caught the woman's shoulder. She howled and fell back.

Gyles slipped beside Santana. Terra pressed forward, finding a desk that was closer to the next gunman. Erika slid along the floor and stopped at a stack of metallic crates that stank of raw meat.

"This is wild," Gyles muttered, not sensing the irony of his words.

"You're telling me." Santana grinned as she broke cover and headed toward the panther cage. The beast spotted her, tracking her with its gaze as Santana made for the front of the cage.

"Cover me!" Santana yelled as shots closed in on her.

Terra, Erika, and Gyles jumped into action. Despite how clumsy Gyles had become in the wake of his time with the Order of the Scythe, it appeared that returning to action brought back his sharpness. They worked as a unit, keeping the quivering scientists at bay while Santana aimed the pistol at the lock and shattered the U-bolt.

The door opened a fraction. Santana swung it wide open, cooing to the panther. "Come on, gorgeous. You're free."

Terra flashed her a look of concern.

Erika yelled, "Are you crazy? What are you doing?"

The panther growled, a low rumble snaking up its throat. Its amber eyes fixed on Santana as it prowled forward, teeth bared. Despite its fearsome appearance, it was beautiful, sleek muscles working to keep it silent as it stalked forward.

"Santana?" Gyles called, ducking as someone fired in his direction.

The panther was inches from Santana. Its nostrils flared as it took in her scent. Santana held its glare, confident in what she was doing, although a tiny niggle gnawed at the back of her mind.

Hold your position. Trust the process.

The panther's lips peeled back. It loudly growled as it neared Santana, already trying to work the scent with its bestial senses. It butted its head into Santana, pressing against her stomach.

It's trained to kill you.

It didn't attack. The panther took a few long sniffs of Santana, then broke their staring contest and emerged into the open laboratory. It looked around, flinching as a bullet *pinged* nearby, then leaped into action.

The creature was powerfully quick, its frustration at being locked up for who-knew-how-long coming out in one quick bound. It zigzagged, using the tables as leverage to jump as it knocked over expensive equipment and made for the nearest scientist.

Cries of pain erupted as the creature bit into his neck. Another scientist called out and shot, catching the creature in the flank.

Then the scientist was down, Terra sending a bullet straight into the man's chest.

Santana worked the next cage, unleashing the eagle. This time she didn't wait for the eagle to identify her. Instead, the bird launched itself into the air in a flurry of feathers and flaps. It screeched, drawing the enemy's attention who rained gunfire, missing the agile bird as it swooped and dodged in the air.

Santana dashed to the next cage. The hog squealed with excitement as she freed it. She called the others to help, but they'd already anticipated her instruction and were setting animals loose in all directions.

The creatures only took a brief interest in the four uncaging them before they darted off around the room. Some disappeared through open doorways. Others flew up and toward the balcony, disappearing along the hallways that had led them inside. Santana's thoughts strayed to those they'd bound upstairs, hoping that the creatures were more interested in freedom than food.

Then the gunfire ceased. Santana looked around, unable to find more scientists with guns in their hands. A few stood by the walls, hands raised, wanting nothing to do with the shootout. Animals ran excitedly and darted around the desks. The lion sprinted in rapid circles around the room, seemingly chasing the panther in a game of cat and mouse.

Santana drew closer to Terra. "Round them up?"

"The animals?" Terra asked.

"No," Santana clarified. "The remaining scientists. I don't trust them for one second."

"Nor should you," Erika added, joining the pair. "But where can we leave them where they won't get eaten?"

"I saw some lockers over there," Gyles chimed in. He pointed at the far wall where tall metal lockers lined the space. "We could lock them in until we finish. Can big cats break into metal?" He looked uncertainly at the creatures, flinching as a falcon darted near his head.

Santana shrugged. "I guess we'll find out."

"What was in that stuff you gave us?" Erika asked, an impressed look on her face. "They want nothing to do with us."

"It's a special concoction," Santana replied. "I can't tell you its secret. That stays with a little-known pet shop owner and me. What I can say is that smell largely guides animals. All we've done is provide a little perfume that allows us to blend in, masking our natural scents."

"Like how Arnie mudded up in *Predator* to avoid heat detection?" Gyles asked.

Santana raised an eyebrow.

"Exactly like that." Terra grinned.

Santana shook her head. "Come on. Let's round these up before the animals get peckish." Her eyes darted to a fallen scientist nearby, his neck covered in blood, pieces missing. "I mean...*more* peckish."

The cleanup was tough with the animals running around. On more than one occasion, the lion appeared to take a keen interest in Gyles, glowering as it stalked toward him, hackles raised. Gyles followed Santana's instructions and remained still, the lion nudging him with its powerful head before emitting a bored roar and darting off again.

Terra kept her gaze on a door at the far end of the room while Erika and Santana stuffed the last of the enemy into the lockers. Already the animals were interested in what was inside, and Santana only hoped they weren't intelligent or hungry enough to chew through the metal doors.

She glanced toward a nearby chimpanzee who was studying the locking mechanisms with determined eyes.

One for later...

"Satisfied?" Terra asked as Santana joined her once more.

"As much as I can be." She followed Terra's line of sight. "What's waiting ahead for us?"

Terra drew a long breath. "More of the same. Only, this time it's different." She didn't elaborate.

"Helpful," Santana replied.

Gyles and Erika joined them in the center of the room.

"Are there more of them ahead?" Gyles asked.

"More of the same, but different," Santana replied.

Erika raised an eyebrow. "Clear as mud."

"Let's get this over with." Santana followed Terra as they made for the door.

CHAPTER TWENTY-SEVEN

Santana could already tell that they were walking into a trap when Terra opened the door.

A small passage led straight to another room, this one fitted with a large deadbolt. Only, the deadbolt was open.

The door stood slightly ajar, and as they neared the room, Terra slowed them down, mouthing, "They're inside. With guns." She mimed a machine gun, drawing a grin from Erika and Santana.

Terra tiptoed to the door, then removed something from her pocket. She crouched low to the ground, taking the object and rolling it through the crack in the door.

She stepped back with her weapon ready. The others filed behind her as a small *pop* sounded, followed by a series of disgruntled shouts. A couple of shots fired at the door, kicking it open several inches. They bided their time before Terra stuck her arm around the door, her gaze piercing through the walls. She fired once. The shot hit. A woman cried out in pain.

She fired again, another shot flying true and hitting its target.

A deep voice called, "Enough! Enough!"

"Lower your weapons," Terra commanded. "We're armed and loaded. Lower your weapons and surrender, now."

"Fine!" the voice shot back. The wounded grumbled and groaned.

Terra filed in silently through the door. The others followed, staying close as she expertly navigated through the smoke. She kept her aim to the center of the room, waiting for the fog to clear. A dark shape waited for them, slowly coalescing as the smoke thinned.

Darius Letterman.

"You've caused quite the ruckus," Darius announced, eyes locking onto Terra's. "Didn't I tell you that you wouldn't like the line of inquiry you searched down?"

"We heard," Santana replied. "We're used to hearing tall talk from small people in this city. All bravado, no execution."

Darius smirked. "You look good for someone who should be dead."

"You look good for someone who *will* be dead unless you choose to comply," Terra interrupted. "I'm placing you under arrest by order of the City of Atlantica."

Darius held her stare, then slowly erupted into a bout of deep, guttural laughter. His face creased, hands finding his stomach as he sat back in his chair and let the laughter take over. The smoke continued to clear until they could see the others in the room.

A man and a woman sat against the wall, the man clutching his hip, the woman her thigh. Another guard was on the right side of the wall next to a set of lockers. They looked as if no one had used them in some time.

"You think we're coming with you?" Darius returned. "You've marched into our quarters—our *private* quarters, I might add— and you think you're going to walk out of here with me in tow?" He cocked his head. "I'm afraid you're mistaken, Officer."

Santana held up her tranquilizer gun. "What about me? Would you come with me instead? I won't allow you the liberty of protesting your case at the station. I'll straight up ensure that you get cast into the jungle, and only the animals will know the location of your body."

A strange look came over Darius, then. "Yes…you do seem to have a way with the creatures, don't you? Funny how no one else managed to escape the prowess of my creations. No one else escaped the claws of the impossible attacker."

"Marsupial lion," Gyles added. "It was a marsupial lion."

Darius scoffed. "Correct." He rose to his feet, sweeping his arms around the room as he spoke. "A feat of incredible science. A creature not only forgotten by time but forgotten in mind, too. A beast capable of amazing acts of violence. A fierce predator in a harsh world, scrapping for its place in the food chain." He cast a look at Santana. "Sound familiar?"

"Sounds like every Atlantican asshole I've ever met," she replied.

"Precisely," Darius praised. "What better avatar to introduce into this concrete jungle? What better beast to twist to our purposes and remove our enemies? All we need to do is set the creature on the hunt, remove the threat while they're in their private quarters, and we get away scot-free. God, I love this city."

"Unfortunately, we took out your beasts," Terra stated. "Sorry to tell you, but two are dead, and one now has a new mama."

A flash of anger appeared behind Darius' eyes. "*That's* where you've put my baby? You've donated her to someone else?"

"Temporarily," Santana replied. "Who knows how long we'll keep her alive."

Darius narrowed his eyes at them, growing red as anger roiled his gut. "Where is she?"

"Get your hounds on the scent," Santana replied. "Find her yourself."

Darius banged his fists against his desk. "Enough. I've had it with your interference, Miss Sokolov. Miss Kris. We end this here, and we end this now. I'm through with you escaping the clutches of our nets."

He motioned to the man standing by the lockers. The man banged his fist against the metal. A loud reverberating clang sounded before a familiar call hit their ears.

Marsupial lions.

The man opened the locker door revealing access to a long passageway. The creatures stalked out of the tunnel, jumping gracefully into the room.

Terra turned her weapon on the creatures. Santana felt Gyles and Erika stiffen. She held out a hand to them, indicating for them to stay still.

Darius beamed. "Yes… Say hello to my pretty girls."

Three lions filed out, then four. They padded onto the ground, ears twitching as they reacted to a clicker in the man's hand. Santana had seen these devices before, used to train dogs to their owner's commands.

"Once we fathomed the formula for one, we didn't stop there," Darius explained. "Years of research went into this project. Years of toying with DNA until we found the closest match we could glean for these beauties."

Wonder filled his eyes. "Oh, and how beautiful they are. A powerful beast of yore revived for the modern world. We added a few…nuances of our own. Increased their intelligence. Allowed them the sense to be trainable. That didn't make the process any easier, but at least we stood a chance.

"These beauties come from a time when obedience wasn't a critical component of survival. The first mistress we birthed was untrainable—a complete chaotic creature born of bloodlust and prowess. But we perfected the formula. Over the years we've watched these babies grow into powerful accomplices. Our mini assassins to rival even the great power of the Red Countess. Who could detect us? Who could bring us in and hold us to account when it's the creatures that did the killing?"

He grinned triumphantly as the lions sat side-by-side, ears attentive.

"You've got it all figured out, haven't you?" A hint of false admiration came through in Santana's voice. "You've done well. The patience and skill it takes to train a creature like that. A creature driven by its nose and its hunger… Even I'm impressed."

"Thank you." Darius chose to ignore the sarcasm. "A long process indeed, but one that pays dividends. Our enemies fall dead at our heels, and there's nothing anyone can do to stop us."

The man clicked. The heads of the lions turned to face him.

"I have a question," Terra announced.

Darius cocked an eyebrow. "Go on, then. You might as well get it out before you become chow for my beauties."

"Well, it's two questions, really," Terra clarified. "First, why the victims? What did they do to you? Why go through such great lengths to train a small army of creatures to take out your victims in the night?"

"Nothing," Darius replied. He laughed. "Absolutely nothing."

"I'm confused," Gyles stated.

"It's easy, my friends," Darius replied, strolling around the room. "What is it that all Atlanticans—I mean true, cold-blooded Atlanticans—need more than anything else in the world?"

A silence lingered.

"Deniability," Erika muttered at last and scowled.

"Precisely," Darius replied. "You don't kill someone yourself. You pay an expert. Get someone else to do your dirty work. That's how it goes. That's the way to keep your history as clean as you can. Disconnect from the crime."

"So you're an assassination service?" Terra asked.

Darius laughed, hands clutching his stomach. "You could look at it like that. We receive large injections of cash to remove… problems." He grinned. "Second question?"

Terra smirked. "If *you're* the one in control, then why is it down to your friend to work your clicker?"

She glanced at the man who stood at the side, back straight, eyes fixed forward. The lions all stared up at him, awaiting their next command.

Terra appeared to hit a sore topic. Darius' smile wilted. "He works for me. By proxy, they work for me. Without my know-how, without my leadership, none of this would've been possible."

"But who's using the clicker?" Santana pressed, enjoying the flush on his cheeks. "Who's got them under their thumb?"

Darius clenched his fists. He stormed over to his desk, then ripped open the drawer. He produced a second clicker and held it up. "Here. They're mine, dammit." He clicked three times, and the lions turned their attention to him. With another click, they growled, saliva pooling at their lips. "Enough talk. I'll demonstrate the power of the lion and my control over the damned things."

He took a small clear bag from the drawer and removed a single hair from the packet. Santana's smile faded when she noticed the similarity between the hair he showed to the lions and hers. Had they somehow gotten her scent from her apartment?

"Now," Darius cooed, eyes turning to Santana. He clicked once and pointed at Santana as the lions sniffed the sample. "Kill."

The lions turned to Santana, growls sounding from their throats. A moment later, they sprang at her.

CHAPTER TWENTY-EIGHT

"Santana! Look out!" Terra cried as the beasts lunged at her.

Santana went down in a flurry of brown and blonde fur. Their weight pressed upon her, shoving her back to the floor. She smelled dirt and animal musk as their growls grew and they sniffed her body.

Somewhere out of Santana's sight, Terra shot. The man cried out as he slumped to the floor. She heard Darius shouting but couldn't understand the words.

Santana remained still, praying against all odds that her plan had worked. She thought back to Emily's hidden room, remembered their conversation as Emily had trialed and concocted the animal scents then and there. It was a mixture of all scents that creatures within the marsupial line found repulsive. Smells that neutralized the threat from the wallaby, the kangaroo, the wombat, and more.

Those creatures were the descendants of the gene pool from which these lions sprang. Santana could only hope the living memory that existed in each animal cell could identify threat and friend.

Santana gritted her teeth as sharp canine teeth caught on her clothing. The lions sniffed, hunting for the scent their master had unleashed but were returning nothing. Their growls filled Santana's ears, but there were no bites. There were no chomps or tearing off her flesh.

One by one, they eased back, sniffing the area around Santana like hounds hunting for the fox.

Santana slowly sat up, finding an enraged Darius on the other side of the desk. She rose to her feet, hand gripping her bullwhip as she addressed the large man. "Call them back. Send them somewhere safe. It's over."

"No…" Darius protested. "No…I won't…" His thumb worked vigorously on the clicker, whipping the lions into a frenzy of confusion as they circled Santana, Terra, Gyles, and Erika, growling and barking at them. "They're mine. They *will* kill. I command it!"

Santana cracked the whip at Darius. The clicker flew from his hand. The lions turned to her, startled by the sound.

Santana moved fast, vaulting onto the desk. Terra held Darius at point-blank range, warning him with his eyes not to move a muscle as Santana worked the whip, cracking at the feet of the lions and driving them back. They huddled by the wall, growling and snapping their teeth, but fear held them back. They wouldn't advance.

She continued her work, the whip crackling like electricity as she rounded them up and guided them toward the chamber they'd entered from. Erika slowly followed them, and as they started jumping into the passageway one by one, she readied herself by the door.

With a final *crack* of the whip, they were gone. Erika locked the door behind them. The room fell quiet.

Terra strode toward Darius, the large man withering beneath her gun. "Darius Letterman, I'm arresting you on charges of unlawful animal cloning, accessory to murder, and, I'm sure, many more charges along the way. You have the right to remain silent. Anything you say can and will be used against you in a court of law. You have the right to speak to an attorney and to have an attorney present during any questioning. If you cannot afford a lawyer, we will provide one for you at government expense."

Darius glared at Terra. "You have no jurisdiction down here."

"No," Terra admitted. "I don't. But remind me once we get up top, and I'll repeat it."

She slapped handcuffs around his fat wrists and pulled him away from the wall. Santana hopped off the desk, finding herself looking at a computer screen that was still illuminated and littered with several emails.

Her eyes went to a word that, in their moment of madness, had escaped her mind.

"Kobra."

"What is it?" Gyles asked, noticing Santana's interest in the computer.

Santana turned to Darius. "Your client. Who is it?"

"*Clients*," Darius returned, hissing the word.

"Don't bullshit me." Santana tapped the words on the screen. "You work for Kobra."

Darius stiffened.

Terra joined Santana as she stared at the screen. Next to the word was a small image of a cobra, poised to strike. Only where the eyes should've been was a black cross.

"I don't know *anything!*" Darius protested, but it was already too late. Terra had her gaze locked on the email, the AI inside her head analyzing the information and drawing whatever it could to track them down.

After a moment, she turned her gaze to Santana. "Got it."

"Just like that?" Santana asked.

"Just like that," Terra confirmed. "Erika, Gyles, are you going to be okay dragging the fat lummox back to surface level?"

Erika and Gyles exchanged a glance.

"I suppose," Gyles replied.

Erika rolled her eyes.

"Let's get out of here, then," Terra commanded. "I'm sick of the stink of animal, and I don't trust that hidden door."

Santana faced the place the lions had vanished through. "What about the lions?"

"What about them?" Terra asked. "We can't draw them out ourselves. They'll be safe here until I can call for backup. We'll have a team come and collect them before they can do any harm."

Santana hesitated.

"What is it?" Terra asked, confused by Santana's pause.

"I'm just thinking..." Santana replied. "There's no way they would've been able to bring these creatures in the way we came. There must be another entrance."

Terra straightened, scanning her gaze around them. "I can't see anything in here."

Santana gave a soft sigh, then motioned for Erika and Gyles to do as Terra requested. "Keep your eyes peeled."

Darius didn't make their job easy, and on several occasions, Santana held herself back from utilizing her tranquilizer darts to keep the man still. She'd rather not waste the solutions, and lugging a man the size of Darius when he was unconscious would've been harder for Gyles and Erika, but still...

"What have you *done*?" Darius exclaimed as they emerged into the large pit-like lab.

The animals had begun to calm, with most of them camping out by the lockers where Santana's team had stashed the scientists. The chimpanzee was still working on the locks, but its attention had moved a couple of lockers down. Some of the creatures looked their way as they entered, and there was a great clattering from the balcony as others busied themselves in the kitchen.

"Must be feeding time," Santana offered.

"There!" Terra exclaimed, pointing at a passageway past the row of lockers. "That way leads out."

"How can you possibly know that?" Erika asked. "Seriously, what are you not telling us?"

Gyles gave her a thankful look, as though the question had been plaguing him, but he'd been too scared to ask.

"Not now," Terra replied.

"When?" Erika barked back.

The panther shifted its gaze to Erika.

"Fine… Lead the way," Erika stated. "Oh captain, my captain."

Terra walked ahead, careful not to rile the animals and draw too much attention. There was no door blocking the passage, and as they filed through, they heard the sounds of more animals up ahead. Santana tallied their number, making a mental note of the breeds and species so she could send down the relevant contacts to rescue the animals the moment they made their escape.

The passageway was long, with rooms sprouting from the walls. There were bedrooms with basic cots. A couple of bathrooms smelled as though no one had cleaned them in some time. There were storage closets and supply rooms…

"This way," Terra ordered, taking a hard right.

The ground began to snake upward, wide enough for a car to pass. There were tire tracks in the mud despite the lack of vehicles. Erika and Gyles huffed as they fought against the gradient, and soon they reached a dead end.

"Fuck…" Gyles muttered, dropping his half of Darius.

Erika, unable to hold him by herself, let go. Darius groaned as he collapsed to the ground. "You sons of bitches."

Santana narrowed her gaze at the wall. There was nothing significant that she could see, only packed earth. It appeared as though the tunnel had only been half-constructed, and there was no way out.

"Terra? Tell me I'm not seeing what I see," Santana offered.

Terra shook her head. "You're not seeing what you see." She turned to Darius and dug in one of his pockets.

"I usually have to pay for a happy ending," he crooned with a sickening grin.

She produced an ID card, then dealt a swift kick to his face. Darius quieted as his eyes rolled back in his head.

Terra returned to the wall and waved the card on the right-hand side. After a moment, a *beep* confirmed the card.

Terra chucked the card back at Darius. "There's a security panel built inside the wall," she explained as a mechanical lock sounded and hydraulics kicked into action. "Pretty smart."

The wall shifted, subsiding into the floor. A flood of light barraged them, and they were all forced to shield their eyes with their forearms. Terra drew her gun and aimed it ahead, blinking against the onslaught.

Santana instinctively drew her gun. Erika and Gyles followed suit, each of them turning their head away as the rumble of engines reached their ears.

Santana could vaguely make out the group of men and women waiting for them. They stood in a line, one figure spearheading the operation. Behind them, black SUVs shone their high beams at the group. She discerned a set of pillars around them and high concrete ceilings. She wondered if they were in a parking garage of some kind, although she had no idea where in the city they were.

"You thought that you'd be able to cause such a disturbance and I wouldn't find out about it?" a soft, feminine voice asked. Something wrapped around her neck, but the light blocked Santana from getting a proper look. "You know what they say in this city, don't you? Word spreads like wildfire."

"Who are you?" Erika adjusted the gun in her hand.

Santana already knew who this was. Judging by the way Terra looked at her, she guessed that she knew, too.

The woman took a step forward, the men and women behind her aiming their weapons at the group.

"Oh, but you know who I am, don't you, Miss Sokolov?" Her head turned to Terra. "Miss Kris."

"Kobra," Gyles gasped behind them.

The woman who called herself Kobra chuckled softly. "Well done. Well done, indeed." She drew a long breath. "Boy, don't we have a lot to discuss."

She snapped her fingers, and her people ran forward. She took a swift step back, and before Santana, Terra, Gyles, or Erika could get a clean shot at her, they had her covered.

Terra shot first, determined to sweep through the crowd and get them out of this situation. Santana joined her, firing several bullets and catching the enemy in the chest and throat. Gyles and Erika joined the assault, but there were too many of them.

The attackers rushed the quartet, swallowing them in blackness. Santana fought against them, throwing punches, launching kicks, but hands gripped her limbs and wrestled her to the ground.

She turned to the side, barely able to make out Gyles and Erika, who were already under the group's control. Terra fought valiantly, her limbs moving as if they weren't hers, sending blow after blow at the enemy.

Then she was down, too. Santana had enough time to see the trickle of blood trailing from Terra's lips before something rough and scratchy covered her head, and the lights went out.

CHAPTER TWENTY-NINE

Their captors indelicately shoved them inside the vehicles.

Santana kept her ears open, using her other senses to track what was happening around her. She believed that they'd divided the group, taken them each into individual vehicles. As the SUV rumbled along, the radio played a series of hip-hop hits that Santana didn't care for, the men and women in the car with her jovially rapping along and laughing as though they were teens at a frat party.

The journey was smooth, but it was long. Santana wondered where they were, whether they were on the outskirts of the great city, or if these people were simply trying to disorientate her by circling until Santana lost all direction and had no hope of finding them again.

Eventually, the vehicle slowed, and Santana heard the *crunch* of tires on gravel. The engine cut. The doors opened. Hands roughly pulled Santana out, and her feet scrambled to find purchase on the ground.

So much for finding a hobby, Santana thought, her mind straying to Taylor Yungheim and the drink they'd shared in his office. A simpler time.

Santana was guided along the path and through a doorway into a building. They dragged her down a set of stairs, and the only saving grace Santana gained was that she thought she heard Terra arguing with her captors.

She never did know when to shut her mouth.

Then Santana was thrown into a room. Her knees hit concrete. Dust kicked up into her mouth. Someone grabbed the sack on her head, and Santana blinked as her eyes adjusted to the light.

She was in a square cell, a single door the only escape. There was a small barred window with which she could see out, but otherwise, all was gray concrete.

"Welcome to your new home," a man with arms as thick as his neck crooned. "Get comfortable. You'll be here some time."

"Why don't you just kill me?" Santana asked.

"Tempting." The man waved his rifle. "But I have orders."

The man chuckled and turned his back to Santana.

She lunged at him, her aching legs struggling to adjust as she jumped. Her hands wrapped around his neck, and he fought to shake her off. She clamped her thighs around his waist, fighting for purchase. Outside, two more guards heard the scuffle and came to his aid, grabbing Santana and fighting to release her.

She slipped down his body, hands scrambling across his waist, one hand digging into his pocket.

A swift boot to her side sent her flying. She skidded to the wall with a dazed expression as a tall, athletic woman aimed her rifle at Santana's face.

"No," the man ordered, lowering her weapon. "Remember your orders."

"It could be an accident," the woman snarled. "We can make it look like she forced us to."

"No," the man repeated. "Kobra needs her...*alive.*"

The woman reluctantly lowered her weapon. She shook her

head, then swept a quick kick at Santana. It caught her in the side of her thigh, and her leg went dead.

Santana curled up into a ball.

"Leave her," the man instructed. "We'll come back to check on her soon enough." A grin appeared on his face. "Oh, you've got so much ahead of you, Sokolov. Kobra has big plans for you…"

They closed the door behind them, leaving Santana alone in the gloomy dark. The only light source was the remnants of rays leaking through the barred window from the fluorescents outside.

Santana sat up straight, groaning as her aching body flared with more pain. They hadn't been gentle with her, and judging by the small patches of blood on her clothing, the lion's wound had opened again. She shivered softly, the concrete room sapping any possibility of warmth as she rested her head against the wall and recovered her breath.

She cocked her head and listened as the sounds of scuffles nearby alerted her to the presence of more guards. Among it all, she could make out the pained cries of Gyles, somewhere in a nearby cell, perhaps?

After a while, all went quiet. Santana racked her mind, trying to process all that had happened, wondering what the hell she had to offer someone like Kobra. Why her? What was Kobra trying to achieve, other than destroying her enemies by hiring out a service that eliminated targets with the use of highly-trained exotic species?

It was all so confusing.

There were so many unanswered questions.

She thought of the animals she'd uncaged and wondered how they were going to survive and get the care they deserved. She patted her side, noting the absence of her cell phone and whip, as well as her pack.

"Oh, Santana…" she muttered. "What the hell have you gotten yourself into now?"

Santana sat motionless for some time, listening to the sounds of the world outside her cell door.

Occasionally she closed her eyes, only to be awoken by the *clap* of footsteps on the bare floor. She listened for signs of the others, but after a few initial outbursts from a struggling Erika, followed by the sounds of a beating, nothing came.

Time passed slowly. Guards provided Santana with water and meager food provisions, ignoring the bulk of Santana's questions as she asked for an idea of when she would be leaving. Why were they keeping her here? Surely it would make more sense to get it over and done with?

That wasn't the way of the morally corrupt. Atlantica ran on a power system, and Santana knew that Kobra was biding her time, demonstrating who was boss and attempting to break them down. She wondered why Terra hadn't been more vocal. As an officer of the AJS and fitted with the latest data and tech inside her skull, surely she could've figured it all out, a way to escape.

Santana fondled the item in her pocket. She had yet to determine the time for its use.

Another hour might've passed. It could've been two. Santana rose to her feet and stretched her legs. She padded around the cell, keeping an eye on the window as guards checked in to keep an eye on her. On her fiftieth lap, or so it felt, Santana paused by the window and looked outside.

The dimly lit corridor stretched in either direction. Two guards strolled up and down it. One of the guards was a woman of around thirty, her hair tied into a high ponytail. The other was a man who appeared to be in his early twenties. There was a cherub-like look to his face, and his cheeks pouched from overeating.

Santana stayed at the bars as they passed her.

"I'd sleep it off if I were you," the woman offered. "It'll pass quicker."

The man simply stared at her.

When the guards had put as much distance between Santana and her cell as possible, Santana fished the item from her pocket and blindly located the keyhole, keeping her gaze fixed on the approaching duo.

The key fit snugly in the hole. She grinned, her little stunt with the guard upon entry paying dividends as she twisted the key slowly and unlocked the door.

She'd bided her time, knowing that the guards were most alert straight after a capture. Now they would be more relaxed. Hell, they might even be bored.

Santana pocketed the key but kept the door shut. She waited for the woman to approach once more.

"Still there?" the woman asked. She rolled her eyes with a pitying expression. "I'm telling you, take a seat. You'll only waste your energy—"

Guilt flooded Santana as she threw the door open, smacking its surface into the woman's face. The woman flew back, her nose exploding with crimson.

Santana stepped out from the cell and turned to the man who'd drawn closer. He looked shocked as he fumbled for his weapon. Santana threw the key at his hand. The metal smacked against his knuckles. She ran at him, throwing herself into the air and drop-kicking his chest. The man went down, smashing his head against the concrete floor.

Hands clawed at nearby bars on the windows. Terra's smiling face appeared. "Santana, behind you."

Santana turned her head as the woman aimed her gun her way. She quickly crossed to the man and hid behind him, using the guy as a human shield. He was out cold, eyes closed. Santana used his arm like a puppet to point his pistol...

They held their positions, neither woman shooting.

"Put the gun down," Santana whispered, her voice carrying through the corridor.

The woman touched a finger to her nose, her eyes ablaze. "Go to hell."

"Please," Santana offered, a touch of emotion in her words. "I don't want to hurt you. You don't have to do this."

The woman glanced behind her. Santana noticed a set of stairs leading up. "I do."

"No," Santana replied. She had seen a hint of goodness in the woman. The woman had cared about her comfort in the cell. "You don't. Get into the cell and give me your weapons. When all of this is over, we'll get you. You'll be safe."

Santana slowly reached toward the key that lay on the floor nearby. The woman bristled. Santana continued, tossing the key up for Terra to catch.

The door unlocked. Terra opened it slowly, head peering around its edge.

The woman looked between them. "I can't...my son...the things they said they'd do..."

Terra raised her hands, emerging from behind the door and standing behind Santana. "Kiera..."

"How do you know my name?" Keira burst out, eyes wide. "Who are you?"

"Calm down." Terra took over. "I'm from the AJS. I know you from your case files. Your son...Ethan, right?"

"Yes," Kiera offered.

"We can take you and Ethan into our protection program," Terra stated. "Help us escape, and we'll keep you two safe from harm. Santana's right. You don't need to be on this side of history."

Kiera hesitated a moment, her hand shaking. She lowered her gun as sobs racked her body .

Terra crossed cautiously to Kiera, hands in the air. Santana dragged the unconscious man into the cell and locked it behind her.

Terra helped Kiera stand. "You've made a wise choice. Get inside, and we'll make sure you remain out of harm's way."

Kiera shook her head, wiping a tear with the back of her hand. "No."

"No?" Terra parroted.

"I'm coming with you," Kiera replied. "You want out of here? You take me. I can lead you through this place."

Terra turned to Santana for confirmation. Santana nodded, then turned her attention to the other cells.

Erika was ready and waiting at her door. She looked disheveled, her hair unkempt, and there was a fresh red lump on her cheek. She limped as she walked out of the cell and commented, "Took your time."

Gyles was asleep in his cell, but for a haunting moment, Santana thought she'd found him dead. He lay curled in the corner, body barely moving, eyes closed. She had to shake him to wake him up.

"Santana?" he asked sleepily.

"Get your ass in gear," she returned. "We're getting out of here."

Together, they bunched in the corridor, looking toward the staircase. Keira looked uneasily between the group of them. "You know this is a suicide mission, right? If you want out of here, you're going to have to be prepared to cross a whole ocean of bad."

"I'm sure we've been through worse." Terra threw a glance at Santana.

"Wait here," Keira stated. "I'll head up and grab some weapons. You're not going to get far without them."

She turned to leave. Terra clutched her arm. "I don't think so."

Kiera frowned. "You don't trust me?"

Erika scoffed.

Terra answered, "No. We've just met you, and you work for the other team. Of course, we don't trust you."

"You're going to arouse suspicion following me up there," Kiera protested. "I won't be able to get anything for you to use."

Terra twisted her lip and held up the woman's pistol. "I'm fine." She jerked her thumb at Santana, who held the other. "She's fine. I think, by all accounts, it's you who's going to suffer."

"And us," Gyles mumbled.

Kiera sighed, realizing she wasn't going to win the argument. "Okay, but stay close." She checked her watch. "Let's get a move on. Guards switch in twenty minutes."

"Stay quiet." Kiera pressed her ear to the door.

Terra exchanged a glance with Santana, accompanying it with a headshake. Terra knew the place outside was empty, but they couldn't tell Kiera that.

"Okay, I think we're clear." Kiera opened the door.

They entered a passageway made of stone. Modern sconces lined the walls with wires connecting one to the other. Kiera ushered them forward, taking a set of turns that would have dizzied Santana if she'd tried to figure them out by herself.

There was a hum of activity around them. They passed wooden doorways with people muttering to each other inside. Kiera didn't bat an eyelid as they passed, and Santana began to wonder how many more prisoners they had here.

What the hell is *this place?*

When they reached yet another fork in the corridor, Kiera held up an arm. Footsteps came from somewhere nearby, and she pressed her back to the wall while motioning for the others to do the same. "Grunts," she muttered.

"Four of them," Terra replied.

Kiera cast her a strange look. "Yes."

Terra shifted closer. "Let me get to them."

Kiera looked set to argue. Terra held up the gun.

Terra took the position closest to the oncoming group. Their footsteps grew, the men muttering among each other, occasionally chuckling. When they neared, Terra confidently stepped out, stopping the men two feet from herself.

She pointed the gun at the center man's chest. "Good evening, fellas. Hands in the air, please. We'll take your weapons and any other provisions you might have now."

The men looked at the gun, smiles growing on their faces. "One versus four, darling? I don't think so."

"Two," Santana announced, stepping out behind Terra with her weapon drawn. "Do as she says."

They cast uneasy glances at each other. The man on the right looked ready to reach for his weapon. Santana drew closer, turning her aim on him.

"You don't know what you're getting into," one of the men offered.

Gyles and Erika appeared, backing up the two women.

"No," Erika stated. "*You* don't."

Gyles turned to Kiera. Kiera appeared beside him.

"Five versus four, I think that makes it," Terra stated.

"Kiera?" One of the men remarked. "What is this?"

Kiera's cheeks flushed. "Freedom."

Terra took advantage of the momentary distraction, meeting the front man's cheek with her fist. His head rolled back as he stumbled into his comrades.

While they fumbled to catch him, Santana cracked the pistol butt on the temple of another man. Gyles and Erika raced forward, diving into the fray as they worked to subdue the group. Kiera remained behind them, casting her gaze to the tunnels for any sign of reinforcements.

The men were soon unconscious, with only Terra sustaining a

numbing blow. She rubbed her arm and grimaced. "Haven't had a dead arm since kindergarten."

"I find that hard to believe," Erika offered.

They stripped the men of their weapons, Terra beaming as she caressed the barrel of a rifle. Together, they dragged the men to the nearest empty room, closing the door behind them and hoping that they would remain unconscious long enough for them to escape.

Santana tossed Kiera a pistol.

Kiera caught the gun with a confused expression.

"What are you doing?" Erika hissed. "She's the enemy."

"No," Santana replied, holding Kiera's gaze. "She's not. If she's with us, she needs to be armed. I have a feeling things are going to get crazy up ahead."

Kiera nodded with a fleeting smile. "You have no idea."

They continued along the corridor, Kiera taking tactical turns to keep them from encountering more groups of guards. Eventually, they reached another set of steps that wound back on itself and climbed at least three stories high.

As they neared the top, Kiera slowed them. Terra joined her side, her head shaking. "You weren't kidding."

They had reached an enormous underground warehouse, the ceilings rising to an easy sixty feet. They couldn't see the walls on either side of the room, and rows upon rows of metal shelves stuffed with boxes stocked the center.

Machines made their way around the space, helper vehicles working to fulfill orders and deliveries as they collected boxes and took them to an unknown location. Dotted around the room were workers dressed in black with weapons holstered to their sides as well as batons.

"What the hell is this place?" Santana asked.

Kiera scanned the way ahead. "What does it look like? It's a warehouse."

"What do you supply?" Santana pressed.

Kiera turned back to her. "You want a lesson in business, or do you want to get the hell out of here?"

"I want an answer," Santana replied firmly.

Kiera rolled her eyes, then ducked back out of sight of a group of men walking past. "Kobra is a distribution company specializing in…bespoke equipment for developers."

"What?" Terra asked.

"We fulfill orders for clients," Kiera replied. "You know…stock things that would otherwise be…inaccessible. You guys were down there with Letterman. You saw what they were up to, right?"

"You're talking about cloning?" Gyles asked.

"Kind of." Kiera composed herself. A bead of sweat glistened on her forehead. "Look, there are businesses around the world—many of them localized to Atlantica—that deal in…unsavory areas of expertise. Kobra is an organization that collects the objects that others can't get hold of and distributes them around the city."

"You're talking contraband?" Terra asked.

"Correct." Kiera continued, "Weapons, drugs, circuitry, and computer parts that contain information other people shouldn't have. We help people where they need it, and we do it well."

"We?" Erika nudged.

"Kobra," Kiera replied with a glare. "I'm not out of here yet."

"What connection does that have with Letterman?" Santana asked.

"Cloning is a specialist process," Kiera stated. "How do you think they bypassed the ICG to build their systems and get to work? Kobra. We provided the parts they couldn't get elsewhere. We have moles inside the ICG, Tynamo Inc, the AJS, and more."

Terra's eyebrow cocked. "The AJS?"

"Of course." Keira brushed away further inquiry by adding, "Now. Let's go."

She broke from cover and sprinted to an area of shelving that was free of product but provided shelter from the workers' eyes. She waved the others over.

They made a break for it, moving quickly as a unit. When they reached Kiera, she craned her neck up to look farther up the aisle. "Hold still."

They obeyed, each of them searching for signs of danger. When the staff member left, they ran farther up the aisle, dodging out the way of several strange machines that were driving up the passages.

They reached the end, hiding behind a large box that could easily have contained a car. Voices laughed and joked around. Santana spotted a camera above the doorway that was in Kiera's line of vision.

"We're being watched." She pointed. "Look, how are we going to get past the security cameras?"

The green light blinked, but they remained out of sight.

"On it," Terra replied. She closed her eyes for a moment, head lowered as she internalized her thoughts. The others watched her with bewilderment until a few moments later, she opened her eyes and announced, "Done."

The green light turned red.

"What the hell?" Erika grumbled. "Are you a superhero?"

Kiera's mouth hung open.

"No time to explain," Terra replied. "Focus on the job at hand."

"Okay, but you owe me an explanation if we get out of this," Erika stated.

"When," Santana corrected.

"We'll see, princess." Terra smirked.

They waited a few minutes before the place cleared enough for them to run. They sprinted into the open, using the body of a tall, wide machine with track wheels to cover them for part of the distance. They approached locked metal security doors with a key card panel. Kiera swiped her card, and the twin doors slid open.

Someone shouted something after them, but they kept moving forward, the doors closing behind them.

The ceilings in this room were low, and Kiera darted toward an open doorway. Posters lined the room with employee information, and somewhere far off, Santana thought she heard someone screaming.

She exchanged a look with Terra. The AJS officer had noticed.

They sprinted to the right, following yet another long corridor. This time the place was brighter, with more furniture and decorations. Now the place looked fit for offices and staff. Only when they jumped up another set of stairs two at a time did they slow.

"Act natural," Kiera told them. "We have two more floors to climb, and you're free."

"We're free, you mean," Gyles corrected.

"Right," Kiera replied.

They passed a group of technicians in white coats. Santana flashed back to the strange animal enclosure beneath the abbey, hoping that they wouldn't come across more animals being tested and experimented on.

The technicians threw them glances but paid no mind. They continued around the corner.

"Almost there," Kiera whispered.

They reached a final set of stairs. Santana kept an eye on the security cameras, finding that each of them showed static red lights now rather than the blinking greens. Whatever Terra was doing, it was working.

Santana was about to take a step up when she froze, her heart beating fast.

"What is it?" Erika asked. "Santana, come on."

"Just a little way more," Kiera offered. "We may struggle with the front guards, but I know a way that can…"

"Shhhh," Santana stated, raising a finger as she scanned the area. "Did you hear that?"

Terra nodded, her eyes trained to a spot that Santana couldn't see. "You're not going to like this."

"What?" Santana asked.

"Guys, come on," Kiera hissed, urging them on as a group of men and women with guns appeared from the corridor to the right.

"Go ahead," Santana replied. "I'll catch up."

She darted off in the direction Terra was staring. Terra added, "*We'll* catch up," before setting off after Santana.

Kiera paused with Erika and Gyles. The men and women cast them strange looks, and Kiera took off up the stairs.

Erika hesitated, then ran to join her. Gyles reluctantly hopped up the stairs and followed them both.

CHAPTER THIRTY-ONE

Santana sped down the corridor with Terra in tow.

Terra was fast, catching up to Santana as she paused at the next intersection of corridors and cocked her ears. Terra continued running, deciding the direction for both of them.

"I thought we'd be able to get you out of here without you playing Tarzan," Terra called. A group of people far behind them down the corridor turned their way with interest.

"Why is it always Tarzan?" Santana pumped her arms. "Why does no one ever go for Jane?"

The sound came again—the groan of an animal in pain. Santana had heard that sound many times beneath the canopy of jungle greenery and a sky speckled with stars as the hunter chomped on its prey and completed the circle of life.

They weren't in the jungle now, and this wasn't your usual state of affairs.

The sound grew closer, and Terra guided Santana confidently onward. They approached two men with coffees in their hands, and AKs slung over their shoulders. Santana and Terra were too fast for them, bowling into them like pins and sending their coffees spraying. They swooped down to disarm the men, then took a sharp right.

The groaning grew ever louder. Terra stopped outside a set of metal double doors. She turned to Santana. "You ready?"

Santana nodded.

Terra placed her thumb on a fingerprint security panel. Again that strange hum came from her metallic thumb, and Santana wondered what sorcery was in her prosthetic digit.

The panel confirmed their entry.

The doors slid open.

Terra and Santana stepped inside.

It was one of the strangest rooms Santana had ever witnessed. The place was large, with a desk in the center and several computer monitors lined along its surface. The walls held oil paintings of several creatures. Santana recognized animals who had long since faded from the realm of existence. Some of the pictures were the size of a postage stamp, and others were on canvases the size of people.

The floor was bare wood with several animal-skin rugs lining its surface. Santana saw a bear, a jaguar, and a wolf that had been skinned and found their final resting place on the floor. A woman stared at the back wall with her fingers laced behind her back.

Santana could understand why. The back wall was made entirely of glass so thick that it warped the exhibit's contents on the other side. Through the wall, she saw rocks and trees and several fallen logs covered in deep scratches and grooves.

The door closed behind them.

Santana and Terra took a few steps closer to the woman. She was slender, with a tactical vest adding some bulk to her top half. Black combat pants clothed her lower half, and she'd pulled her hair back into a ponytail similar to Terra's and Santana's.

In the corner of the office was a glass terrarium with a cobra resting inside.

"Kobra," Santana announced.

The woman nodded without turning. "You've found me."

The pained groaning sounded once more, and this time Santana stepped forward wide-eyed as she spotted the poor creature.

A marsupial lion stood on the other side of the glass. This one was different from the others, at least one-and-a-half times the size of its brethren and with a shaggier coat of fur. It looked as though it hadn't cooked properly in the lab. Its eyes were darker, its teeth sharper, and its maw wider.

Santana had seen feral animals before and had been alarmed at their rugged appearance compared to their domesticated counterparts. This creature was no different.

The creature snapped at a group of three people in thick, protective suits who were jabbing it with electric prods, driving the creature into the corner. Foam dripped from the lion's mouth, and even through the small, letterbox windows of their helmets, Santana could detect the sick glee in their expressions.

Kobra glanced over her shoulder and offered Santana a smug grin. "Wild. Untameable. Oh, we've tried. Many times we've tried, but she won't have it. No matter what we do, she only causes problems."

"What is she?" Terra asked, unable to help herself. The AK she'd confiscated pointed at Kobra's back.

"She's the mother," Kobra replied. "The one that all the others sprang from. The first of her breed. Only, this one was simply a test, a point of focus to learn from. She's beautiful, but she's useless. She's already slain ten of my team, so now it's time for her to die."

Santana bristled. "You can't kill her because you don't like what you've created."

"Can't I?" Kobra replied. "I hardly think you're in any position to offer an opinion here." Her face soured as she turned her attention back to the squealing creature. "You're a prisoner in *my* realm, and as such, you should respond accordingly. I can do what I like, and I *will* do what I like, for I am the Kobra."

"You're Kelly Osmond Braxton," Terra stated.

A cold pause washed over the room. Kelly adjusted her hands behind her back. "You are correct. Although, those who are wise will address me as Kobra."

"Kelly Osmond Braxton," Terra continued, undeterred. "You're under arrest."

"Says who?" Kelly finally turned to face them. "You're a prisoner in my domain."

"If that were the case, we'd still be in our cells," Santana replied.

"If you were still in your cells, my creature would still be roaming free around her exhibit," Kelly stated.

Santana frowned. "What do you mean?"

Kelly grinned. "You think you can break free of my prison without me finding out about it? Oh, Santana, you're dumber than you look.

"I had such great plans for you, the wild girl from the Atlantican jungle. I've heard of your prowess with the creatures of this world. I've studied you, seen evidence of your reputation. If anyone could tame this beautiful creature, I knew it would be you."

Santana glared.

"We could have killed you," Kelly stated. "We could've killed you all back there when you captured Letterman. After all, you cut off one of our primary links to our restoration program. A program that *I* designed and Letterman built for me."

Terra took a step forward.

"It was all working so well, too." A sad look washed over Kelly's face. "Letterman takes all the fall, assumes all the risk of the operation, and I pay him and set him loose on my targets. A degree of separation between victim and murderer. It's how we survive here in Atlantica."

"Why those targets?" Terra asked. "Why Brian Felkins? Why Hilary Hopkins? Why the others?"

Kelly rolled her eyes. "Because I can? Because they were all former employees of my operation, deserters and traitors who decided to run off and were threatening to blab to the AJS or, worse, one of those animal groups that report into the ICG. I wasn't going to have it.

"Do you know how long it takes to birth a creation of such beauty? An impossibility into this realm?" She turned back to the glass, pressing a hand against it as the lion erupted into a fit of squeals and collapsed to its stomach.

"I made him send me the mother. When they determined that she was useless, I brought her to me, set on fixing the problem." She sighed. "But my mother was right. Some problems don't have a solution."

Terra kept the rifle trained on Kelly, taking another step forward. She removed a set of handcuffs with one hand. "Make it easy, Kelly. Come with us, and we can get you out of here unharmed. We don't want to cause a riot. This can end the easy way."

Santana raised her pistol. "It's over, Kelly."

But was it over? Kelly remained remarkably calm, given their current position. Even now, with two guns aimed at her, Santana got the horrible feeling that there was something they were both missing.

Something scuffled outside the door. Terra glanced over her shoulder and frowned. "Now, Kelly."

"I don't think so," Kelly replied. "You see, all I have to do is open those doors and a dozen of my people are ready to take you with them and return you to your cells."

She cocked her head. "Maybe we'll dispatch you. That might be better. Although..." She groaned, a toddler unable to reach their favorite toy on a shelf. "I want my baby trained."

The lion had stopped moving, the three in their protective suits turning to Kelly to await further instructions.

"Maybe I should end it all…" Kelly muttered.

"No," Santana replied. "You can't kill an animal in cold blood."

"Didn't you kill two of her babies last night?" Kelly raised her eyebrow.

"We were under attack," Santana replied. "Self-defense is leagues apart from cold-blooded murder. She's an innocent creature. Let her go."

"No." Kelly made up her mind. She drew a long breath. "It's time. She's already caused more chaos than she's worth, and if I lose any more men, I'm going to have to go on another recruitment drive." She snapped her fingers, then nodded to the others in the exhibit.

They nodded, lowering their electric prods and reaching for their guns.

"No!" Santana shouted, taking a step forward. "If you won't free her, then I will."

She shot at the glass. The report was like a thunderclap. A large spider-web crack appeared next to Kelly. She flinched and stepped out of the way before chuckling. "That glass is nearly ten inches thick. Good luck shooting your way through."

The people inside had stopped, attention turning to the site of the bullet. Satisfied that they were safe, they drew their weapons.

"Maybe I can help, then." Terra turned her AK to the glass and pulled the trigger. A volley of bullets rained from the barrel of the gun, the room exploding into a thunderous din. Kelly threw herself to the floor. Santana gritted her teeth and joined the assault with her pistol.

The glass cracked. Then it shattered.

Shards rained to the floor.

It unleashed all hell.

CHAPTER THIRTY-TWO

"Noooo!" Kelly screamed as the wall crashed down. She shielded herself, much of the glass raining on her body.

Terra released the trigger, finding then that as the glass had crashed, several of the bullets had torn straight into the exhibit, and two of the three people behind the glass were now lying on the floor, unmoving.

The third turned his weapon on the pair and pulled the trigger. Terra strafed to Santana and shoved her to the floor. She rose to her knees and shot back, one of her bullets finding its way through the visor window and filling the helmet with blood.

"Fuck," Santana groaned, getting to her feet. A moment of silence passed in the room.

"Are you okay?" Terra asked.

"I'm better than they are." Santana nodded at the fallen. Her eyes fell on the lion. "Stay here."

"What are you doing?" Terra replied.

"Checking that the mama is okay." Santana pointed at Kelly. "You do the same with her."

She ran toward the lion as Terra turned her attention to Kelly, rifle pointing at the woman's back.

Santana's feet *crunched* on the glass. She slowed her advance, careful not to alert the creature even though it wasn't moving. She stepped into the exhibit, boots now on earthy ground. She padded closer with her pistol pointed at the beast.

The men and women in the suits were dead, there was no doubt about that, and it seemed that the lion was, too. She knelt beside the creature, marveling at its size. Its fur was coarse and long, its monkey-like tail curled under its body, nestled by its stomach.

Santana laid a hand on the lion's flank. There was something there, soft but beating. She pressed her ear into its fur and heard the faint heartbeat that lingered.

"It's okay, girl," Santana soothed. "You're safe now. We can get you somewhere better than this place. Somewhere you can truly call home."

She placed her hands beneath the lion, attempting to scoop it into her arms. The creature was too heavy, she couldn't guess at how many pounds, but there was no way it was going to budge.

She turned to find Terra straddling Kelly, pulling her hands into the cuffs. Despite the dire situation, Kelly was smiling—actually smiling—and soon Santana learned why.

"Doors, open," Kelly commanded.

The twin metal doors slid open, and a half-dozen men and women filed inside. It took a moment for them to register the chaos, their eyes scanning across the broken glass, the unconscious lion, and the woman straddling their boss on the ground.

They reached for their weapons.

Terra was faster, drawing hers and assaulting them with a barrage of bullets. She aimed around them, scaring them back, letting them know that caution was advisable and that she wasn't one to fuck with. Santana ran to join Terra and dove behind the desk. Together they fought back the tide of bodies, although their hands still appeared around the door frame and shot blindly into the room.

Bullets embedded themselves in the tree trunks. Dust kicked into the air. "They're going to kill the lion!" Santana called, teeth gritted as she blinked through the malaise and kept them distracted.

"Cover me," Terra shouted, diving to the side of the desk. She sprinted for the doors, soon pressing herself against the walls beside them. She shot at the people she could see, and their sounding grunts confirmed their fall.

Terra shifted closer to the door, and a hand snatched her collar. A dark man with bulging muscles pulled her into his grip with a pistol held to her throat. "Enough! Drop your weapons."

"Don't listen to him, Santana," Terra called. "Shoot."

He pressed the gun harder into her throat. Santana saw the pain on Terra's face and the fire in her eyes. "Santana, shoot!"

Santana hesitated, holding her gun to them. The gunfire died as three more emerged behind the man, holding their aim at Santana.

"It's over." Kelly grinned from beneath her. "You've lost."

"Put the gun down," the man demanded. "Or your friend gets turned into soup."

"You're going to blend me?" Terra replied. "Strange way to die."

The man wasn't amused and adjusted his grip on her collar. Terra cleared her throat, then let her gun slip from her hand with a strange glint in her eye.

Kelly laughed on the floor, an oddly choked sound.

"Do as he says." Terra made a strange motion with her head.

Santana frowned, then took a step to the side, removing her weight from Kelly. She dropped the gun, confused by the awed look coming over those who had Terra captured. Their eyes grew wide, mouths falling open as they stared at Santana.

What did I do?

A rumbling growl sounded from behind. Santana turned on the spot to find the lion hiding among the shadows of the branches. She could only make out the glint in its eye, the *hunger*. Its fur bristled as it poised to leap.

"Get her!" the man commanded.

At the first shot, the lion exploded into action. It leaped toward Santana, paws raised, claws extended, mouth open to reveal its dagger teeth.

Terra took advantage of the distraction and elbowed the man in the stomach. He dropped his weapon, then staggered off-balance as Terra shoved him into his pack. They fought to regain control as the lion roared and Santana crippled them with shots to their shoulders and knees.

Santana took a step aside as the beast crashed onto Kelly. The lion's jaws locked around the flesh of her back and tore into her while Kelly tried to crawl away on the bed of glass. Its claws made quick work of her, leaving behind a messy pool.

Santana slowly stepped back until she was against the wall. The lion focused its attack, mouth and fur matted with blood. When Terra fired again, it raised its head, launching toward the door.

"Terra, move!" Santana shouted.

Terra jumped to the side as the lion finished her work for her, batting at the guards with her paws and fighting until every last person was still.

Santana and Terra moved to the center of the room, gaze fixed on the creature. After a minute, it stopped its attack and turned to face them.

Its eyes bore into Santana's. Its lips peeled back into a sour growl. There was no trace of brown or blonde on its face, only crimson. As Santana froze, waiting to see the creature's next move, her mind flooded with thoughts of the predatory creatures she'd encountered over the years. Every one of them, no matter their species or breed, held that same primitive look that had helped them last on this planet for years. No matter their appearance, size, or genus, hunger looked the same in every creature.

So did understanding. So did appreciation.

The lion stalked toward them, its head low as its powerful shoulder blades shifted. It bared its teeth, and Terra took Santana's hand in hers.

"We could kill it," Terra offered, her other hand adjusting on her AK.

"No." Santana didn't offer further instruction.

The lion was within inches now, sniffing their clothes and the smattering of blood, glass, and sweat. Santana was sure that some of Emily's potent scent remained, but it wouldn't be a full cover. This creature could sniff the true Santana. This creature was primal, primitive, and uncontrollable.

The lion snapped its jaws, nuzzled its head past Santana and Terra, and pushed them apart as it wove between the two.

"Santana?" Terra repeated.

"Hold…"

The lion performed a circuit of the pair, then put a little distance between them. It turned toward them and unleashed an almighty cry, the strange sound of a panther yowling and a bear growling, then turned and fled from the room.

Santana and Terra breathed a collective sigh of relief. The coppery smell of blood hung in the air. They heard screams of alarm as the lion made its way through the corridors.

Terra cast a glance back at the mess that was once Kelly Osmond Braxton. "What do we do now?"

Santana gave a long exhalation. "We follow the lion to the exit so we can get the hell out of here." Something in the corner of the room caught her eye. A small metal cabinet showed several dents from ricochets, and the door hung loosely open. Part of a coil looped out of the cupboard, and behind it, the strap of a backpack. Santana opened the cabinet and collected her effects, handing the other confiscated goods to Terra. Santana took her phone and dialed a number.

CHAPTER THIRTY-THREE

The lion had proven to be everything that Kelly had respected and feared—a prime killing machine.

They only had to follow the trail of blood through the corridors to find the exit. With the lion's fine-tuned sense of smell, she had worked her way up the stairs where Santana and Terra had broken from Kiera, Gyles, and Erika, and after a short distance, daylight flooded their eyes.

The air was cool with a fine mist hanging low. They exited into a tarmac yard bordered by barbed wire-topped chain-link fencing. Beyond the fence was the Atlantican jungle, the large trees hanging low over the fence and a single dirt track leading there.

The lion was nowhere in sight.

"Fuck…" Santana muttered.

"What?" Terra asked.

Santana glanced at her phone, then dialed again. "Cancel the operation," she stated. "The target has escaped." A wry grin crept on her face as Sandra's voice sounded, repeating her order before ending the call.

"What was that?" Terra asked.

Santana looked out at the forest. "I thought Sandra might be able to help contain the lion again, to give it a home with its children, safe behind bars, but…"

"But the lion deserves to be restored into the wild?" Terra finished.

Santana nodded. "The Clone Kings…E.R.N.I.E.…the ICG, all wanted the same thing, to restore the populations to the wild and give the creatures a fighting chance of survival in the modern world. We can give that to this marsupial lion, give her a chance to see the world and discover if there's a place where she can survive."

"But there's only one. She won't last long out there."

"Shouldn't we give her the chance to try?"

Terra considered this. "What if she gets into the city?"

"You think she'll go back to civilization after all she's been through?" Santana waited for a response from Terra, but she remained silent. "We can keep an eye on her. I'm sure you can keep track of reports of wild animals. If she becomes a problem, we'll deal with her. But shouldn't we give her a chance to prove herself?"

Voices sounded from the building behind them. From the outside, it looked like a simple outpost, a single-story building with a corrugated iron roof. Down below, they both knew different.

"We should leave," Terra offered.

Santana nodded. "What about the others?"

"We'll find them." Terra had a knowing look in her eye.

They commandeered a nearby SUV after Terra located a hidden spare key. The vehicle ran on Atlanticore, which made hotwiring a potentially explosive idea. They made it to the chain-link gates and passed a security post with two dead men inside. A short distance into the forest, Terra pulled the SUV over and whistled.

Kiera, Gyles, and Erika emerged from their hiding places in the trees.

"I thought we'd lost you," Gyles called. "The lion... It..."

"We know," Santana interjected.

They climbed inside the SUV. Terra hit the gas.

"What the hell happened back there?" Kiera asked.

Santana and Terra exchanged a glance.

"We'll fill you in real soon," Terra replied.

"Let us catch our breaths first," Santana added.

Somewhere nearby in the jungle came the cry of a marsupial lion, followed by an eruption of birds taking wing into the sky.

CHAPTER THIRTY-FOUR

The vodka soothed as it burned down Santana's throat.

The room had a golden cast as the setting sun fell low over the forest and spilled in through the floor-to-ceiling windows of Taylor's office. There was a strange sense of calm as Taylor studied Santana. Her feet were on the desk, and a couple of scrapes and bruises showed on her arm from the last few days of adventure.

"Am I right to believe that you didn't take my advice?" Taylor grinned.

Santana considered this, swirling the vodka in the glass. "I wouldn't say that I found a hobby so much as I found a job that needed doing."

Taylor shook his head.

"Not in the wilds," Santana clarified. "I caught up with an old friend."

Taylor looked out over the top of his glasses. "Caught up with a friend? Is that where you got all those marks?"

"We caught up in our way," Santana replied. "I did it, though. I took the week off any venture into the jungle for you or other clients. You should be proud of me."

"I'm not sure I believe you." Taylor chuckled.

"Believe what you like."

The desk was once again littered in scattered papers and heavy books that lay open with yellowed leaves showing. Faded illustrations filled the pages, and words bled into each other on the ancient parchment. Santana noticed an image of something that looked eerily familiar.

"What's that?" She leaned forward and swept a few pages out of the way to get a clearer look.

"What does it look like?" Taylor asked.

The image showed an oval pendant with basic inscriptions—the same one that had come to Santana after her mother passed. An identical match to the one someone stole, and a private investigator named John "Dick" Chambers recovered. The jewelry she'd hidden in the apartment where a man named Gyles was exploring listings for a new place where he could invite his gal pal.

"The pendant…" Santana muttered, turning the page and finding an image of an old sailing compass—a sextant—carved from gold. There was a hole in the center that was the perfect shape to fit the golden oval of the jewelry.

Santana looked up at Taylor. "What have you found? What is this?"

Taylor smiled, a smug look in his eye. "You're going to be a very happy lady," he stated. "We may have found the key to unlocking the secret of your mother's pendant, and it's hidden within the pages of this book."

"You can't be serious." Santana got lost in the book, eyes glued to the pages, mouth agape as she turned the leaves and tried to soak in the information.

A hand reached out to hers, steadying it on the page. The fingers were wrinkled, nobbled with bone. "Santana…there's more."

Santana looked up.

Taylor's eyes were wide and dazzled with excitement. "We think we've found him, Santana. We think we've found Archie."

Santana's heart raced, and her gaze locked with Taylor's as she sought to understand what he was telling her.

Finally, after all these weeks, she'd have something positive to tell Valentina Winters. Finally, she'd be heading back into the jungle.

Finally, they'd uncover the mystery of her mother's pendant.

Her gaze turned to the endless sea of green as a thousand thoughts crossed her mind at once.

Somewhere deep in the jungle, the lion roared.

AUTHOR NOTES MICHAEL ANDERLE
NOVEMBER 12, 2021

Thank you for not only reading this story but these author notes as well.

I am in Las Vegas for the 20Booksto50K® 2021 Vegas conference for indie authors, and I am exhausted.

Not as bad physically as I might have thought from the serious amount of travel I've been doing. No, my physical exhaustion comes from my body waking me up at 4:00 in the morning (religiously) and not sleeping enough.

I'm tired mentally and emotionally because I've had almost 2 weeks of being 'on' both here in Las Vegas at the show and previously in the UAE (Sharjah Book Fair) as 'Michael Anderle – Author and Publisher' and I'm ready to go into hiding, again.

Becoming Michael Anderle – *hermit* has a good ring to it.

One of the highlights of this week at the conference is the time I get to spend 'in person' with those I work with here at LMBPN. One of the LONGEST (Well, technically the longest) partner in crime helping build this crazy company is Stephen (Steve) Campbell.

Steve is one of the happiest, most upbeat individuals I know, and I just enjoy the hell out of getting to work with him. Being with him in person working is a constant energy infusion. I'm not so sure Julie - his incredible wife - agrees with me in all things Steve, however.

For example, Julie laughed out loud when she found out I named Steve' Zen Master Walking®' in my author notes. Pretty sure her experiences with Steve don't mirror my experiences with Steve. I'm ok with that. I work with a great version of Steve, and he has been consistent for years.

Just like this year at 20Booksto50k® Vegas where we help other authors learn this business of publishing.

Now, for those who don't know Steve Campbell at all, here is an interesting fact.

I got introduced to him through a podcast he did once upon a time called The Author Biz. In fact, the white-haired-wonder (I give him a lot of names in my author notes) has a picture and archived versions of his podcasts.

Since Steve reviews these author notes before they go into the book(s) then right about now he is probably wondering why I'm pulling these shenanigans by bringing him up.

Are you Steve?

>>>>> Yes I am. I'm wondering how I can cut all of this out, but then Michael's author notes would be just "thanks for reading the books" and "I'm really tired." <<<<<<<<

Well, the answer is I value the hell out of our relationship – it means the world to me, and I thank you, Steve from the bottom of my heart. And… my appreciation will be forever memorialized…so long as you don't delete these words.

>>>>>And I can say the same about you, Mister Anderle. (aka, the author with hair that may soon be as white as mine.) What began as a great working relationship quickly morphed into a genuine friendship that I greatly value.<<<<<<<

I hope that those of you who are starting your business have a partner in crime like I do. Steve might be the older, wiser, and more knowledgeable one between the two of us.

But that doesn't make Steve any less fun to work with ;-)

Ad Aeternitatem,

Michael Anderle

CONNECT WITH THE AUTHOR

Connect with Michael Anderle

Website: http://lmbpn.com

Email List: http://lmbpn.com/email/

https://www.facebook.com/LMBPNPublishing

https://twitter.com/MichaelAnderle

https://www.instagram.com/lmbpn_publishing/

https://www.bookbub.com/authors/michael-anderle

www.ingramcontent.com/pod-product-compliance
Lightning Source LLC
Chambersburg PA
CBHW020418110726

47899CB00006B/2031